FLYING TIME

FLYING TIME

A NOVEL

Donna Esposito

DONNA ESPOSITO

ISBN: 1533467544
ISBN 13: 978-1533467546

CreateSpace Independent Publishing Platform
Charleston, SC
www.CreateSpace.com/6028494
Available from Amazon.com and other retail outlets

For the Greatest Generation
May longer and longer shadows never obscure them.

PART I

LAURELMONT

CHAPTER 1

The glint of sunlight on metal caught her eye, and her hand shot out to grab it almost before she realized what it was. She turned her hand over and slowly opened her fingers as if releasing a delicate butterfly; indeed, her treasure did have wings. A heart-shaped piece of Lucite lay on her palm. Embedded in the clear acrylic was a brass collar insignia: a propeller with wings. "South Pacific" and "1943" were crudely engraved in the metal above and below the insignia. She could hardly believe her luck at finding such a prize. The box of junk in which it was buried contained broken watches and costume jewelry, so she guessed it could not be too expensive.

"How much?" she asked nonchalantly, hoping her face did not betray her excitement.

"Oh, how about fifty cents?" the vendor replied.

"Sold," she said, as she dug into her change purse and pulled out two quarters. She stuffed the plastic heart into the pocket of her shorts and walked away from the row of tables toward a bench under a willow tree near the parking lot. She and her father had been coming to this flea market every Sunday for the past few years, but this was definitely the best treasure she had ever found. She pulled out the heart to examine it more closely. It was clearly

3

handmade. She looked up to see her father coming toward her.

"Done already, Clare?" he asked. "Me, too. Find anything good today?"

Clare held out her hand to show her father the heart.

"That's quite a find," he said. "A real piece of history. That's the insignia of the Army Air Forces. Some pilot must have made that for his sweetheart during the Second World War. The clear plastic was probably from the canopy of a crashed airplane. Did you pay very much for it?"

"Just fifty cents," she replied.

"Oh, that was a bargain. I got two stamp albums and several interesting coins. I expect they'll sell pretty quickly."

Clare Carlyle's father owned a coin and stamp shop on the main street in town. It did not make very much money to live on, but he enjoyed finding unusual items and matching them up with the right collector. Since they lived above the shop in a building inherited from Clare's maternal grandparents, their expenses were few, and he could indulge his hobby. Mr. Carlyle had been an accountant but never really enjoyed it. When Clare's mother died nine years ago and her grandparents followed soon after, Mr. Carlyle decided to leave the now too-large house in the suburbs and move into the building that had once housed his in-law's bakery. He began thinking about the empty shop downstairs and how much he would like to work for himself. After talking it over with Clare, her father decided to pursue his dream of being a rare coin and stamp dealer. He first opened the store part-time and then full-time when he found he could make a go of it.

Clare loved looking at the new stamps and coins

coming in every day. She liked the ones from exotic places best, filled with tiny images of tropical birds and unfamiliar plants. She found each country on the globe that sat on her desk and read about it in the worn set of encyclopedias on her bookshelf. As a young girl, Clare wondered if she would ever see these curious places and meet the unique people who live there. As she got older and began to think about her future, the idea of becoming an anthropologist appealed to her. Her father always supported her ideas, even if they seemed impractical. He encouraged her to find colleges with strong anthropology programs and was pleased when she was accepted at Penllyn College. Clare had done very well in her first year, as her father knew she would. Proud as he was of her achievement, he was nevertheless glad to have her home for the summer. It was lonely without her, and the Sunday expedition to the flea market was just not the same.

Clare and her father walked back to the car. They drove toward town with their treasures, the open windows wildly blowing Clare's dark auburn hair. Mr. Carlyle looked at his daughter and thought she was fortunate to have inherited her mother's good looks. However, he was glad Clare had chosen Penllyn, one of the few women's colleges left. At least he did not have to worry about her being distracted by boys during the school year.

They pulled the car into the narrow alley behind their home. Mr. Carlyle went directly to the shop while Clare climbed the stairs to their living quarters. The apartment was furnished with antiques that had been in the family for years. Clare remembered the modern furniture that filled the split-level they had left in the suburbs. At first she had not liked the old furniture and hardwood floors of the apartment, but now she appreciated their connection to the past and could not imagine living in a new, plush-carpeted house with furnishings in the latest style.

Clare went to her bedroom and fished the charm out of her pocket. That was what she decided it had to be: a sort of good luck charm or talisman. It was too large to be a pendant and did not have a hole for a chain. The plastic felt warm and smooth in her palm, comforting like a Native American worry stone. She set it carefully on her nightstand and wondered how anyone could have gotten rid of it. It was her good luck charm now, and she would take it wherever she went. The motion roused her orange tabby cat Reggie from his nap on her bed. He stretched, rubbed against her hand, and then jumped down and ran toward his food bowl in the kitchen. Clare followed him and realized it was time for her dinner as well as Reggie's. She gave the cat some food and started to boil water for the capellini she and her father would eat later. In a few minutes, she heard her father ascending the stairs. He came in looking very pleased and announced that one of the coins he had found would bring several hundred dollars from the right collector. When the pasta was ready, they sat at the mahogany dining table and discussed their flea market finds over dinner.

"I wonder who made the charm," Clare mused. "And who did he make it for? And why didn't she keep it? Even if she's not alive any longer, surely she must have had some relative who would have wanted to keep it."

"Those are interesting questions, Clare, but impossible to answer," her father replied. "Thousands of men served in the Pacific during the war. It would be impossible to trace it to just one person unless there were an identification number on it."

"There isn't. The only marks are 'South Pacific' and '1943.' I guess it will stay a mystery, but I'm glad I found it. I'll treasure it more than the original recipient, I'm sure."

After dinner, the pair settled in their living room, with Clare sprawled out on the sofa and her father in his armchair. Although they had a television, they rarely used it except to watch old movies and preferred to pass the evenings reading or listening to music. Clare's grandparents had left behind a large collection of books and even more records. The records were mostly from the 1940s and 1950s. Some were big band albums, and some were recordings of Broadway musicals. Although she sometimes listened to popular music, Clare found she preferred the old standards. She could tell Glenn Miller from Benny Goodman, and she knew all the words to musicals like *Oklahoma!* and *The Sound of Music,* which was rare for someone her age. Her favorite was *South Pacific* with its exotic location and dramatic story set during World War II. When she saw the movie for the first time, she knew then that she wanted to travel there someday. She read any book on the region she could find, including the book *South Pacific* was based on, *Tales of the South Pacific* by James A. Michener. She was surprised to find that it was quite different from the musical and, in fact, even better. The slim volume was so descriptive that it was easy to imagine what life must have been like for some of the men and women who served in the Pacific during World War II.

On this night, Clare was reading Margaret Mead's *Coming of Age in Samoa.* Although she knew its veracity was controversial, she found it interesting and thought it might be helpful for her anthropology courses in the coming semester. After an hour of reading, she noticed that her father was dozing in his chair. She was getting tired, too, so she decided to go to bed. She would need to get up early for work the next day. She had spent the last several summers working at the town library, shelving books or checking out reading materials for the patrons. It was an ideal job for her; she got to see all the new books that came in and take advantage of all the activities the library had to offer.

Clare got into bed, and Reggie jumped up to his position on her pillow. Before she turned off the light, she took another look at the charm on her nightstand. *I wonder who made this*, she mused. *They must have had some story to tell.* With that thought, she switched off the light and drifted off to sleep.

CHAPTER 2

The sun was just coming up when Reggie awakened his mistress. The cat was so punctual that Clare did not need to set an alarm clock. She fed him breakfast and then went to take her shower. She dressed quickly, pulling on a clean pair of blue jeans and selecting an emerald-colored blouse someone had once told her brought out the green in her hazel eyes. When she went to the kitchen for breakfast, she found her father was up, too, and making some coffee. She made scrambled eggs for both of them, and they read different sections of the newspaper while eating. When Clare went to her bedroom to get her purse, she noticed the charm on the nightstand and stuffed it into her pocket.

Clare started off on her walk to work. It took her about fifteen minutes to walk there leisurely, less if she hurried. Today she had plenty of time and even stopped at her bank's ATM to withdraw some money for lunch. Some days she packed a lunch, but when the weather was fine, it was so nice to take a walk and eat in one of the little restaurants in town. Clare put the two twenty-dollar bills the machine had dispensed into her wallet and resumed her walk to work. She arrived at eight-thirty, half an hour before the library opened to the public. She let herself into the modern building with her key, a privilege not usually granted to summer employees. Since she had worked there for so long, the rest of the staff saw her as more than a nineteen-year-old home from her first year of college.

Mondays were a slow day at the library. Few patrons came to check out books. Clare's assignment for Monday mornings was to shelve the large pile of books returned over the weekend. This was a relaxing task, and she looked forward to working in the stacks uninterrupted for several hours. As she made her way through the Dewey Decimal System and then the fiction shelves, her mind wandered. She thought about her classes in the upcoming semester and wondered if she would like them. She wondered if she would be able to study abroad or maybe participate in one of the field trips offered periodically by the Anthropology Department at Penllyn. Clare wondered if she, like Margaret Mead, would someday write books about foreign cultures that someone else would place on the shelves at the library.

The cart full of books dwindled until Clare finally shelved the last one. She glanced at her watch and saw that it was just past noon. She told the head librarian at the circulation desk that she would be taking her lunch break. Clare got her purse and a tote bag containing the sections of the newspaper she had not read at breakfast. She did not mind eating alone, but she had to have some reading material for company.

Clare strode off down Main Street toward a cluster of shops and eateries. She had a few minutes to decide which restaurant to patronize and would probably pick whichever one was not too crowded. She had walked that way countless times before, past buildings constructed at the beginning of the twentieth century or even at the end of the nineteenth. Every building was designed with care and some architectural flourish, unlike the boxy, mundane buildings cropping up outside of town. She walked past the old five-and-dime store and glanced appreciatively at the Art Deco touches around the doors and windows. It housed offices now but was unmistakable in its original use. Likewise, the former department store's exterior spoke of a different era. It, too, had recently been converted to office space. City Hall, the courthouse, and the bank were still functioning in their original locations, their neo-classical façades lending a stately presence to a street that was beginning to look a bit tired. The old theater had closed a few years back, but Clare had been fortunate enough to see a movie there before its demise. Even in its shabby state, it was clear it must have been a palace in its heyday. A barbershop, shoe store, and candy store also stood empty.

The downtown had certainly seen better days. Clare often imagined what it must have been like decades before, bustling with activity and opportunity. That kind of promise had encouraged her grandparents to open a bakery there when they arrived from Italy, knowing little English and having even less money, but possessing an abundant desire to work hard and create a successful life for themselves. The nearby factories and the steel mill supplied all the customers a bakery could want, and the business was a success. All of Laurelmont was a success, in fact, for many decades, until one by one the factories closed, relocating their operations overseas. The closing of the steel mill was the final blow, and many other businesses failed in its wake. Because it was the county seat, the town survived; some businesses requiring office space did move in to fill the voids, but the town was a shadow of its former self.

Clare passed a few empty shop fronts before coming to a break in the buildings. Wedged between two brick structures was a silver-colored diner in Moderne style. Its streamlined profile pointed the way to a future it never reached; the diner had been closed for as long as Clare had lived in Laurelmont, its windows getting grimier and its once-shiny exterior more and more tarnished as the years passed. Clare cast it a rueful glance as she walked past, deciding to have lunch at the pizza place on the corner. She was nearly past before she realized that the diner looked different today; the neon sign in the window flashed "OPEN." Clare stopped in her tracks and stared at the flickering sign. She looked up at the large neon sign over the building that proclaimed "Flying Time Diner." Above the name, also in neon, was the image of a globe with an old twin-engine plane, like a DC-3, circling around it. Both signs were dark. But the windows did look somewhat cleaner than before, she thought. Clare walked back to the door and peered in. There were people inside. She pulled on the handle, and the door opened toward her. Inside there was a long counter with a row of red stools and a cash register at one end. A sunburst-patterned chrome backsplash on the wall behind the counter framed the grill, soda and coffee dispensers, and glass cases for displaying pies and other baked goods. A few tiny booths with the same red leatherette upholstery as the stools were in front of the windows that faced the street.

Clare was astonished. Since her father was a member of the chamber of commerce, he usually heard about any new businesses opening in town. Surely he would have mentioned it to her if he knew the diner was reopening. After taking in the scene, Clare realized a waitress was standing behind the counter looking at her.

"Anywhere you like, dear. Do you need a menu?" the waitress questioned.

"Yes, please," Clare answered and sat down on one of the stools. The restaurant had a few other patrons. A man was sitting at the far end of the counter engrossed in the newspaper, and a couple sat in one of the booths.

When the waitress came nearer to hand her the laminated menu, Clare could see that the woman was really quite elderly. She was a bit taller than Clare and a little plump with white hair and a lined face, but her blue eyes were still clear and sharp. Clare imagined that the woman must have been very attractive when she was young.

After examining the menu, Clare decided to play it safe with a cheeseburger, French fries, and a Coke. There were already hamburgers frying on the grill, so it was just a few minutes before the waitress came back with her order. This time Clare noticed some faded stitching on the woman's white uniform. The name "Nell" was embroidered in pale blue thread to the left of her lapel.

Clare pulled the newspaper out of her bag and began reading while she ate her cheeseburger and fries. The food was good, the kind of simple fare one expects from a diner. When she finished, the waitress gave her a handwritten bill. The meal was inexpensive, and she did not even have to break one of the twenty-dollar bills from the ATM. Clare left the money by her plate, along with a tip, realizing her lunch hour was almost up. She would have to rush to make it back to the library on time. Although she knew the head librarian would not be angry if she were a little late, her own work ethic made her hurry out the door.

Glancing at her watch, Clare began to retrace the footsteps that had brought her to the diner for lunch; she really did not like to be late. In her haste, she did not notice a woman walking toward her on the sidewalk. She brushed the woman's arm with her own and quickly apologized. The woman seemed more surprised than annoyed. She stared at Clare a moment before she continued walking past.

Clare came to the candy shop and was nearly thrown off balance as the glass door opened in front of her.

Two boys ran out, each grasping a brown paper sack in one hand and an oversized lollipop in the other. They continued up the street and paid no notice to Clare. Startled at the narrowly avoided impact with the door, she paused a moment. *The candy shop has a new owner, too,* she thought. *No, that's impossible.* She had walked past on her way to lunch not quite an hour before. The windows were dark as always then, she was sure. She looked through the large plate glass window. Shelves held glass jars full of penny candy. A glass case held fudge. Two teenage girls who looked about five years younger than Clare were motioning toward the fudge they wanted to an elderly, balding man in a white apron behind the case. He packaged their candy and held out the parcel as the taller of the two girls paid him. Clare stared dumbly at them as they left the shop. She had never seen them at the library before; she was sure of that. And they were dressed up, in some kind of costume, she supposed. Both girls wore blouses and skirts with white socks and saddle shoes. They turned to look at her, too, first staring at her jeans and then at her sneakers. They looked at each other, shrugged, and then headed off with their fudge.

Clare glanced at her watch again, realizing she would definitely be late now. When she looked up, she noticed a car pass her on the street. It was large and black, its streamlined profile moving slowly. A moment later another car passed. This one was blue but shaped similarly with a long, rounded hood and small passenger compartment. *There must be an antique car show somewhere,* she thought. When a third such car passed, Clare noticed it did not have the classic car license plates she was accustomed to seeing on automobiles of that vintage. Before she could reflect on this, the door to the candy store opened again, and the balding man in the apron stepped out.

"Are you all right, miss?" he asked her. "You seem

lost."

"No, I'm not lost," Clare replied. "I was just surprised to see your store open."

"Well, why wouldn't it be open? It's been open six days a week for the last fourteen years."

Clare stared at him blankly.

"Are you sure you're all right, miss?" he questioned again.

"But, but ... ," she stammered. "Your store wasn't open this morning or at all for the past nine years!" she cried.

"Miss, I can tell by your clothes that you're not from around here. I think you must be a little disoriented from being in a new place. I can assure you that my store *has* been open. When I opened it in Twenty-nine it did seem like a bad idea. People told me I was a fool, but I wouldn't give up. And I soon found that people always have a little money left for some candy, even in the hardest times. And now with the rationing and all, people want a little escape even more, even if it's just some penny candy. Did I say something wrong, miss? You look upset."

Clare felt dizzy, as if her legs would give out at any moment. She felt the arm of the man around her shoulder, and he led her inside the shop. He sat her down on a wooden chair behind the counter. He opened a glass bottle of Coca-Cola and offered it to her.

"Here, drink this. I thought you were going to faint for a moment there."

"I did, too," Clare replied weakly.

"Are you hungry? Can I get you something to eat?" he asked.

"No, I just ate lunch at the diner."

"Oh, good. Well, then you met Nell. She's a beauty, isn't she? And so friendly, too. Why don't you sit here a moment until you feel better. Here, have a root beer barrel. They always make me feel better," he said, pressing the candy into her hand. "Since you're new in town, I ought to introduce myself. I'm Martin Tolliver,"

"I'm Clare Carlyle," she replied, shaking the man's hand.

"And where are you from, Miss Carlyle?" Mr. Tolliver asked.

Clare started to say she was from Laurelmont, but something made her blurt out "Schenectady" instead. It was one of those places everyone has heard of because it has a funny name, but no one really knows where it is or knows of anyone who actually lives there.

"Oh, Schenectady. I had a cousin who visited there once, but I've never been there myself. Well, welcome to Laurelmont. Are you just passing through, or are you here to stay?" Mr. Tolliver questioned.

"I'm not sure," Clare replied.

"Well, if you decide to stay, I'm sure Nell can help you out. And be sure to come in and visit again."

"Thank you, Mr. Tolliver. You've been very kind," Clare said as she rose and made her way to the door. She left the shop just as a group of children eagerly rushed inside. Now she was not entirely surprised to see the red, white, and blue stripes of the barber's pole spinning as she walked past the barbershop and noticed a man having his hair cut inside. The marquee of the theater, though not lit up in the daylight, did proclaim that evening's feature: *Casablanca.* Clare set off toward the library again in a daze, her mind racing to explain the curious transformation of downtown Laurelmont.

As she passed the theater, she suddenly comprehended the situation. She laughed aloud with relief and a little embarrassment. *Of course,* she thought, *how could I not have realized it right away? A motion picture crew must be using the town to film a period movie!* Clare had heard of other towns being used for movie locations, so it seemed plausible. *Laurelmont is an excellent choice. Blocking off the streets to local traffic, hiring extras to play the townspeople, and setting up the empty stores gives a very convincing picture of the early 1940s. Still, the crew had worked so quickly, in just the time I was eating lunch, to transform the street … And that "Mr. Tolliver" was very good at staying in character. He must be a fine actor. Hollywood can certainly work magic,* Clare mused.

Clare was sure her tardiness would be excused by the head librarian, and she started walking back again but now at a much more leisurely pace. The windows of the old department store were dressed with mannequins wearing the sharpest styles. The five-and-dime was lit up, its windows full of sundries and a lunch counter visible on one side. Clare passed City Hall, the courthouse, and the bank, all looking better than they had in years. As she turned the corner to reach the library's entrance, she stopped in her tracks and felt her blood run cold. She looked upon a grassy field with several park benches. The modern building of glass and concrete was not there.

CHAPTER 3

Several moments passed before Clare realized she was sitting on one of the benches in the grassy lot where the library had stood. She had managed to seat herself before briefly fainting from the shock of what she saw – or did not see. No Hollywood movie crew could remove all traces of the library building where she had worked for the past four summers. It seemed one explanation remained: the one she had first entertained and then quickly rejected when talking with Mr. Tolliver. She pulled the newspaper from her bag. The date on the masthead now read June 14, 1943. Clare tried to wrap her mind around this seemingly impossible fact. She did not believe in time travel, and yet she now seemed to be fifty years in the past. There was nothing she could see to contradict this. *Perhaps I've been hit by a bus? Maybe I'm in a coma, and all this is just in my mind?* That explanation did not comfort her any more than time travel did. Whatever had happened, it was not going away, and it had started when she left the diner.

Clare decided she had to return to the diner to undo this strange turn of events, so she strode back down Main Street again. Now she realized that *she* was the one wearing a costume, as women dressed in sedate skirts and blouses, some of them even wearing hats and gloves, gave her odd

18

glances as she passed. No women were wearing pants, and even the few men she passed were not wearing blue jeans. Her white sneakers looked out of place, too. Even her shoulder-length straight hair looked out of style, as if she had missed her appointment at the beauty parlor. She began to feel self-conscious and quickened her pace. When she arrived at the diner, she saw that the neon globe and airplane sign was lit up. The chrome exterior sparkled. The diner looked as if it had just rolled off the assembly line.

Clare opened the door to find the diner much more crowded than when she ate lunch. All the booths were filled and most of the stools were, too. Patrons sat drinking coffee and eating in front of the glass cases now filled with an array of pies, cakes, and pastries. Chrome gleamed everywhere.

Behind the counter stood a tall, raven-haired beauty with eyes the color of the summer sky. Her starched white uniform bore the name "Nell" in sapphire-colored embroidered script. Clare was surprised and not surprised at the same time.

"Anywhere you like, dear. Do you need a menu?" Nell questioned.

"No, I'm not staying. Thank you, anyway," Clare replied. She turned and left the diner, confident the scene outside would return to normal. She was shocked to see an old Chevy truck traveling down the street and two men in Army uniforms walk by. She pulled the newspaper out of her bag and saw that the date still read 1943. Dismayed, she turned and entered the diner again.

"I knew you would be back! No one can resist Nell's pies!" the waitress beamed as she cleared off a place at the counter for Clare, who saw nothing else to do but sit down.

"Apple, blueberry, or Boston cream?" Nell asked.

"Blueberry," Clare answered, and Nell placed a slice in front of her. She also put down a sturdy ceramic mug, which she filled with coffee.

"Thank you," said Clare.

"You're welcome, Clare," Nell replied, smiling. Clare looked at her with astonishment.

"Don't look so surprised," Nell continued. "I was expecting you. Mr. Tolliver came in to tell me you're new in town and might need some help. Have you got a place to stay tonight? A job?"

Clare had not thought so far in advance. She supposed she might need somewhere to spend the night. Then she thought of her father. He would be beside himself with worry if she did not come home.

"I'm not sure yet," Clare replied. "I might need a place to stay, and I definitely don't have a job" she said, thinking about the empty lot where the library had stood.

"I heard Mrs. Harrigan saying she has a room open in her boarding house. It's on Hamilton Street, a left just past the courthouse. As far as a job, I know the factory is hiring. I see you've already got a uniform. Did you work in a factory before?"

Clare looked down at her jeans and sneakers and reddened. "No, actually I worked at a library."

"I doubt Mrs. Brooks needs any help at the library, but I'll let you know if I hear about anything. Do you know anyone in town at all?"

"No," Clare said, supposing she did not know anyone.

"I must introduce you to my sister Kay. She's about your age and can show you around. I guess I never properly introduced myself, now that I think of it. I'm Nell O'Neill," she said, extending her hand. Clare took the shapely hand and noticed a small heart-shaped gold pendant around the woman's neck. A smaller mother of pearl heart decorated the pendant with a tiny gold anchor in the middle. Nell realized where Clare's gaze had fallen and proudly held out the pendant. She opened it, revealing it to be a locket with pictures inside. On the right was a young man in a sailor's uniform, and on the left was a tiny photo of Nell and the same young man, standing arm in arm.

"That's my beau Johnny. He's in the Navy. Somewhere in the Mediterranean, but he can't tell me where, of course. Do you have a sweetheart?"

"No," Clare replied truthfully.

"That's hard to believe," Nell said. "If you did something with your hair and wore some fashionable clothes, I'm sure you'd have all the fellas you could handle. McCall's Department Store is having a sale, and Madam Price's Beauty Parlor is very reasonable. Kay can take you there," Nell offered.

"Thanks, maybe," Clare said weakly. She was a little embarrassed by the turn the conversation had taken, but no one else seemed to be listening to them. She finished her pie, and Nell laid the check down on the counter. Clare picked it up and saw that the pie was twenty cents and the coffee was five cents. She reached into her pocket for some change but pulled out the charm instead. She had completely forgotten about it. The brass insignia gleamed, and the Lucite was unscratched. Not wanting to come up with an explanation for it, Clare shoved it back in her pocket before Nell noticed. She brought out a few coins and placed a quarter down, along with a nickel for a tip.

Nell collected the money and said, "If you don't have any plans, you should come back for dinner. The blue plate special is macaroni and cheese tonight. And Kay will stop by after work. I'd like you to meet her."

"Thanks for all your help, Nell. I'll see you at

dinner, and I'm looking forward to meeting your sister," Clare said politely, although she hoped she did not see her for dinner and would not meet her sister.

Clare exited the diner once more, certain that her world would return to normal this time. However, she still saw the "antique" cars and the "costumed" people and was overwhelmed with dismay at this unbelievable situation.

CHAPTER 4

Clare began to wonder if she would have to resign herself to this new life. But first she would go home. *Maybe that will do the trick*, she thought hopefully. She walked along the street to her home, optimistic she would see the sign for rare coins and stamps in the storefront window as always. From a distance, the building she called home looked the same as usual, the lower part housing the shop and the upper floors the living quarters. When she got nearer, she saw with a curious mixture of disappointment and delight that loaves of bread filled the windows. The painted sign above the door read "Salerno Bakery," named, she knew, for the town her grandparents had emigrated from in Italy. She stood back a distance and watched several customers enter the store empty-handed and exit carrying loaves of Italian bread, some round, others long. Each time the door opened, the rich aroma of freshly baked bread wafted out into the street. *Could it be possible that my grandparents are really inside*, Clare wondered. She wanted to go in and see, but she now felt self-conscious about her attire. Then she reasoned that her grandparents were recent immigrants, and perhaps would be dressed strangely themselves. Feeling more confident, she strode up the steps and into the store.

A large glass counter was filled with bread of all shapes. A smaller case held an assortment of pastries, cookies, and even cannoli. The interior of the shop was warm and neat as a pin. A large map of Italy hung on the wall next to a door that Clare knew led to the room with the oven and worktables. Prints of Italian paintings graced the other walls. A small man with dark hair and a pencil-thin mustache stood behind the counter. Clare recognized him at once to be her grandfather. She supposed her grandmother was in the back room tending to the oven. If it really were 1943, then her own mother had not yet been born, so there would be no children to take care of yet.

"May I help you, miss?" the man said with an Italian accent.

Clare realized she could not just stand there gawking, so she pointed to a small loaf of bread and said, "That one, please."

As her grandfather packaged the bread in a paper wrapper, Clare caught a glimpse of a woman in the back room kneading dough on a wooden table. She was petite with soft brown hair and green eyes. She looked up from her work and smiled at Clare. Clare smiled back and wondered if the woman realized they looked quite similar. She would have liked to stay and watch them but could think of no pretext, so she handed her grandfather a dime and left the store, the loaf of bread under her arm.

As she walked down the steps of the store, an orange cat appeared from the alleyway. "Reggie?" Clare questioned incredulously. The cat rubbed against her legs, and Clare knelt down to pet him. He purred and flopped over on his back for Clare to rub his belly. She obliged him for several minutes until the cat rose and sat on the steps, meticulously licking himself. *Maybe cats do have nine lives,* Clare pondered, as she thought about the day she had found Reggie in the alley a few years ago. Clare hoped he might follow her as she walked away, but the cat continued his grooming.

Clare decided to go back to the park where the library had been to sit and think about what to do. She positioned herself on a bench and began absently picking at the bread, breaking off little morsels to throw at a pigeon that materialized out of nowhere. Soon a crowd of birds had formed at her feet, pecking at the crumbs she threw and cooing happily. Then it occurred to her how strange she must look to the people who passed her. It was not bad enough that she was dressed in such a peculiar manner, but she was also wasting food in a time of rationing and victory gardens. She shoved the rest of the bread into her bag, and the pigeons eventually scattered. *If I have to stay here, then I have to learn to fit in*, Clare resolved. And she did not see any other option but to stay. She remembered the boarding house that Nell had mentioned and decided that she should rent a room there. She opened her wallet, and to her relief, the two twenty-dollar bills were still there. She did not know how much a room would cost, but she hoped it would not be too much given how little the food she purchased had been.

Gathering up her belongings, Clare made her way over to Hamilton Street. She hoped she would be able to spot the boarding house and was not disappointed when she came upon a large three-story brick house with a sign hanging from the roof of the front porch reading "Harrigan's Boarding House." Underneath, a smaller sign read "Vacancy." Clare walked up the steps to the porch and rang the doorbell. After a few moments, a plump woman with curly, salt-and-pepper hair opened the door.

"Hello, dear. How may I help you?" the woman inquired.

"I'm interested in renting a room," Clare replied.

"Wonderful! Come right in and let me show it to you. It's just upstairs."

Clare followed the woman through the open door and into a large parlor with a fireplace, a burgundy velvet divan, and several armchairs upholstered in flowered prints. It was bright but very old-fashioned, even for 1943. A dining room with a long mahogany table was to the left, and a curving staircase lay ahead. Clare followed the woman up the stairs, continuing past the second floor and up to the third floor. There was a corridor with four doorways leading from it. The woman went to the farthest door on the right and opened it to reveal a small room.

The room contained a twin bed with a nightstand next to it, a chest of drawers on one wall, a dressing table on the opposite wall, and a chifforobe next to the window across from the bed. The furniture, a matching set, was in Art Deco style with a dark walnut veneer finish. On the bed was a worn pink chenille bedspread. Mrs. Harrigan pulled back the heavy curtain covering the window, and Clare could see that the walls were covered with faded pink floral wallpaper.

"It's a small room, and it doesn't have a closet. I hope it's big enough for you. The rent is five dollars a week. That includes the linens and use of the kitchen, parlor, and washing machine. You'll share a bathroom with the three other tenants on the third floor. There are also three tenants below plus myself," Mrs. Harrigan explained.

"It's perfect," Clare exclaimed, grateful she had enough money for the rent. "I'm Clare Carlyle. From Schenectady," she said, knowing the questions would be coming.

"And I'm Mrs. Harrigan, of course. I'm sure you'll be wanting to settle in and change out of your traveling clothes. You must have left your bags at the train station. Do you need any help with them?" Mrs. Harrigan questioned.

"No, I'm fine. Thank you very much. I'll be back in a little while," Clare said, glad that the older woman had come up with her own explanation for Clare's clothes and lack of luggage.

Clare followed Mrs. Harrigan back down the stairs. She gave Clare a key to the front door and told her she could pay the first week's rent when she returned. Clare walked out into the sunlight again and headed back downtown. She would have to return with some bags and appropriate clothing, which meant a trip to McCall's Department Store.

CHAPTER 5

Clare pulled the brass handle of the heavy glass door toward her and stepped into the hushed interior of McCall's Department Store. Before her lay the glass cases of the jewelry department with the women's clothing off to one side and the shoes off to the other. She saw the sign for the elevator at the back of the store and made her way toward it, hopeful a store directory would be near. A placard next to the elevator enumerated the various departments and where they could be found. The men's and children's clothing were on the second floor, while housewares and other necessities were in the basement. The elevator door opened, and a neat older gentleman stepped out and motioned for Clare to enter.

"Which floor, please?" the elevator operator asked.

"Basement, please," Clare responded as she stepped into the car. The man followed her, closed the door behind them, and pushed the brass lever of the elevator controls to take them to the lowest level. In a moment the bell rang, signaling their arrival, and the man opened the door for Clare. She emerged into a brightly lit space containing shelves full of dishes, pots and pans, towels, curtains, bedspreads, and everything else one could need for a home. Clare studied a map near the elevator door and found the luggage section. She passed by displays of festively-colored dinnerware, glassware in every hue, and an assortment of kitchen implements until she found herself next to a section of suitcases and other baggage. She picked up a medium-sized suitcase made of imitation leather. It was only six dollars, so Clare decided to buy it. She returned to the first floor again and headed toward the women's clothing department.

A well-dressed, matronly woman approached her and asked if she required assistance. Clare figured she did need some help.

"Yes, please," she answered. "I'm looking for some new clothes. A few skirts and blouses, I guess."

"Certainly," the clerk replied. "We have a large selection of stylish clothing for young women." She led Clare to several racks weighted down with an array of garments. The woman scrutinized her closely and then picked out a few cotton skirts and blouses. She led her to a dressing room and opened the door. Clare stepped in to try on the clothing. She pulled off her jeans and unbuttoned her green blouse. The first skirt she tried on was khaki and close-fitting. The saleswoman had a good eye, as it fit her perfectly. Next she put on a pale blue skirt that was a little fuller than the previous one. Last, she tried a simple black one. The blouses, one a soft yellow, one white, and one ivory, also fit her well. She looked at the price tags and saw that each blouse was two dollars and each skirt was three. She admired herself in the mirror until she looked down at her white socks and sneakers. She would need shoes, too. Clare emerged from the dressing room with her new outfits.

"How did the clothes fit, miss?" the saleswoman asked.

"Very well, thank you," Clare replied. "I'll take

them all, but I need to pick out some new shoes, too."

"Yes, I was going to suggest you visit the shoe department, if you hadn't mentioned it," the woman said, looking down at Clare's sneakers. "I'll hold your purchases at the counter until you're ready."

Clare thanked the woman, left the suitcase she had been carrying with her, and headed toward the shoes. The display was not large, but there was one rack with a sign that proclaimed "No Ration Stamp Needed!" As she did not have any ration stamps, Clare focused on this rack. A young woman came over to help her.

"Can I get your size for you?" she questioned. Clare was not sure if shoe sizes had changed over the years, so she asked if the woman could measure her foot. The woman obliged, although she could not stop staring at Clare's sneakers. "I'll show you what we have in your size that doesn't require ration stamps," she said as she disappeared through a door to the back room. After a moment, the young woman returned carrying several pairs of shoes. Clare tried on a pair of white canvas pumps and a few others also made of fabric. She picked out a black pair, the white canvas pair, and a beige pair. Each was three dollars. She tallied up her purchases, realizing she would be spending thirty dollars. *That's cutting it close*, she worried. *I'll definitely have to find a job tomorrow.*

As Clare walked back to the clothing department with her new shoes, she passed a display of hosiery and undergarments. She figured she had better pick out some of that, too. When the saleswoman totaled Clare's purchases, she owed McCall's Department Store twenty-eight dollars. Nell had been right; the store was having a sale, and Clare breathed a little easier with twelve dollars left in her wallet. She left the store with her bags and ducked into an alleyway to put her new wardrobe inside the suitcase.

On her way back to Mrs. Harrigan's, Clare decided to stop in T.F. Kingsley's Five-and-Ten-Cent Store. A bell on the door tinkled, announcing her entrance. The store was not as grand as McCall's had been or as quiet or as clean. Wooden shelving and glass-fronted counters displayed a variety of inexpensive goods. Signs hung from the ceiling alerting shoppers to the location of each department: toiletries, stationery, candy, notions, toys, housewares. To the right of the door was a long lunch counter. Some children sat toward one end eating sundaes and milkshakes. Clare took a fabric shopping basket from a wire rack near the door. She went to the toiletries section and picked out a pink-handled toothbrush, some Pepsodent toothpaste, a bar of Ivory soap, and some Drene shampoo. Noticing a display of cosmetics, she selected a tube of Tangee lipstick and a tiny bottle of Evening in Paris perfume. She passed by the stationery section on her way to the cashier and impulsively picked out a small hardbound notebook and red Bakelite mechanical pencil.

The cashier was a young woman near Clare's age with dark hair and a fair complexion. She picked up each item carefully to note the price, entered the amount in the cash register, and placed everything in a brown paper bag. The total came to four dollars as the cash register clanged open. Clare paid and left the store.

Using her new key to open the great oak front door, Clare entered the boarding house and found Mrs. Harrigan and another middle-aged woman listening to the radio in the parlor.

"Hello, Clare. This is Mrs. Nelson from the second floor."

Clare went over to the seated women and introduced herself. Then she gave Mrs. Harrigan five dollars for the first week's rent.

"Will you be joining us for dinner?" Mrs. Harrigan asked.

"No, thank you," Clare replied, remembering Nell's suggestion to come back to the diner to meet her sister.

"Maybe tomorrow. You should go get settled in your room," Mrs. Harrigan advised. "You must be tired after traveling so far."

Clare excused herself and climbed the stairs to the third floor. She opened the door to her room and found that Mrs. Harrigan had placed a set of rose-colored towels on the bed for her to use. Alone, she was able to inspect her new lodgings more carefully. Everything in the room, the furniture, the bedspread, the drapes, a little rag rug on the floor next to the bed, was well-worn, and yet Clare realized everything was immaculately clean with no trace of dust or dirt. She opened the door to the chifforobe and hung her new skirts and blouses inside. She placed her shoes in the bottom of the large compartment and then put her new undergarments in the top drawer. She arranged her purchases from the dime store on the dressing table and sat down on the stool to look at herself in the mirror. She felt some relief to see the familiarity of her own face staring back at her.

Pondering her reflection, Clare could think of no rational explanation for what had happened, and yet it *had* happened. *I've got to try to make the best of the situation*, she told herself. She felt a hint of pride that she was handling this new reality so well and also a hint of excitement. Clare had often wondered what life had been like during World War II, and now this was her chance to find out.

Clare thought back to her first days of college. Up until now, going away to college had been the most exciting thing that had happened to her. As much as she loved her father, she was thrilled to be gaining independence and felt her life was finally beginning when she said goodbye to him in front of the old stone buildings of Penllyn. On her first night in the dormitory, there had been a meeting to welcome all the freshmen. Each girl had to describe herself with an alliterative adjective to create a sort of mnemonic device for everyone to remember. As the girls went around the circle and she was introduced to a succession of laughing Lauras, dainty Dianas, and smiling Suzannas, Clare struggled with what to say. Clever Clare had first come to mind, but she knew that would not win her any popularity contests. Perhaps she should say "clueless" to endear herself to the other nervous freshmen? When her turn came, she blurted out "Courageous Clare." A few girls smirked or rolled their eyes, but she probably would not have been friends with them anyway. But *was* she courageous? She really did not know but hoped she could be. People had told her she had been very brave when her mother died, but she did not see how. What else could she have done? No, she had never had an opportunity to discover if she really had courage. Perhaps she would now.

After some minutes, Clare roused herself from her reverie. She decided to change into one of her new outfits for dinner so that she did not draw too much attention to herself. Clare put on the yellow blouse, khaki skirt, and beige pumps. She admired herself in the mirror and then sat down again. She applied the Tangee lipstick and put a tiny dab of perfume behind each ear. But something was not quite right. Her straight hair had certainly looked out of place, yet she had no idea how to style it in the rolls and curls she saw the other women wearing. Growing up without a mother, she had missed out on a lot of instruction in the art of hairstyling and make-up. *Oh well,* she thought, *maybe I will have to go to the beauty parlor after all.*

CHAPTER 6

Clare opened the door of the diner and saw that it was quite crowded for dinner. Nell spotted her and waved her toward one of the small booths. Sitting in the booth was a dark-haired young woman whom Clare recognized immediately as the girl from the five-and-dime.

"Clare, this is my sister Kay," said Nell.

"Oh, I knew it had to be her! We met at the store today, Sis," Kay interjected. "Welcome to Laurelmont."

"Thank you, Kay. It's very nice to meet you. Everyone in town has been so nice to me," Clare replied.

"Nell tells me you're from Schenectady. Are you just passing through, or are you going to stay awhile?"

"I'm not exactly sure yet, but I have a feeling I might be staying for some time," Clare responded.

"So you're on your own? How old are you?" Kay asked.

"I'm nineteen. How old are you?"

"I'm eighteen. I just graduated from high school. I still live at home with my parents. I had wanted to do something exciting, maybe join the WAVES or something, but my parents didn't like that idea, so I'm stuck working at Kingsley's. But it's a swell job, really. What did you do before you came to Laurelmont?"

"I just finished my first year of college. At Penllyn."

Kay's eyes grew wide. "Gosh, you've been to college?" she asked. "You must be a genius. Or rich. What did you study?"

"Oh no, I'm not a genius, and I'm certainly not rich," Clare protested. She had forgotten that it was unusual for women to go to college in those days. "I want to study anthropology, but I mostly took basic courses the first year, so I haven't learned too much anthropology yet."

"Are you going back in the fall?" Kay asked.

Clare had not thought about this before. She could not very well show up at Penllyn and expect to take classes. "No, I don't suppose I am," she replied with obvious disappointment.

"Well, maybe after the war?" Kay suggested.

"Yes, maybe." Before Clare could ponder this any longer, Nell, who had returned to the counter at the start of their conversation, now came toward them carrying two heaping plates of macaroni and cheese.

"Two blue plate specials, on the house," she said as she set one heavy china plate in front of each girl. The white plates had a red stripe around the rim, and Clare briefly wondered why it was always called the blue plate special.

"Oh, thank you, Nell, but I insist on paying," said Clare.

"Nonsense! You've been my best customer today. This is the third time you've been here. Besides, I have a feeling we'll be seeing a lot of you."

"Yes, I guess so," Clare said with a bittersweet smile. She dug into the mountain of macaroni. It was hearty and creamy, and she felt instantly better. It really was comfort food.

"So what are your plans now?" Nell asked.

"I still haven't decided what to do. I guess I need to

find a job."

"Oh, I just found out that Judy is quitting her job at Kingsley's!" Kay exclaimed. "She and Joe are getting married, and she's following him to Pensacola for training," she added. "I'm sure that you could have her job if you wanted. Just come down to the store tomorrow when it opens, and I'll put in a good word for you with Mr. Winston."

"Thank you, Kay," Clare replied. "I'll definitely think about it."

"Please do! I know it doesn't pay as well as a factory job, but we could have a lot of fun together. And the other girls who work there are swell, too. Except for old Mrs. Dietrich. She's kind of scary," Kay said with a giggle. "So, do you have a boyfriend?"

"No," Clare replied, surprised that Nell had not already filled her sister in on this detail. "Do you?"

"I've got five fellas!" Kay exclaimed proudly. "One sailor, one SeaBee, a Marine, a soldier, and a boy in the Coast Guard."

"Wow!" Clare replied. "You just need a pilot for a complete set." With that remark, she saw Kay's cheeks redden and her face fall. "Did I say something wrong?" Clare asked.

"She had one of those, but it didn't work out," Nell explained.

"I'm sorry," Clare apologized, truly regretful that she had hurt her new friend.

"It's all right," Kay answered. "You couldn't have known. He was a lot older than me. I thought it was serious, that he wanted to marry me, but my parents said that he only wanted one thing. They said a man from an upper class background like him would never really want to marry a girl like me. I guess they were right. He stopped answering my letters. I haven't heard from him in a couple months, so I gave up writing, too."

"Oh, but what if … well, what if something happened to him, and that's why he never wrote back?" Clare asked.

"My letters never came back. They get returned if the guy is killed or missing," she said matter-of-factly. "He probably met some South Seas beauty, some Dorothy Lamour type. I guess it's all for the best. He wasn't even Catholic. My parents weren't happy about that, either. Oh well. This way I can write to as many fellas as I want and not feel guilty about dancing with all the men at the USO club. Oh, you have to come with me to the dance on Saturday! It's your patriotic duty! You do dance, don't you?"

"Yes, I guess so. That sounds like fun," Clare said with some trepidation. She was suddenly grateful for the ballroom dance class she had taken at Penllyn to fulfill the physical education requirement. They had spent a week on swing dancing. At the end of the semester they held a dance and invited the ballroom class from nearby Glenmere College to come. This had been Clare's first opportunity to practice her steps with a male partner. Since there were only girls at Penllyn, they had to take turns leading and following. She hoped she could remember the steps.

"We'll have a grand time! You dance with the boys for half the night and serve coffee and doughnuts for the other half. It's at the YMCA, but it's serving as a USO club for now. A lot of different guys come through here on their way to training or to go overseas. So you almost never see the same boys twice. You're not supposed to give them your address, but all the girls do. You'll have a whole bunch to write to before you know it."

"That sounds swell!" Clare said, trying out the dated

expression. She instantly felt foolish, but Kay did not seem to notice.

"So which bands do you like? Artie Shaw is my favorite. But Harry James really sends me, too!" Kay exclaimed.

"I suppose Glenn Miller is my favorite," Clare replied, trying to remember if he had already disappeared by now.

"Oh, it was so patriotic of him to join the Army Air Forces. I hope they won't let him go anywhere that's too dangerous, though."

"I hope not, too," Clare said, concluding he was still in the United States.

Nell reappeared at the table and asked the girls if they wanted some dessert. Clare declined, surprised to see that she had polished off the whole plate of macaroni and cheese during their conversation.

"Do you want to go to the movies tonight?" Kay offered.

Before Clare could respond, Nell answered, "Kay, I'm sure Clare is very tired from her travels. Maybe you had better let her settle in tonight."

Clare realized that she was indeed tired from her temporal journey. "Thank you, Kay, but Nell's right. I think I will head back to my room. We'll go another night."

"And you will come to the store tomorrow, won't you?" Kay asked.

"Yes, I promise. It was so nice to meet you. And thank you, Nell, for the wonderful dinner." With that, Clare rose from the booth and left the two sisters chatting about what movie to see. Clare pushed open the door of the diner for the fourth time that day and optimistically strode out into the twilight. Her hopes were dashed when she saw that the marquee of the theater was lit up, proudly proclaiming that the Laurelodeon was open for business.

As she walked back to her room, she reflected on how kind and helpful everyone had been to her. It was so different from what she was used to. It was not that people in her own time were mean or unpleasant, really; it was just that people did not get involved anymore, did not want to talk to a stranger. She considered Kay's suggestion of getting a job at the five-and-dime. *Perhaps I should look at the factory, maybe be a "Rosie the Riveter,"* she thought. *That seems like more important work. Or maybe I should join the WACs or the WAVES or the WASPs. That would be more important still. But what if something happens to me?* Could *something happen to me? Could I die before I'm even born?* This was too much to contemplate now. She would try the dime store for a while and see what other opportunities arose after that, she decided.

She let herself into the boarding house once more and again found Mrs. Harrigan seated by the radio with Mrs. Nelson and this time a third woman who was introduced to her as Mrs. Ellis. Clare bid the ladies good night and ascended the stairs to her room. She decided to get ready for bed and took her toiletries into the bathroom so she could brush her teeth and wash up. It was just like being in the dorm at college, she observed, but with fewer people sharing the bathroom.

When she returned to her room, she undressed, realizing she did not have a nightgown. *I'll get one tomorrow,* Clare thought, and in the meantime put on a slip she had bought at McCall's. Clare settled down onto the bed and switched on the white milk glass lamp on the nightstand. She was used to reading before she went to sleep, but she had no book. Then she remembered the little notebook she had purchased from Kingsley's. She opened it and began to write with the mechanical pencil. Her eyes felt heavy as she concluded her improbable record of the day's events. As she began to doze, a thought came to her. She recalled reading once that an elaborate dream that seemed to last for hours was really only a few minutes of effort by the unconscious mind. *Of course,* she thought happily. *This has all been a dream! Why hadn't I realized that sooner?* She would awaken the next morning in the present day, refreshed and ready to begin the week. With that comforting thought, she snuggled down in the crisp white sheets under the chenille bedspread and fell into a deep slumber.

CHAPTER 7

Clare opened her eyes a crack, reaching out with one hand for Reggie's furry form. It was brighter than usual, so he had not awakened her on time. When her hand did not encounter the cat beside her, she opened her eyes fully, only to see an unknown room full of strange furnishings before her. She sat bolt upright with a startled cry. In an instant, everything came flooding back to her: the diner, Mrs. Harrigan's Boarding House, Nell and her sister Kay. She crept out of bed and peeked out the window. Outside she saw two children pulling a red wagon. A woman wearing a hat and white gloves walked past. In the distance she could see smoke rising from the immense chimney of a factory. Clare turned from the window and slumped down on the floor with her back against the wall. It had not been a dream, after all. She drew her knees up to her chin and sat with her arms around her legs for a few minutes trying to grasp what had happened.

However improbable it was, she appeared to be stuck in 1943, and there was nothing to do about it. Clare's thoughts turned to her father and how worried he must be. She had never stayed out all night long before, and she knew he would be frantic. The idea of him all alone and looking for her was almost too much to bear, but what could she do? She really did not understand how time travel could even work. *Perhaps time isn't passing in the same way in the present day, and no one has even missed me?* That thought cheered her, and after a few minutes, she got up and went to the chifforobe. She took out the blue skirt and white blouse and went into the bathroom. There was no shower, so she washed her hair in the claw foot tub and then filled it with water for a bath. When Clare was dressed, she returned to her room and finished getting ready. She checked her watch and saw that it was almost nine o'clock. She decided there was no time to go to the diner for breakfast, so she went downstairs thinking she would leave for Kingsley's right away.

The smell of coffee and freshly baked bread greeted her as she descended the stairs. She followed the aroma down to the kitchen, which she had not seen the previous day. Sitting at a large red and white enamel-topped table were Mrs. Harrigan and another woman Clare had not met before. She was not nearly as old as the other ladies Clare had already met, perhaps just in her late thirties, sturdily built with blonde hair and a ruddy complexion. Mrs. Harrigan introduced her as Mrs. Kaminski, who was deftly rolling out dough that she spread with a layer of poppy seeds and then rolled up and placed in the oven. Several finished loaves were already cooling on the counter.

"Please call me Anna," Mrs. Kaminski said with a slight accent. "Did you ever try poppy seed bread?" she asked.

"No," Clare admitted, "it smells wonderful!"

"Then you must try some," Anna said, cutting off a piece of the swirled loaf. Clare tasted the golden crust and rich filling still warm from the oven.

"Oh, it's heavenly!" Clare exclaimed.

"Anna is the best baker I know," Mrs. Harrigan

interjected.

"Oh, no," Anna protested. "It's nothing special. Very simple to make. I'll show you how sometime."

"Thank you," said Clare. "I'd like that very much, but I'm afraid I have to run now. I'm looking for a job today."

Both women wished Clare luck as she left the kitchen. Mrs. Ellis was knitting in the parlor, and Clare bid her a good morning before she departed. It was a fine summer day outside, and the morning sun felt good on her bare arms and legs. Soon she arrived at Kingsley's Five-and-Ten-Cent Store and went inside. She stood inside the door looking around for a moment before Kay rushed over to her.

"You came!" she cried. "I was beginning to worry you had changed your mind. I told Mr. Winston about you, and he wants to meet you. Oh, but didn't you forget something?" Kay said, looking at Clare critically.

Clare looked down self-consciously and then back at Kay questioningly.

"Your hair," said Kay. "You forgot to fix it! I could understand about yesterday because you were traveling, but today ... ," her voice trailed off.

Clare inadvertently passed a hand over her hair. Yes, she had forgotten about it.

"You can go in the ladies' room to fix it before you meet Mr. Winston," Kay suggested.

"I don't ... well, I ... ," Clare stammered.

"You don't mean you don't know how to, do you?"

"Yes, that's it," Clare confessed. "I've never been very good at things like that."

"Your hair is pretty enough to wear down, but I think I'd better help you," Kay said, leading Clare toward the ladies' room. Before she knew it, Kay had produced some bobby pins and was rolling up sections of Clare's hair. After a couple of minutes, Kay led her to the mirror and turned her to face it. Clare was shocked to see her hair styled in an elaborate array of rolls; she barely recognized herself.

"What do you think?" Kay asked.

"It's … wow, you're really good at that," Clare answered.

"Thanks!" said Kay. "I'd like to be a beautician someday."

"I definitely think you've got talent. Thank you for helping me."

"It's my pleasure. I'll give you some styling lessons later. But now let's go meet Mr. Winston," said Kay, leading Clare out of the ladies' room and toward the back of the store. In the rear left corner of the store was a small enclosure with a door and windows. Kay knocked on the door, and a distinguished-looking man in a dark suit with graying hair and a mustache emerged.

"Hello Mr. Winston, this is my friend Clare Carlyle who I was telling you about," said Kay.

"Ah, yes. Thank you, Miss O'Neill. It's very nice to meet you, Miss Carlyle. Please come right in," he said, motioning for Clare to join him in his office.

"Thank you, Mr. Winston. It's very nice to meet you, too," Clare said as she entered the small room. Kay left them and returned to her post at the cash register.

"Miss O'Neill tells me you're new in town and looking for a job. Tell me more about yourself. Did you graduate from high school?" Mr. Winston asked.

"Oh, yes. And I've had one year of college."

"College? Will you be going back?"

"No, not right away but maybe someday. In the meantime I'd like to find a job in Laurelmont."

"Do you have any retail experience?"

"Yes, actually my father owns a coin and stamp shop, and I've helped him out a lot. And I've worked at the library for the past few summers," Clare added.

"Excellent. It sounds like you're used to helping people find what they want. When can you start?"

"Right away, I suppose."

"Very good. You can start today. I'll have Mrs. Dietrich show you around."

"Oh, thank you so much, Mr. Winston! I really appreciate you giving me a chance."

Clare followed Mr. Winston out of his office and toward the linens and notions section. A heavyset, severe-looking woman in her late fifties was stationed at a cutting table surrounded by bolts of fabrics.

"Mrs. Dietrich, this is Miss Carlyle. She will be taking over Judy's position. Please get her settled," Mr. Winston said, shaking Clare's hand and turning back toward his office.

"Please follow me, Miss Carlyle," Mrs. Dietrich said, leading Clare toward a door marked "Employees Only." Inside, a wooden table and four chairs occupied the middle of the room, and a row of gray metal lockers lined one wall.

"You may use this one," the saleswoman said, pointing out an empty locker on the end. She opened a small closet and took out a purple pinafore. In yellow lettering it bore the inscription "T. F. Kingsley's 5¢ and 10¢ Store." Clare put the smock on over her blouse. Now she was dressed just like Kay and Mrs. Dietrich.

"You will be responsible for the housewares, toys, and stationery departments. You will ensure that the displays are tidy and fully stocked at all times. You will help all the customers in those departments to select the appropriate items for their needs. You will work from nine o'clock until five o'clock each weekday and have a half-hour break for lunch. Do you have any questions?"

Clare realized she did not know how much she would be paid but did not want to ask. "No, Mrs. Dietrich. No questions yet," she said with a smile.

Following the woman back to the sales floor, Clare went over to the housewares section to familiarize herself with the inventory. She looked over the array of kitchen implements, linens, and cheap, but stylish china. Everything was so colorful compared to the utilitarian items she was used to seeing. Potato peelers and rolling pins sported red or green painted handles. Tea towels had stylized leaping deer, flowers, or Mexican scenes of cacti and sombreros. The dinnerware was a rainbow of plates, teacups, gravy boats, and platters. Clare guessed the cheery colors were a small measure to combat the memories of the Depression and the strain of the war. She straightened a few stacks of dishes and then made her way over to the stationery department. She neatened piles of notebooks and writing paper and studied the different types of pens and bottles of ink on the shelves. Next she examined the offerings of the toy department. There were jacks, marbles, small celluloid trucks, paper dolls, and an assortment of Mickey Mouse and Snow White items. After a few minutes, she spotted a customer in the housewares section. It was a young woman of about her own age pushing a baby carriage.

"May I help you?" Clare asked brightly.

"Yes, I'm looking for some new juice glasses. Can you show me what you have?" Clare led her to a display of glassware and pointed out a few different styles. The woman chose a Scottie dog pattern, and Clare helped her carry six glasses to the cash register where Kay totaled up her purchases.

The morning wore on, and Clare assisted a slow but steady stream of customers in finding fountain pens, ladles, refrigerator dishes, and the like. Around noon, Kay came over and asked if she wanted to have lunch.

"Sure, but who will take over for us?" Clare asked.

"Ginny from the beauty department will take care of your areas, and Peggy from the candy counter will handle the cash register. And we'll fill in for them when they have lunch at one o'clock." Kay led Clare over to the other departments and introduced her to the two women. Both were in their early twenties and looked very stylish to Clare.

"Let's just eat at the lunch counter today," Kay suggested. Clare agreed but wondered if she were missing an opportunity to return to her own time by not going to the diner.

The girls sat down on the green stools of the lunch counter. Clare ordered a grilled cheese sandwich and a vanilla-flavored Coke, and Kay ordered a bacon, lettuce, and tomato sandwich with a root beer. Polly, the lunch counter attendant, made their sandwiches and chatted with the girls for the rest of their break. They returned to their stations, and at one o'clock Clare also kept an eye on the beauty department. A man in an Army uniform asked her for some help choosing a perfume for his girlfriend, and Clare tried them on for him until he settled on Tabu. The day passed quickly, and she found observing the customers quite interesting. *Perhaps I'll be learning some anthropology after all,* she thought.

At five o'clock, Mrs. Dietrich came over to Clare and told her she was dismissed for the day. Clare returned to the locker room to retrieve her purse and put her pinafore into her locker. Kay came in then to do the same.

"Do you want to have dinner at my house?" Kay

asked. "My mother's making a pot roast tonight – a real treat now that meat is rationed! She asked me to invite you."

Clare wondered again if she ought to go to the diner instead but decided that it would be rude to decline the invitation. "I would love to. That's so kind of your mother," she replied with a smile.

Clare followed Kay to her home a few blocks away. It was a double house with the O'Neill family living on the right side and another family on the left. Kay moved a red bicycle lying in the front walk out of the way.

"That's my brother Eddie's. He's always leaving his things around," Kay explained as she led Clare into the house. The smell of the roasting beef greeted them as they entered the front parlor. It was modestly furnished but tidy.

"Is that you, Kay?" a voice called from the kitchen.

"Yes, Mother! And I've brought Clare with me," Kay said as they walked through the dining room and into the kitchen.

"Wonderful!" Mrs. O'Neill exclaimed as she wiped her hands on her apron. She was an older version of Nell and Kay with the same blue eyes and dark hair, although Clare saw touches of gray as she got closer.

"Mrs. O'Neill, it's so nice to meet you. Thank you for inviting me to dinner. May I help you with the cooking?" Clare asked.

"Heavens, no," she replied. "Everything is in the oven and will be ready in half an hour. You girls go and relax after working all day."

"Come on, I'll show you my room," Kay said, leading Clare back through the dining room and up the stairs. The bathroom was at the top of the steps, and three doorways opened onto the hallway. The first room clearly belonged to Kay's parents, and the next was a boy's room that Clare supposed was Eddie's. At the end of the hall was a large room with two twin beds.

"This is my room," Kay said as they entered. "Well, mine and Nell's. But after she gets married I'll have it all to myself."

Kay motioned for Clare to sit down on Nell's bed, and she sprawled out on her own. A single nightstand with a small lamp sat between the beds. On Nell's side of the nightstand was a framed photograph of the sailor Clare recognized from Nell's locket. Kay's side was bare, but Clare did see a magazine clipping of Frank Sinatra taped to the mirror above Kay's dressing table.

"So how did you like your first day at Kingsley's?" Kay asked. "Mrs. Dietrich wasn't mean to you, was she?"

"No, she was fine. I had a good day. It was kind of fun, really, arranging the shelves and helping the customers. Thanks for getting me the job."

"I think it would be more fun if we had more male customers, but we'll see plenty of boys at the dance on Saturday. You'll still come, won't you?"

"Of course. I'm looking forward to it."

"Do you know what you'll wear?" Kay asked.

"No, I hadn't thought about it," answered Clare, truthfully. "Can I go like this?"

"Umm, I suppose you could, but a nice dress might be better. You can borrow one of mine. I think we're about the same size," Kay said.

"Oh, thanks, Kay! You're a lifesaver," Clare said gratefully. She was not sure when or how much she would be paid, so she did not want to spend any more money than necessary.

Kay rose from the bed and opened the closet door. She peered in and pulled out a dark green chiffon dress.

"How about this one? It never really suited me, but

I bet it would look swell on you."

"Oh, Kay, are you sure? It's beautiful."

"Of course, I'm sure. You can try it on after dinner. And I can show you how to do your hair."

"That would be swell," Clare answered, disguising her apprehension about the lesson.

The girls spent the next few minutes examining Kay's record collection until they heard her mother call them to dinner. As they descended the stairs, the screen door slammed, and Kay's brother Eddie ran past them to the bathroom to wash his hands.

Dinner was waiting on the dining room table, and Mrs. O'Neill motioned for Clare to take a seat next to Kay. Eddie ran downstairs and took his position across from the girls. The screen door opened again, and Kay's father came in carrying his black metal lunchbox. Mrs. O'Neill greeted him with a kiss on the cheek and took the lunchbox into the kitchen. Mr. O'Neill took his place at the head of the table.

"Well now, who is this pretty lass? Would this be the fair Clare who I've heard so much about?" Mr. O'Neill asked.

"Yes, Pop, Eddie, this is my new friend, Clare Carlyle."

"It's a pleasure to meet you both," Clare said. "Thank you for having me to dinner. Your family has been so kind to me."

Mrs. O'Neill served everyone a slice of pot roast, and then carrots and boiled potatoes were passed around the table. Although the food was delicious, Clare tried not to eat too much, conscious of the fact that this was an extravagant meal for the family.

"And how do you like Laurelmont, dear?" Mrs. O'Neill asked. "Will you be staying long?"

"I like it very much, thanks to Kay and Nell. It's because of them that I have a job and a place to stay," Clare answered. "I suppose I could be here for quite a while."

The conversation turned to the day's events. Mr. O'Neill recounted his day at the factory, and Kay told her family about the people she saw at Kingsley's.

"Eddie, what did you do with yourself today?" his father asked.

"Bobby and I went looking for scrap metal. We collected a bunch of cans and some old tire rims," Eddie explained.

"You've done that almost every day this summer. I'm very proud of you, Eddie," his mother said.

"I'm not. That's just kids' stuff. I want to really help. Like kill some Japs. I sure hope the war isn't over before I'm old enough to fight."

"Good heavens, Edward Francis O'Neill! How could you say that? I'll have no more of such talk from you again," Mrs. O'Neill scolded.

"How old are you, Eddie?" Clare asked.

"I just turned fourteen," he answered, "and I can't enlist until I'm seventeen."

"I don't think you have to worry, Mrs. O'Neill," said Clare, reassuringly. "The war will be over by then."

"I hope you're right, dear, but I just don't know. How can you be so sure?"

"I just have a feeling, I guess," Clare replied.

"You're awfully optimistic, Clare," Mr. O'Neill said. "We've only made a little progress in the Pacific, and there's still all of Europe to free. The last thing I want to see is my boy in uniform, but I won't be surprised if it comes to that."

"I know we have a lot of tough times ahead, but I just can't help feeling that it will all be over in about two more years."

Mr. and Mrs. O'Neill smiled at Clare indulgently. Why should they believe her, after all? Things did look awfully bleak, she supposed.

Clare and Kay helped Mrs. O'Neill clear the table. Then Mrs. O'Neill announced that she would serve dessert. She returned from the kitchen carrying a molded gelatin salad, glistening and jiggling ever so slightly. Clare was not especially fond of Jell-O, but she politely ate the portion Mrs. O'Neill served her.

"Mrs. O'Neill, everything was wonderful," Clare said. "I can see where Nell gets her talent from."

"Oh, thank you, dear," Mrs. O'Neill answered. "It's a pleasure to have you here. And it's nice not to have an empty chair at the table. Nell's been working so hard at the diner that I feel like we hardly see her."

"She's saving up for when she and Johnny get married," Kay explained. "She had a letter from Johnny today. He says he's doing swell and hasn't seen any action yet."

"He's a fine lad, that Johnny McMurphy," Mr. O'Neill added. "From a good, Irish Catholic family. A hardworking, salt-of-the-earth type. Just the kind of man you want for a son-in-law," he said, looking hard at Kay, who began to blush.

"Now Tom, there's no need to start that again," Mrs. O'Neill chided. "Why don't you kids run along now."

Eddie rose from the table and dashed out the front door scarcely before his mother finished the sentence.

"May I help you with the dishes, Mrs. O'Neill?" Clare asked.

"No dear, you and Kay go and enjoy yourselves."

Kay and Clare went back up to Kay's bedroom.

"Do you want to try on the dress now?" Kay asked.

"Sure," Clare answered. Kay removed the green dress from the closet, and Clare took it with her into the bathroom. She put it on, but she could not see how it looked in the small mirror over the sink. Clare walked back into her friend's room just as a Jimmy Dorsey record began to play. The opening notes of "Green Eyes" greeted her as Kay turned around to see her.

"You look marvelous!" cried Kay. She pulled Clare over to the vanity mirror. "Look!"

"Oh," gasped Clare. She twirled around to see how the fabric moved and involuntarily began humming "I Feel Pretty" before reminding herself to stop, as the song had not yet been written.

"The boys will be falling all over themselves to get a dance with you."

"Are you sure you don't mind me wearing it?" Clare asked.

"Of course, I'm sure. It never looked that good on me anyway. Now shall we do your hair?"

Clare returned to the bathroom and changed back into her clothes. She sat down at Kay's dressing table while Kay stood behind her.

"Did you like your hairstyle today? I could teach you how to do that now."

"It was beautiful, but maybe it's a little too fancy for just going to work. Maybe something simpler?"

Kay took the bobby pins out of Clare's hair, and the rolls fell back down to her shoulders.

"Something simpler? How's this?" Kay asked, parting Clare's hair far to one side and sweeping it over to cover one eye.

"I think I'll leave that one to Veronica Lake," Clare said, laughing.

"I'll try again," Kay said, positioning herself

between Clare and the mirror so Clare could not see herself. After a few minutes, Kay stepped away to reveal Clare's hair in a simple pageboy style.

"That's perfect!" Clare said, beaming. Kay showed her how to style it and curl the ends under. "I hope I'll be able to do that myself tomorrow."

"I'm sure you'll do just fine. And if not, I can help you at work," Kay answered.

"You've been such a dear, Kay. I can't thank you enough."

Clare and Kay spent the next hour listening to the radio and paging through magazines. It was almost dark when Clare announced that she had better go home. As she was leaving, she thanked Mr. and Mrs. O'Neill, who were now sitting on the front porch swing. It was a lovely evening, and she enjoyed the walk back to Mrs. Harrigan's. She let herself inside and climbed the stairs to the third floor. It had been a long day, and she was happy to relax in her room. She took the charm out of the pocket of her skirt and placed it on the nightstand; it was the first time she had noticed it all day. Then she retrieved her notebook from the drawer of the dressing table and jotted down the day's events.

Clare realized she had made no attempt to return to her own time at all that day. She resolved to try harder the next day; she would visit the diner as often as she could. She had to find a way back. Or did she? She had to admit that she was beginning to enjoy herself, and she was pleased that she had fit in so well. Fortunately, no one had asked her too many questions about her past. Everyone had just accepted that she was a young woman on her own, and no one was overly curious about her. Clare guessed this was because so many people were traveling to new places because of the war. She was grateful for the ready explanation for her sudden appearance in town.

As she got ready for bed, Clare reflected on her evening with the O'Neills. A family dinner was not something she had experienced for a very long time. It was not something she liked to dwell on, but she did miss having a complete family. Yet even when her mother was alive, her family was not like the O'Neill family; she had never known what it was like to have brothers or sisters around. Kay was beginning to feel like a sister to her or what Clare imagined having a sister might be like.

CHAPTER 8

The next morning, Clare was awakened early by the sound of her alarm clock. She had been sure to set it the previous evening as she had come to accept that Reggie would not be waking her up. She washed, dressed, and then tried styling her hair in the manner that Kay had shown her. She had some success and felt she looked appropriate enough not to draw attention. Making good on her resolution of the previous evening, she left the boarding house without eating breakfast and headed straight to the diner.

At the diner, Clare found Nell already behind the counter, looking pretty and fresh even after what must have been a long night.

"Good morning, Clare. How was your first day of work?"

"It was swell! Kay's helped me so much, and everyone at Kingsley's was so nice. And your parents were so kind to have me to dinner. I'm sorry you weren't there."

"I'm sorry I missed it, but I'm working as many hours here as I can while Johnny's away so we can get married and buy our own home right away when he comes back," Nell said as she poured a cup of coffee for Clare.

"I saw the portrait of him in your bedroom. He's

very handsome. And your parents sure like him.""

"Yes," Nell said. "I'm lucky I fell for a guy my parents like so much. We've known each other since grade school, and our mothers play bridge together. Kay hasn't been so lucky, but she'll find the right guy someday," said Nell, turning back to the griddle to attend to some pancakes.

Clare ordered scrambled eggs and toast. She read a newspaper that was lying on the counter while she ate her breakfast and watched Nell flirt with some elderly men who must have been regulars. Clare noticed it was almost time for work, so she paid her bill and told Nell she would see her later. As she placed her hand on the handle of the door, she realized she felt an apprehension unlike her previous exits from the diner. This time it wasn't that she would *not* return to her own time but that she *would*.

Nevertheless, Clare pushed open the door and stepped out. She felt a tiny sense of relief as two men in fedoras hurried past. She made her way to Kingsley's. Kay and Ginny were just getting there, too. The three young women went inside together and put on their purple smocks. Mrs. Dietrich unlocked the main door, and a steady stream of customers flowed in. The morning flew by, and Clare suggested to Kay that they have lunch at the diner. They both had hamburgers, and Nell was too busy to talk to them much. Again Clare emerged from the diner and was happy to still see Kay beside her.

The rest of the day was uneventful, and Clare wandered around the store getting to know the stock and the other employees better. She helped make several sales, and she thought she even saw the hint of an approving smile from Mrs. Dietrich. When the store closed, she decided to sit outside in the park and read the newspaper before dinner. There was not a lot of war news that day but instead many human interest pieces and articles about local men in the service. Clare searched her memory for what events had already happened and what would happen next. She vowed to study the newspaper every day and keep up with exactly what was happening in the war. She found it very interesting in an abstract sort of way; she did not feel as if she were part of what was happening. To her it was more like watching a movie that she knew had a happy ending. It was hard for her to comprehend that the pictures and names she saw in the paper were real people who might or might not survive the war.

After an hour, Clare returned to the diner for dinner and took a seat at the counter.

"Back again? That's the third time today," Nell exclaimed.

"Well, I guess I just can't get enough of your cooking. Is there a special tonight?" Clare asked.

"Of course! Tonight it's my famous chicken croquettes."

"I'll have to try them, then," Clare answered.

In a few minutes, Nell brought her a plate of golden fried chicken croquettes, shaped into rounded cones and topped with gravy. A small bowl of pickled beets accompanied them. Clare ate the food slowly as she surreptitiously observed the other patrons, studying what they wore, how they styled their hair, and how they talked, if she could catch snatches of their conversations. When she finished, she really did not feel like departing just then. Although she was no longer hungry, Clare ordered a bowl of rice pudding. She ate the pudding distractedly, first picking out the plump raisins and then the creamy rice one grain at a time. After a while, she decided to leave, as Nell was busy with other customers. She bid good night to Nell and felt the same trepidation gnawing at her as she opened the door. The streetcar clanged as it made a stop, and Clare sighed with relief.

It was still early, so Clare decided to go see *Casablanca* at the Laurelodeon. Of course, she had seen it before on television but never on the big screen. She paid the five-cent admission fee and found a seat in the balcony. The red velour seat was much more plush and comfortable than when she had seen a movie there shortly before the theater closed. Before the house lights dimmed, she admired the palatial interior of the theater, which had a Moorish theme and a dark blue ceiling with gold painted stars to simulate the night sky. Soon the theater darkened, and a hush fell over the audience. Before the feature played, a newsreel was shown with updates on the progress of the war. Then the movie started, and Clare watched the familiar scenes play out with rapt attention.

After the film ended, Clare walked back to the boarding house, which was dark at that late hour. She let herself in and went upstairs. Before going to sleep, she made another entry in her journal. It was her third night now in this strange room that was beginning to feel like home. Clare wondered if she would ever find her way back. Clearly just going to the diner was not enough. As much as she liked Nell and her cooking, Clare decided there was no point in going there three times a day. Even worrying about how to get back seemed futile. She was now resigned to her new life and felt a sense of excitement about what the coming days and months might bring.

CHAPTER 9

The rest of the week passed quickly for Clare, and it was the end of the workday on Friday before she knew it. She was relieved to receive a small check for the four days she had worked and went to the bank to cash it. Fortunately, the bank did not require her to have an account. She had enough money to pay Mrs. Harrigan for another week plus a bit extra for food and a few incidentals. Before they parted after work, Kay reminded Clare that the USO dance was the next evening and suggested that Clare come to her house on Saturday afternoon to get ready.

Clare awakened early on Saturday morning although she had no plans until later in the day. She dressed and went down to the kitchen for breakfast. She ate some cornflakes she had gotten from the corner grocery store with milk that had just been delivered. She was alone for a few minutes until Anna came down wearing an apron.

"Good morning, Anna. Are you baking more bread today?" Clare asked.

"No, not today. I'm going to make pierogi. Have you ever eaten them?"

"Yes, but I'm sure I've never had any as good as the ones you make," Clare said, remembering the frozen pierogi, all doughy and tasteless, she had eaten on occasion.

She watched Anna mix the dough and then begin rolling it out on a floured cloth until it was impossibly thin. She cut some of the dough into squares, placed a spoonful of potato and cheese filling onto each one, carefully folded the dough over to form a triangle, and pinched it together to seal the filling inside. When she had filled all the squares, she cut out circles from the remaining dough and filled them with cabbage or farmer's cheese.

"I promised to make these for a dinner at the church tonight, but I'll save a few for you to try. Come back for lunch," Anna suggested.

"I'd like that very much, Anna. But how can I repay you?" Clare asked.

"Don't be silly, Clare," Anna replied.

Clare went back up to her room and read the newspaper for a while. Then she decided to go for a walk. She set out for the library to see if she could borrow a book. The old library was a narrow brick building with shelves of books on two floors. It was dimly lit even with the morning sun streaming through the windows that faced the street. Clare's soft footsteps were the only sound as she made her way to the librarian's desk where an elderly woman sat behind a nameplate that read "Mrs. Brooks."

"Hello, dear. May I help you?" the librarian asked in a whisper.

"Yes, please. I'd like to apply for a library card. I'm new to Laurelmont," Clare explained softly.

"Ah, very good," Mrs. Brooks answered with a smile. "Just fill out this form."

Clare took out her mechanical pencil and began to write.

"No, dear. Please use ink on the form," Mrs. Brooks said, pushing a fountain pen and bottle of ink toward her. Clare took the pen warily and was immediately sorry she had not bought a pen and ink from Kingsley's to practice with. She had a cheap ballpoint pen in her purse but decided against using it, lest she have to explain where it came from. She wrote her name and address on the form, remembering to write the address of the boarding house instead of her own home just in time. Mrs. Brooks took the form and scrutinized it for a moment.

"Oh, Clare Carlyle. Yes, I heard you just moved here. I stopped by the candy shop for my Walnettos, and Mr. Tolliver mentioned you just arrived in town. I'm glad to see that Laurelmont's newest resident is interested in reading. Now if I could just get the other girls your age to read something besides those movie star magazines. And who is your favorite author, Clare?" Mrs. Brooks asked.

"Oh, James Michener," Clare blurted out without thinking.

"No, I've never heard of him. He isn't one of those pulp writers, is he?"

"No, he's ... I guess he isn't very famous yet. Outside of Schenectady, anyway."

"Oh, I see. Well then, anyone else whose books we might actually have?"

"I like Ernest Hemingway a lot."

"Ah, yes, we have his books. We also have many novels suitable for young women like those of Jane Austen and the Brontë sisters," Mrs. Brooks suggested.

"Thank you, Mrs. Brooks. Maybe I'll just look around if that's okay."

"Sure, dear. You just call if you need me. Quietly, of course."

Clare found the stacks of fiction books. She soon realized she was the only patron in the library, and the hushed whispering had been unnecessary. Nevertheless, she continued to whisper when she brought her selection,

Villette by Charlotte Brontë, to the circulation desk.

"Ah, a fine choice, Clare. I'm sure you'll enjoy it," Mrs. Brooks said as she stamped a date onto the date due card and the pocket that had contained it. She also gave Clare her new library card, made of heavy green cardstock.

"Thank you, Mrs. Brooks. It was very nice to meet you," Clare said as she put the book into her tote bag and left the library. She next strolled over to McCall's Department Store and picked out two inexpensive cotton nightgowns. She would have liked to purchase more clothing but thought she had better wait until she got paid again.

Walking back to the boarding house, Clare decided to make a detour to the Salerno Bakery. The smell of bread greeted her as she neared the shop. When she entered the store, she saw that this time her grandmother was at the counter helping customers select some bread. It gave Clare a chance to look around the shop while she waited. The floorboards she knew as well-worn were new and did not creak under her footsteps. When the other customers had paid and left, Clare made her way over to the cases to examine the selection. She decided on cannoli and asked for six of them: one for her, one for Anna, and one for Kay and her brother and parents. Her grandmother placed them in a little paper box that she tied up with string. Clare paid her and left, wistfully longing to talk with her and reveal her identity. The ginger cat appeared out of nowhere, rubbed against her legs for a moment, and then went on his way.

When Clare returned to Mrs. Harrigan's, she found Anna still sitting in the kitchen, rolling out a new batch of dough.

"Ah, Clare, shall we have lunch now?" Anna asked as she rose to fill a large pot with water for the pierogi.

"I'd like that, and I brought dessert for us, too"

Clare answered, showing her the box from the bakery. Anna prepared the pierogi and topped them with melted butter. There were a few of each kind to sample. Clare tried one and was surprised to find it light and tasty, not doughy or greasy.

"These are wonderful!" Clare cried. "You should open a restaurant."

"Well, maybe someday. But for now I do sell my breads and some of the other dishes I make to a few of the local restaurants. That's why I'm down here in the kitchen so much," Anna explained. Clare had been wondering about that. She had also noticed that Anna wore a wedding ring but had not mentioned a husband.

"Have you lived here long?" Clare asked.

"It depends what you mean by 'here.' Here in this boarding house for just one year. I moved in when my son enlisted in the Marines. He had just turned seventeen, and I couldn't stop him any longer. Before that, we had a small apartment, but I decided not to stay there by myself. My husband Karol was killed in an accident in the mines ten years ago, and we've been on our own ever since. Karol and I came from Poland almost twenty years ago now."

"Oh, I'm so sorry about your husband," Clare said.

"Yes, it was very hard at first, but at least I had Gregory to keep me busy. Now I just pray that he returns safely."

"I'm sure he will," Clare said awkwardly, realizing she could not be sure of this at all. It occurred to her that the window on the second floor with the flag in it must belong to Anna. The flag had a single blue star on a field of white bordered by red, signifying having a son in the service.

When they had eaten the pierogi, Clare cut the string on the bakery box and offered a cannoli to Anna;

they ate the sweet ricotta-filled tubes of pastry.

"This is very good," Anna said. "Have you eaten these before?"

"Oh, yes, many times. My grandparents were from Italy, and they had a bakery. They used to make them all the time."

"What part of Italy did they come from?"

"Salerno, in the south," Clare explained.

"Salerno? Just like the bakery here. Maybe the Russos who own the bakery know your grandparents?" Anna suggested.

"Oh, I doubt that. They moved here a long time ago, to Schenectady."

"Still, I'll bet the Russos would be very happy to know you. Clara is a very nice lady."

"Yes, she seemed nice in the store. I'll have to introduce myself to her," Clare said, still not sure of what she could say to her grandmother.

Clare helped Anna clean up the lunch dishes and watched her make more pierogi. Then she went upstairs to relax a bit before going over to Kay's house. She took out her new book and read the first chapter. After a while, she decided to get ready to go. She had not thought about the dance too much before this point, but now she was beginning to feel a bit nervous. *I wonder if someone will ask me to dance,* Clare thought. *Or maybe no one will.* She was not sure which idea was worse.

Clare looked at the three pairs of canvas shoes she had purchased from McCall's. None of them really went with the green dress. She decided on the black pair and hoped no one would pay too much attention to them. She reasoned that the boys would probably just be happy to see some women and would not notice something like shoes.

Clare retrieved the remaining cannoli from the

kitchen and walked over to Kay's house. Eddie and some of his friends were playing a game of catch in the yard, and he shyly said hello to Clare when she walked up to the front porch. Clare rang the doorbell, and Kay bounded down the stairs and opened the door.

"Come on in, Clare! I'm so happy you're here," Kay said, leading Clare inside. "We'll get ready together. It's so much more fun to have someone to go with. Nell won't ever go with me 'cause of Johnny. I tell her it's okay just to dance with the boys, but she says no, she'd rather do something like rolling bandages to help out. That's fine, too, but not so much fun. If you can help your country just by having a good time dancing, then why not, I say!"

Clare smiled and handed the bakery box to Kay.

"I brought these for you and your family," she explained.

"Oh, that's swell, Clare. They're from that nice Italian bakery. I'll put it in the kitchen," Kay said, disappearing for a moment.

"Shall we get ready?" Kay asked, pulling Clare up the stairs with her. They went into her bedroom, and Kay put on a Glenn Miller record. She opened up the closet door, and took out the green dress for Clare. Then she selected a robin's egg blue dress for herself. They both changed into the dresses.

"Would you like me to do your hair?" Kay asked.

"Gee, would you, Kay? That would be swell," Clare replied. She sat down at the dressing table, and Kay began to style her hair.

"How's that?" Kay asked after a few minutes of work. Clare admired the bobby-pinned rolls that Kay had carefully created.

"It's fantastic, Kay! Thanks a million." Clare got up, and Kay took her place at the mirror. She deftly styled her own hair in a fashion that was similar but not quite the same. The girls then applied lipstick and a dab of perfume behind each ear. Kay pulled Clare next to her in front of the mirror.

"Look at us! Don't we look like a million bucks?" Kay exclaimed. Clare had to admit they did look quite attractive. As they walked down the stairs, Kay's father came through the front door.

"Oh, excuse me, ladies," he said. "I thought this was the O'Neill's house. I didn't realize I walked into some Hollywood starlet's house by mistake!"

"Oh, Pop, you're so silly," Kay said as she gave him a kiss on the cheek. Clare felt a sudden twinge of sadness. She *would* like to see her own father. What would he say if he saw her dressed up like this? Kay's mother emerged from the kitchen to admire them.

"Don't you girls look lovely? Now you go and have a good time at the dance," Mrs. O'Neill said.

"And don't let those boys get fresh with you," Mr. O'Neill added with a wink.

CHAPTER 10

    Clare and Kay walked the four blocks to the YMCA. Although she had never been inside, Clare knew the building well. They climbed the big marble steps and entered through massive wooden doors.

    "The dance is in the gymnasium," Kay explained. "There are rooms upstairs where the guys can read or write letters or listen to the radio. We girls just stay down here, though, to serve the drinks and doughnuts and dance."

    There were several small tables in the lobby with wooden folding chairs around them. Kay opened one of the heavy doors to the gym, and both girls went inside. A line of long rectangular tables was at one end of the room, and at the other end a group of musicians was setting up their instruments.

    "Oh, there's a real band here," remarked Clare with surprise.

    "Yes, there usually is a few times a month. The rest of the time there are just records, but the boys don't seem to mind too much. Tonight it's Mort Lester and his Laurelhoppers," Kay explained. Clare involuntarily wrinkled her nose and silently hoped they sounded better than their name suggested.

    "They're really very good," Kay said, as if reading

Clare's thoughts. "They have a girl singer, too. Betty Wilton. She's terrific. I think she'll be a big star one day." Clare had her doubts about that, but she did not mention it.

A few other girls had trickled in while Kay and Clare were talking. Kay brought Clare over to them and introduced her. They seemed genuinely friendly to Clare, which surprised her a bit. She thought they might consider her to be competition. Since there were no men at Penllyn, there was always a bit of a rivalry when they met the male students from Glenmere College. Clare reminded herself they were not there to meet men to date anyway, just to cheer them up while they were on leave tonight.

Some of the other young women who worked at Kingsley's arrived, as well as a few salesgirls Clare recognized from McCall's. By seven o'clock, there were about fifty women there: brunettes, blondes, redheads, short, tall, and in-between. Each had obviously paid careful attention to her hair, make-up, and outfit. Clare knew she was not the prettiest girl there, but she did not think she was the most unattractive one either.

A group of three older women in their fifties came in together and made their way to a position behind the tables. Conversations trailed away, and the room became quiet.

"Good evening, girls," one of the women began. "I see some new faces here tonight, so please allow me to introduce ourselves and review the rules for the dance. I'm Mrs. Prescott and this is Mrs. Lincoln and Mrs. Banks," she said, gesturing to the two women beside her. "We are the Laurelmont USO dance committee and will be overseeing everything tonight. The doors will open at seven-thirty, and we'll start serving coffee, punch, and doughnuts. The band will start playing at eight o'clock. We're fortunate enough to have Mr. Lester and his musicians here again tonight. They will play until ten o'clock with a half-hour break. You girls will serve refreshments for the first hour and dance for the second hour or vice versa. Mrs. Banks will explain the rules of conduct now."

"Thank you, Mrs. Prescott," began Mrs. Banks. "And thank you, ladies, for volunteering your time this evening. Naturally, we have a few ground rules that must be observed for tonight's entertainment. First, you must be pleasant and courteous to all men. However, you must not be *too* pleasant. Socializing with the men outside of the dance or making a date with them is strictly forbidden, as is giving the men your address or telephone number." At this Kay gave Clare a wink.

"As you will be dancing with the men, is it permissible to hold their hand when appropriate, but any other physical contact or displays of affection are prohibited. Many of you have brothers, fiancés, or even husbands in the service. Remember that these men are probably somebody's brother, fiancé, or husband. You should treat them how you would want your own loved one treated by a woman in a strange town. Ask them about their hometowns, their families, and their girls. Keep the conversation upbeat, and do not talk to them about where they may be going or what dangers may await them. Does anyone have any questions?"

No one raised her hand, so the girls began dividing themselves up into the group who would dance first and the group who would serve first. Kay said she preferred to serve the refreshments first and Clare agreed. They put on white aprons, and then they busied themselves setting up the trays of doughnuts, punch bowls, and coffee urns. At seven-thirty, Mrs. Lincoln and Mrs. Banks opened the doors to the gymnasium. A crowd of men had already formed in the lobby and began filing inside. The older women greeted each man as he came through the door and pointed him to the refreshments.

Clare was overwhelmed at the sight of so many men approaching. When the crowd got close enough so that she could make out individual faces, she was immediately struck by how young most of them looked. They were boys, really, not men. She was sure many of them were not even as old as she was. Although she had known most servicemen were only in their late teens or early twenties, all the movies about the war featured men like John Wayne and Dana Andrews who were obviously much too old. It was only now, seeing these servicemen, that she fully appreciated just how young they were.

Clare and Kay were stationed together at a punch bowl. A group of three sailors came up to them first. Clare stared at them with amusement; she thought they looked as if they walked off the set of *On the Town*.

"Hello, sailors! Can I get you some punch?" Kay asked as she began filling cups with a big silver ladle.

"Thanks, doll! Save me a dance!" the oldest one said to Kay as he took the cup from her. Kay continued ladling until she noticed Clare was just standing beside her dumbly. She gave her a little jab with her elbow.

"Go on," Kay said quietly, handing her another ladle.

"Sorry," Clare whispered. A large group of GIs was approaching. Clare filled a cup before they reached the table. *Okay, you're on*, she told herself.

"Hi there, boys! Would you like some punch?" she said gaily. She felt a bit silly, but the men responded with enthusiasm. She doled out the punch to an orderly line of Army privates while Kay served a rowdy group of Marines. Finally Clare reached the last man of the line.

"Here you go, Private," she said, handing him a

cup.

"Thank you, miss. It's awful nice of you to do this for us," he said with a grin. Clare paused and looked at him for a moment. The line had moved so fast that she really had not paid much attention to individual men. The soldier in front of her looked to be a bit older than her with fair hair and light eyes. He was slim but muscular with a fine, straight nose and a strong jaw. He was very handsome, Clare decided. All the men were handsome in their uniforms, but this one might have caught her eye even without the uniform. And yet there was something familiar about him. She had not seen him in Kingsley's or around town, of that she was certain, but she felt sure she had seen him *somewhere*.

"Oh, it's nothing, really, compared to what you're doing for us," Clare said, returning his smile.

"Miss, could I have a dance with you later?" he asked.

"Oh, that would be swell," Clare replied, beaming. "I'm Clare. Clare Carlyle."

"I'm Roy. Roy Humphrey," the young man said.

"I'm very glad to meet you, Roy. Now don't forget to find me for that dance."

Roy took his punch and went back to the crowd of men. Clare continued to serve a steady stream of sailors, Marines, and GIs. All of the men were polite, and many were quite attractive, yet she found her eyes wandering to the crowd to see if she could spot Roy. Although he was about average height, maybe five-foot nine, something about his bearing made him stand out from the other men to Clare, and she could not help searching for him.

At eight o'clock, Mrs. Lincoln went to the front of the room to introduce the band. Half of the girls took off their aprons and went out into the center of the gym, which was now the dance floor.

"Wasn't that fun?" Kay asked.

"Yes, the boys were all very nice. And one of them asked me to dance."

"One? A lot more will ask you than just one! Was it the blond one I saw you talking with?"

"Yes, do you know him?" Clare asked.

"No, I've never seen him before."

"Oh, I feel like I've seen him somewhere, but I can't think where."

"I've never seen him in Laurelmont. Maybe you saw him in Schenectady?"

"Maybe," Clare answered, but of course she had not.

"Well, I'm going to take over the doughnuts now. Think you can handle the punch on your own?" Kay asked.

"Aye, aye, Captain," Clare said, saluting.

The lights dimmed slightly, and the Laurelhoppers began playing their first notes. Clare recognized the song as "Moonlight Serenade" immediately. Although Mort Lester was no Glenn Miller, the band did not sound bad at all. The dance floor filled up quickly. Clare scanned the crowd and felt a stab of jealousy when she saw Roy dancing with a pretty redhead. *Oh, Clare, what's the matter with you,* she chided. *He's here to have a good time. Do you really expect him not to dance with anyone else but you?* She was annoyed with herself for the petty jealousy and was glad for the distraction when two Marines came over to her for some punch.

After the first song, Mort Lester introduced the band members to much applause.

"Now, ladies and gentlemen, I'm delighted to introduce the lovely Betty Wilton to sing the next song." Applause broke out again, along with a few wolf whistles, as a beautiful woman with platinum blonde hair wearing a scarlet dress came to the microphone. She began to sing "Don't Sit Under the Apple Tree" in a clear, sweet voice that filled the room. Clare had to admit she was very good. She studied the crowd again. A wave of relief washed over her, followed closely by shame, when she saw that Roy was not dancing with anyone.

"How about some punch?" a sailor asked.

"Oh, yes, sorry. Here you go." When Clare looked back out into the room, Roy was no longer where he had been standing. Then she realized he was at the doughnut table talking to Kay. He selected a doughnut and started walking toward Clare.

"Hello Roy, are you enjoying yourself?" Clare asked.

"The band is swell. Would you like a doughnut?"

"Gee, thanks, but I don't think I'm supposed to. They're just for you."

"Well, I'd like to share mine with you," he said, breaking the doughnut in half and giving her a piece.

"That's awful sweet of you, Roy," Clare said, nibbling on the doughnut. She filled another cup with punch and handed it to him. "Where are you from, Roy?"

"I'm from Toledo, Ohio. Well, I was born in Tennessee, but I've lived in Ohio for a long time. Are you from Laurelmont?"

"Yes, I mean I live in Laurelmont now. But I'm from Schenectady, New York, originally."

"Oh, I've never been there. In fact, this the first time I've been this far east. We're getting closer and closer to the coast. I guess we'll be shipping out soon."

"What did you do in Toledo?" Clare asked.

"I was a welder at the Willys jeep factory," he answered.

"That's pretty important work. You probably could

have gotten a deferment from the draft." The look on Roy's face made her instantly regret saying it.

"I wasn't drafted. I enlisted last year. I want to do my part," he said seriously. "What do you do when you're not serving punch, Clare?"

"I work at the five-and-dime," she replied sheepishly. "I only just moved here, and it's the first job I found, but someday I'd like to do something more important."

"Well, I think your being here is mighty important. It's done wonders for my morale," Roy said, grinning. A small group of soldiers came toward them. "I'd better let you get back to doing your duty."

Clare served the men and watched the dancers. She soon saw Roy jitterbugging to "Sing, Sing, Sing." He was a good dancer, and he expertly twirled and turned his attractive partner. Any feelings of jealousy Clare had were now drowned out by insecurity about her dancing ability.

After the band played for about forty-five minutes, Mort Lester announced they would take a half-hour break. The lights brightened, and the dancers dispersed. The girls who had been dancing made their way back to the serving tables and donned their aprons again. Kay returned to Clare at the punch bowl.

"Are you having a good time?" Kay asked.

"Sure, swell," Clare answered.

"Your private is a nice young man," Kay said. "I saw him talking to you a lot."

"Yes, but he danced with a lot of other girls. And he's a good dancer. Maybe he'll dance with me once and not want to dance with me again."

"Oh, Clare, don't be silly. Look, here he comes now."

"Hello, Clare," Roy said.

"Hi Roy, this is my friend Kay."

"Yes, we met at the doughnuts," he answered.

"Oh, of course. Would you like some more punch?" Clare asked.

"No thanks. Honestly, I don't even like punch, but I just wanted to talk to you." Clare felt herself blushing and turned to see that Kay was no longer beside her. "Do you think you're done serving punch now?" Roy asked.

Clare looked around and saw that the other girls who had been serving had taken off their aprons and were beginning to mingle with the men. "I guess it's okay," she said, untying the apron and folding it on the table.

"Do you want to sit in the lobby until the music starts again?" he asked.

"Sure," Clare answered, and she followed him out of the gymnasium and into the lobby. One of the small tables was vacant, and Roy pulled out the chair for her. *How polite,* she thought. *Men don't do that anymore.*

Once they were seated across from each other, Clare found herself staring at him, first at his face and then his uniform. The tiny crossed rifles on his collar insignia indicated he was in the infantry.

"Is everything all right, Clare? You're looking at me funny."

"Oh, Roy, I'm sorry. It's just that I feel like I've seen you somewhere before."

"Well, I know I've never seen you before, Clare. I'm sure I'd remember if I had."

"You're a very good dancer," she said, changing the subject.

"Thanks, Clare. Do you like to dance?"

"Yes, but I don't get to very often, so I'm afraid I might not be as good as the other girls."

"Aw, Clare, I'm sure that's not true. Can I ask you

how old you are?"

"I'm nineteen. How old are you?"

"I'm twenty-one. Do you have a sweetheart?"

"No. Do you have a girl back home?"

"No, there's no one special in Toledo."

"Do you know what you want to do after the war?" Clare asked.

"No, I dunno. I don't know if I'll want to go back to welding, but I don't know anything else."

"Well, you could go to college," Clare suggested.

"Oh, I don't think I could afford that. No one in my family has been to college, anyway."

"But the government will pay your tuition. Lots of guys will go to college that wouldn't have had the chance otherwise. You know, the GI Bill ... "

"Yeah? I never heard about that. How do you know so much about it? And who's this GI Bill, anyway?" Roy asked.

"No, not *who*. It's a new law. Or it will be soon, I guess. I, uh, I think I read something about it in the newspaper."

"Well, that would be nice. I'll have to think about that."

From the gym they could hear the musicians begin tuning their instruments again. Mrs. Lincoln announced that the music would resume momentarily.

"Shall we go dance now?" Roy asked.

"I'd love to," Clare answered, and Roy took her hand and led her back into the gymnasium. They made their way to the middle of the dance floor. Clare was pleased to hear the opening notes of "Frenesi" as Roy took her in his arms. He had a strong lead, and Clare had no trouble following as they fox-trotted around the room, deftly avoiding the other couples. When the last notes faded, Roy released her from his embrace, and they applauded enthusiastically.

"You're a wonderful dancer, Clare. You were just pulling my leg about not being good."

Before Clare could respond, a sailor approached them. "Mind if I cut in, pal?" he said to Roy. Clare looked at Roy, hopeful he would refuse.

"Go ahead, sailor. Just bring her back in one piece."

The sailor took Clare's hand. Before she knew it, he was twirling her around to "In the Mood."

"I'm Sal, doll. What's your name?"

"Clare. Where are you from, Sal?"

"I'm from Brooklyn. Can't you tell?" he said with a strong accent.

By the end of the song, Clare was breathless. As they applauded, she saw that Roy was on the other side of the room; he had just finished dancing with Peggy from the five-and-dime. Before she could catch his eye, a tall Marine with two stripes on his arm came over to her. She danced with the corporal to "Maria Elena," happy for the slower pace of the song. When it ended, a sergeant who wore the propeller and wings insignia of the Army Air Forces on his uniform, the same insignia as on Clare's charm, approached.

"May I have this dance, miss?" he asked politely.

"Sure thing, Sergeant," Clare replied. Roy was nowhere in sight now. "Are you a pilot?" Clare asked.

"Oh, no. I'm a waist gunner on a B-17. I'm hoping to finally get some action after all this training."

The band played a lively instrumental version of "Boogie Woogie Bugle Boy." The airman skillfully led her through steps she had not even learned in her class at Penllyn. The men all knew how to lead. It was much easier than dancing with the boys from Glenmere had been, and

Clare felt more confident now. When the song ended, she was happy to see that Roy, who had been dancing with Kay, was now near her again.

"May I cut in, Sergeant?" Roy asked the gunner.

"I suppose so, Private," he replied reluctantly.

Although she had enjoyed dancing with all the men, Clare felt a thrill when Roy took her hand again. Betty Wilton began singing "I Had the Craziest Dream." Clare smiled as she gazed into Roy's blue-gray eyes. *Goodness, I am having the craziest dream,* she thought. She was sorry when the song ended, and a sailor appeared at their elbows to take her away, but she could not refuse him. After a few more dances, she again found herself partnered with Roy. This time Betty sang a rousing version of "Bei Mir Bist Du Schön." This was Clare's first jitterbug with Roy, and his turns and twirls left her breathless and dizzy. She leaned against him slightly when the music stopped, and he put his arm around her. After the applause died down, Mrs. Lincoln returned to the position in front of the band again.

"Ladies and gentlemen, our evening is almost over. Before we hear our last song from Mr. Lester and the Laurelhoppers, we want to thank you all for coming tonight. And on behalf of the citizens of Laurelmont, we wish you boys good luck and thank you for your service to our nation." Mrs. Lincoln retreated from the microphone to a round of polite applause, and Betty Wilton took her place there for the final number. A GI approached Roy and Clare.

"Mind if I cut in, buddy?" he asked Roy. Clare looked anxiously at Roy and felt him tighten his grip on her arm.

"Sorry, pal," Roy said. "Not this time." He drew Clare close as Betty began singing "I'll Be Seeing You." Clare rested her head on Roy's shoulder and hoped that the song would never end. But of course it did. The lights came back on, and the couples slowly left the dance floor.

"Gee, Clare, I had a swell time tonight," Roy said. "This was the best time I ever had at one of these dances. I'm awful glad I met you."

"Me, too," Clare replied as they walked back to the lobby of the YMCA.

"Clare, can I ask you something?"

"Sure, Roy. What is it?"

"Would you write to me? I think I'm going overseas real soon, and it would mean an awful lot to me."

"Of course, Roy. But I'm not allowed to give you my address."

"That's okay. I can give you mine."

Clare reached into her handbag and tore out a piece of paper from her little notebook. She handed it to Roy along with her pencil. He took the paper and pencil and wrote:

Pvt. Roy W. Humphrey
15102940
Co. G, 2nd Battalion
7th Infantry Regiment, 3rd Division
c/o PM, New York, NY

Clare took the paper with the address from Roy. Suddenly she had an idea.

"They said we're not supposed to tell you where we live, but they didn't say anything about where we work!" She wrote down her name and the address of Kingsley's on Main Street. Reflexively she wrote down the Laurelmont zip code and then scratched it out. She was pretty sure they did not have those yet.

"Thanks, Clare. Can I ask you something else?

Would you send me a picture?"

"I'll try, Roy. I don't have one, but I'll try to get one taken for you." Before Roy could respond, two soldiers came up to them.

"There you are, Trigger. We've got to get going now," one of them said.

"Looks like he found himself a honey. Give him another minute," the other one said, and they walked a few paces away.

"Trigger?" Clare asked.

"Yeah, like Roy Rogers's horse. Plus I'm pretty handy with a rifle, so it stuck."

"Wouldn't it be easier just to call you Roy?"

"Sure, but everyone's got a nickname, and I guess I like it better than 'Toledo' or 'Blondie,'" Roy explained with a laugh. "Well, I suppose I gotta go now. Goodbye, Clare."

"Goodbye, Roy," she said, and he started to turn away. "Roy?" He stopped and turned back to face her. Without thinking, Clare stepped toward him and kissed him softly on the lips. "Please be careful, Roy," she said. He looked surprised but pleased. Then he turned and ran toward his waiting buddies. Clare looked around to see if anyone had noticed. None of the other girls were paying attention, she realized with relief. She did not know what had come over her. It definitely was not like her to go around kissing men she had just met, but she was not sorry she had done it.

Clare walked back into the gym and donned her apron again. The men had left, and the musicians were putting away their instruments. She began to help clean up, slowly picking up empty cups and half-eaten doughnuts. Kay made her way over to Clare.

"There you are, Clare. Did you have a good time tonight?" Kay asked.

"Uh-huh."

"You spent a lot of time with that private."

"Uh-huh."

"Is that all you can say now?"

"Sorry, Kay. I'll tell you all about it later."

"This sounds like a good story. We'll stop by the diner for a milkshake. You can tell me everything then," Kay suggested. They finished cleaning up, returned the white aprons, and left the YMCA building.

Although it was almost eleven o'clock, the streets were still lit up as they walked to the diner.

"Well, look at you two!" Nell exclaimed when she saw them. "Did you steal any hearts tonight?"

"Not me, but I think Clare did," Kay said, and Clare felt her cheeks redden. "Two chocolate shakes, Sis." Nell mixed up the milkshakes and set them down in front of Kay and Clare.

"Okay, now tell us everything," Kay said. Clare looked around and saw that they were the only people in the diner.

"Well, I met someone. His name is Roy, and he's a private in the infantry, and he's from Ohio, and he was a welder before the war. That's about all I know. And he's a real good dancer."

"He was," Kay agreed. "I danced with him once. I think he just wanted to dance with me so he could ask me about you, though."

"He did? What did he ask?"

"He wanted to know if it was true that you really didn't have a sweetheart. And I told him it was true, as far as I know, anyway."

"So what does he look like?" Nell asked.

"He has blond hair and light eyes. Not too tall but not short, either. A handsome face."

"Yes," Kay agreed. "But how about that Marine corporal I saw you dancing with? He looked like a young Gary Cooper, don't you think?"

"I suppose so. He was nice. They were all nice. But there was just something about Roy. Plus I can't shake the feeling that I've seen him somewhere."

"So how did it end?" Kay asked.

"Well, he asked me if I'd write to him and if I'd send him a picture."

"And did you say yes?"

"Yes. And I kissed him."

"He kissed you?" Kay asked, her eyes widening.

"Well, no. I kissed him. He was just about to leave, and I stopped him and kissed him. I don't know what made me do it. I've never done anything like that before. I mean I've kissed boys before, but not someone I didn't really know."

"Clare, did anyone see you? You could get in big trouble for that. They wouldn't let you come to the dances anymore," Kay warned.

"I know. I don't think anyone saw me. And it won't happen again. I'm sure of that."

"Well, that sounds like quite an evening, Clare. So are you going to write to him?" Nell asked.

"I suppose so. But I don't know what to write about. I barely know him."

"If you know him well enough to give him a kiss, then you certainly know him well enough to write him a letter!" Kay said.

"I suppose you're right," said Clare, laughing. "Well, what do you write about?"

"Oh, I don't know. Nothing serious. Movies I saw. New songs I heard. Things like that. I try to keep it upbeat and never complain about things like rationing. I figure they've got it a whole lot worse than us."

"That's true. Well, I guess I'll think of something. Do you know where I can get my picture taken?" Clare asked.

"There's Pendleton's Portrait Studio on Main Street. But if you want something faster, then there's a photo booth at Goldmiller's Drugstore. It's only a quarter for a sheet of eight." Kay suggested.

"That's a good idea," Clare said. "Would you do my hair for the picture?"

"Of course," Kay answered. "You should wear the green dress, too."

"Thanks, Kay! I don't know how I can ever thank you enough."

"Well, girls, let's go home now," Nell said. "I'm ready to close up for the night." Kay and Clare stood outside while Nell turned off the lights and locked the door of the diner. The neon airplane and globe went dark, and the girls began walking back to the O'Neill house. They were a few blocks away before Clare realized she had not even thought about returning to the future when she left the diner.

The front porch light was on when they reached the O'Neill house, but the lights inside the house were off. Nell unlocked the door, and the girls silently entered the front parlor. Nell went to the kitchen while Kay and Clare went upstairs. Clare changed back into her own clothes.

"Why don't you take the dress home with you?" Kay suggested.

"Gee, thanks, Kay. I'll have it cleaned before I give it back to you. It was awful nice of you to take me with you tonight," Clare whispered. "I had a swell time."

"Me, too, Clare. We'll do it again next Saturday."

Clare walked back downstairs and said good night

to Nell. She left the O'Neill house and returned to Mrs. Harrigan's. The house was dark save for a tiny lamp in the parlor. She let herself in and went up to her room. She quickly threw off her clothes and put on her nightgown. Clare sank down onto the bed. She was too tired to write in her journal, but she did take out the paper where Roy had written his address and put it on her nightstand. She closed her eyes and replayed the scenes of the evening in her mind until she finally fell asleep.

CHAPTER 11

When Clare awoke on Sunday morning, she realized she had nothing to do for the whole day. She supposed most people would be going to church, but she was not accustomed to doing that. The stores would not be open, and there certainly would be no flea market to go to. Instead she lounged in bed and updated her journal with the events of the USO dance. It had begun to seem like a dream to her, but when she saw Roy's address on her nightstand she knew it was real. What could she write to him about, she wondered. She would have to buy some stationery on Monday, but in the meantime she decided she would spend the day trying to compose a letter to Roy.

Clare got up and dressed. She realized she would also have to figure out how to do laundry, but first she started on a draft of the letter. After an hour of writing and erasing, she finally composed something that satisfied her. She did not want to wait until next Saturday to get her picture taken, so she decided she would go to Goldmiller's on her lunch break the next day, even if it meant not wearing the green dress or having Kay do her hair. *I hope Roy won't be too disappointed when he sees how I really look,* she thought.

Next Clare decided to tackle the laundry. She

bundled up her clothes and walked downstairs. The parlor and kitchen were empty; she guessed the other residents were still at church. She found the door to the basement and cautiously made her way down the rickety wooden steps. The basement was dimly lit and dank. The washing machine, an old-fashioned tub kind with the wringer attached, stood in one corner. Clare looked at it closely. It was very different from the modern washing machines she had used. After examining it for some minutes, she decided she would have to watch Anna using it before she would be brave enough to try it on her own. In the meantime, she would wash her clothes out by hand in the bathtub instead. After she had done so, she hung them up to dry outside on a clothesline she found in the small backyard.

Since the day was fine, Clare went for a walk, taking her book and stopping in the park to read. After a few hours, she returned home, as she now thought of the boarding house, and checked on her drying clothes. They were mostly dry, so she brought them inside with her. Several ladies sat in the parlor, gathered around the radio listening intently to what sounded like a soap opera. Clare greeted them but did not feel like staying to listen. She returned to her room and hung up the clothes. She looked at the draft of the letter again, made a few more changes, and then read for a while. Wandering back downstairs, she found Anna cooking in the kitchen. Clare sat down at the table to talk with her. She told Anna about the USO dance, omitting the part about Roy, and Anna told Clare more about her son.

Later Clare went back to her room. She would have to find more things to occupy her time on the weekends. *Maybe I could volunteer to do something more useful*, she thought. She went to bed early that night, looking forward to the next day.

On Monday morning, Clare carefully dressed for work, putting on the yellow blouse and blue skirt. She decided she would need to buy more clothes and a dress of her own next weekend if she could afford it. After a quick breakfast, Clare left for work. She arrived at Kingsley's just as Kay got there, and they walked into the locker room together and put on their pinafores.

"Kay, I'm going to have my picture taken in the photo booth at Goldmiller's today at lunchtime. Will you come with me?"

"Of course, Clare. You changed your mind about getting all dressed up?"

"I don't want to wait until Saturday. I want to send it to Roy right away. How often do you send letters to all those fellas you write to?"

"It depends. Every day for some of them and just once a week for others."

"Maybe I'll try twice a week and see how it goes." Clare was not sure she could think of something to write every day.

At lunchtime, Clare and Kay walked over to Goldmiller's Drugstore. The photo booth was at the rear of the store, and Clare was relieved to see no one else was using it.

"Do you think I look okay?" Clare asked. "I hope Roy won't be too disappointed that I'm not dressed up."

"Don't be silly. You look very pretty. I think the more natural look suits you better anyway. You know, Nell and I were talking yesterday, and we think you look a lot like Gene Tierney."

"Oh, Kay, I don't know about that!" Clare did not know what Gene Tierney looked like, but she took it as a compliment. She combed her hair, put on fresh lipstick, and pulled back the curtain of the photo booth.

"Wish me luck," Clare said as she put a quarter into the coin slot and closed the curtain. A warning light flashed, and the camera snapped the first picture. After eight pictures, she left the booth and waited for a strip of photographs to emerge through an opening on the side. The two girls examined the pictures. Clare's eyes were closed in one photo, but she was pleased with the other seven.

"They look lovely, Clare. Roy will be very happy, I'm sure."

"Thanks, Kay. Say, why don't you get your picture taken now, too? It's my treat. I'm sure all those boys you write to would like a new picture."

"Oh, I don't know ... "

"Come on, I insist," Clare said as she put a quarter in the machine for Kay.

"Thanks, Clare," Kay said when her photos were ready. "Shall we have lunch here?" The girls ate at the small lunch counter of the drugstore. They had a few more minutes left of their break, so they browsed in the magazine aisle. Clare picked up a copy of *Photoplay* and was pleased and flattered to see a picture of beautiful Gene Tierney on the cover, although she was not sure she bore any resemblance to the actress at all.

Near the end of the day, Clare went to the stationery section of the five-and-dime and selected a set of pale pink notepaper with matching envelopes. She also picked out a package of V-mail stationery that folded to form its own envelope. She took them to Kay at the register and paid for them along with a fountain pen and ink. That evening Clare sat down at her dressing table to write her letter to Roy. She read over the draft from the day before, made a few more changes, and then started to copy the text onto the rose-colored paper. When she finished, she read it again to make sure there were no mistakes:

> June 21, 1943
> Dear Roy,
>
> I'm so very glad I met you at the USO dance in Laurelmont this past Saturday. You are a wonderful dancer, and I really enjoyed dancing with you, especially the last dance to "I'll Be Seeing You." Roy, I do hope I'll be seeing you again soon. I've enclosed two pictures that I had taken at the photo booth in the drugstore today. I hope you won't be too disappointed to see that I am not all dressed up and don't have a fancy hairstyle, but this is how I usually look.
>
> I wish we had gotten more time to talk at the dance. I would like to know more about you. Do you come from a large family? Do you have brothers and sisters? I am an only child, but my friend Kay, who was serving doughnuts at the dance, is starting to feel like a sister to me. She was the one who convinced me to come to the dance, and I'm sure glad I did!
>
> Roy, about what I did when I was saying goodbye to you, well, I hope you do not think me too forward. I do not usually go around kissing men I have just met, but it just felt right that I should give you a goodbye kiss. I hope you didn't mind too much.
>
> I will try to write to you often, although I'm afraid my letters might not be very interesting. I hope you will be able to write back to me and tell me that you are well. Please take care of yourself.
>
> Fondly,

Clare Carlyle

Satisfied with the letter, Clare folded it carefully and placed the two pictures she liked best between the sheets of paper. She inserted the folded sheets into the envelope, sealed it, addressed it, and affixed a three-cent stamp to the top right corner. The purple V-for-Victory stamp was in perfect condition, and it suddenly occurred to her how much her father would appreciate the stamp. She felt a twinge of sadness, then guilt when she realized that she really had not thought about her father or her previous life very much for the past few days.

The next morning, Clare dropped the letter in a mailbox on her way to work. She wondered if Roy would write to her or if he had forgotten about her already. She worried briefly that he met a different girl every Saturday night and had a whole harem writing to him.

Clare settled into a routine: working at the dime store during the day, home to the boarding house in the evening, dinner at the diner or with Anna, reading or listening to the radio in the parlor at night. On Friday she was happy to receive another paycheck. As she was opening it, Mrs. Dietrich approached her with another envelope.

"This letter came for you today," she said sternly as she handed it to Clare. It was a letter from Roy.

"Thank you, Mrs. Dietrich. I hope it's all right that this came to me here."

"Normally only the managers receive mail at the store, but I suppose we can make an exception in your case since you may not have a permanent address yet."

"Thank you, Mrs. Dietrich," Clare said, anxious to leave. When Clare and Kay walked out of the store, Clare produced the envelope from her purse.

"Look Kay, I got a letter from Roy! He didn't

forget about me after all!" she said with excitement.

"So what does it say?" Kay asked.

"I don't know. I haven't opened it yet."

"Well, what are you waiting for?"

"I don't know. I think I want to wait until I get home."

"Okay, but you'll tell me what he wrote tomorrow, right?"

"Of course, Kay. I think I want to buy some more clothes tomorrow and maybe a dress. Do you want to come with me?"

"Sure. Shall we meet at McCall's at noon?"

"That's sounds swell. And I promise I'll bring the letter."

The girls walked together until Kay had to turn onto a different street to take her home. Clare continued along until she reached the boarding house. She went inside to her room, placed the letter on her dressing table, and went to dinner. Afterward, she came back and sat down to read the letter. She carefully opened the V-mail and read:

June 20, 1943

Dear Clare,

I hope you remember me from the dance on Saturday night. I wanted to write to you right away since we are shipping out real soon. By the time you get this letter I will be on my way overseas. I had an awful nice time at the dance. I think you are a swell dancer, and I wish I could have danced every dance with you, but it wouldn't have been fair to the other guys.

I hope you will write to me like you said. Letters from home, especially from a pretty girl like you, are what keep us fellows going. I may not be able to write too often, and it could be awhile before you hear from me again, but you shouldn't worry. I hope you don't mind, but I asked my mother to send you a picture of me. She insisted I have my portrait taken the last time I was home on leave. I don't know what she'll do with so many of them, so I thought she could send one to you.

I want to thank you for the good night kiss you gave me – or was that a dream? I will remember that for a long time. I don't think I will have another chance for dancing – or kissing – where I am headed for a while.

Yours truly,

Roy H.

Clare read the letter again. And again. She was pleased with it. She noted that he had lovely penmanship. She felt embarrassed by her own handwriting and wondered why no one from her generation had such nice penmanship anymore. She decided to answer his letter right away, and drafted the text on a scrap of paper before transferring it to a sheet of V-mail stationery. She wrote:

June 25, 1943

Dear Roy,

I was very pleased to receive your letter today. It was the highlight of my week! I hope it will not take too long for you to receive my letters. Thank you for asking your mother to send me your picture. I will be very happy to have it. I can understand why she wanted you to have your portrait taken. She must be very proud of you.

Right now I rent a room in a boarding house. It's very neat and clean, but a little lonely. The other women who live here are very nice, but most of them are a lot older than me, and we don't have too much in common. Sometimes I sit with them and listen to the radio at night. I have one friend here, Anna, who isn't as old as the others, but she is still old enough to have a son in the service. She is from Poland and is teaching me how to cook food from her homeland.

When I moved to Laurelmont I didn't take many things with me, so tomorrow I am going shopping for some new clothes. My friend Kay will come with me to give me some advice. She's very knowledgeable about things like fashion and hairstyling.

Roy, I hope you are doing well. Take care of yourself and know that I am thinking about you.

Fondly,
Clare

Clare mailed the letter to Roy on her way to McCall's on Saturday. When she got to the store, she found Kay waiting for her on a bench beside the door. The girls went inside and spent the afternoon trying on new outfits, hats, and shoes. Clare finally settled on another blouse and skirt, plus two inexpensive cotton dresses. One was a red and white gingham check with a ruffle around the neckline, while the other had a floral print on a yellow background. She felt she could wear them to work or to the dance.

Their shopping complete, Clare and Kay stopped at the soda fountain of Goldmiller's Drugstore for a snack. As they sipped their ice cream sodas, Kay said, "Well, you've kept me in suspense long enough. What was the letter from Roy like?"

In response, Clare pulled out the letter from her purse and handed it to Kay. She read it carefully and gave it back.

"Oh, that's a real nice letter. I get lots of letters, and

most of them aren't as nicely written as this one. You were lucky to meet him. Who knows who you'll meet tonight? You'll have a whole collection of pen pals in no time."

"Gee, I don't think I want to write to a whole bunch of guys. I think Roy is enough for now."

"Well, then you had better not go around kissing anyone tonight."

"I don't think that will happen again, Kay. Well, I'll make sure it doesn't, anyway," Clare said firmly.

After they finished their sodas, the girls went back to Kay's house to get ready for the dance. Clare wore the gingham dress and Kay styled her hair. They arrived at the YMCA and found there would be no band this time, just records. Again Clare and Kay served refreshments, this time lemonade and cookies, to the throngs of young servicemen. When it was their turn to dance, they were twirled around the room to the sounds of Count Basie, Sammy Kaye, and Duke Ellington. Clare had a wonderful time and quickly felt confident dancing. She was relieved to find that she did not feel herself drawn to one man in particular and was not asked to write to anyone.

On Sunday, Clare wrote another letter to Roy and spent the rest of the day relaxing. The workweek passed quickly, and she was excited to find two letters along with her paycheck on Friday afternoon. The first bore Roy's now familiar handwriting. The second, marked "Do Not Bend," had an Ohio postmark. Again Clare waited until after dinner to open the letters. First she opened the one from Roy and read:

June 24, 1943
Dear Clare,
I hope this letter finds you well. I wanted to send you a quick note while I had a moment. I am aboard a

large ocean liner right now. It used to be luxurious, but no more – we are packed in like sardines. But I can't complain too much. The chow is good, and they play records for us and even show some movies. We have just found out where we are headed. I wish I could tell you, but the censor would just cut it out. It's someplace I certainly never expected to see. Let's just say if I wanted a camel, I wouldn't have to walk a mile!

Clare, I was thinking about what you said about the government paying for us to go to college after the war. I don't know if you're right about that, but I hope you are. I think it might be a good idea. I wasn't the best student in high school, but I wasn't the worst one, either. There's nothing wrong with being a welder, but maybe I'll look into what you can study in college. I always kind of liked taking things apart and seeing how they worked. I guess maybe that would be some kind of engineering. Maybe there will be some jobs in that area after the war.

Well, I will close for now, Clare. Take care and don't worry about me.

Yours truly,

Roy

Clare reread the letter several times. She gathered that he must be on his way to North Africa. Clare knew that the fighting was done there, and the next big action would be the invasion of Sicily. She could not remember the date when that would happen but figured it must be soon.

Carefully opening the second envelope, Clare extracted the folded letter within. Between the sheets of onionskin paper were two wallet-sized photographs of Roy taken in a studio. One was a full-length portrait, and he stood stiffly in front of a painted background with a serious expression. He looked trim and dashing in his uniform and cap. In the second picture, a close-up, the hint of a smile played on his lips, and he looked as handsome as Clare remembered him. Clare studied the pictures closely and then read the accompanying letter:

June 27, 1943
Dear Miss Carlyle,

My son Roy asked me to write to you and send you his picture. I have enclosed two photographs taken earlier this year. Roy told me he met you at a USO dance. You must be a very special girl as he has never asked me to do this before. Roy said you were very pretty, plus smart and well-mannered, too. I would like to meet you someday. If you are ever in Toledo, please do look me up.

It's very good of you to entertain the boys at the USO dances. I try to keep busy with my job at the Electric Autolite Company to keep from worrying about Roy and my other son too much. Although I'm very proud of them, I just want them to come back home as soon as they can. I hope you will keep your promise and write to Roy. I know it means a lot to him.

Sincerely,
Mrs. Zetta Humphrey

Clare was now free to stare at Roy's visage and ponder where she could have seen him before. Her mind drew a blank; in the end, she concluded he must remind her of an actor on television or something like that. She resolved to puzzle over it no more.

On Saturday, Clare wrote to Mrs. Humphrey, thanking her for the pictures and assuring her she would continue to write to her son. She then penned another letter to Roy:

July 3, 1943
Dear Roy,

I hope you are doing well. I was delighted to receive letters from both you and your mother yesterday. It was so nice of your mother to write and send me your picture. Two pictures, actually! You look very handsome in your uniform. I hope your trip is over, and you were not seasick at all! I have a pretty good idea of where you are now. It must be very interesting to see that part of the world. I hope I will be able to travel a lot someday, too.

I think your idea of studying engineering is a very good one. I'm sure there will be many opportunities for all kinds of engineers after the war.

Tomorrow is the Fourth of July, and I am going on a picnic with Kay and her family in the park. Then we will watch the Independence Day parade through downtown Laurelmont. I'll be thinking of you and all the servicemen who are fighting for our freedom now with much gratitude. Please take care of yourself.

Fondly,
Clare

That night Clare and Kay went to the dance at the

YMCA, as was now usual. Clare did spend the following day with the O'Neill family, first enjoying a picnic lunch and then watching the parade. Marching bands played rousing tunes while World War I veterans donned their uniforms again and paraded amidst military vehicles that had just come off the factory's assembly line and would soon be headed for combat. It was a stirring sight, and Clare felt a surge of patriotism like she had never experienced before.

Clare proudly showed the pictures of Roy to Kay and Nell, as well as to the girls at the five-and-dime. Everyone agreed that he looked like a very fine young man. Clare placed the pictures in a small, hinged double picture frame she purchased at the dime store and set the frame on her nightstand.

During the week, Clare anxiously read the newspaper each morning looking for word on the invasion of Sicily but saw nothing. On Friday, Clare received another letter from Roy. This time she opened it immediately, rather than waiting, and read:

> *June 30, 1943*
> *Dear Clare,*
>
> *I wanted to write and tell you that my ocean voyage is finally over. I'm sure happy to be on dry land again. As it happens, the land we are on is very dry! I was real excited to find three letters from you when our mail caught up with us today. Thank you for sending the pictures! You look beautiful, just like I remember you. I showed your picture to some of my buddies, and they wouldn't believe you were a regular girl I met at a USO dance. They said you must be a pinup girl, and I was just pretending to know you! I will keep one picture in the Bible my mother gave me and the other one in my helmet*

liner for good luck. That way I can look at you whenever I want!

You wanted to know a little more about me. I have an older brother, James, who has been in the Army for more than two years already. I think he is somewhere in the Pacific. I also have a younger sister, Lucille, who still lives at home. I sure do miss them both. Before I enlisted I used to like to play baseball and go fishing in Lake Erie when I wasn't working at the jeep factory. Sometimes my pals and I would take the train to Detroit or even Chicago for the weekend. Have you ever been to Chicago? We could have plenty of fun there, going dancing at all the nightclubs.

Well, it's almost time for dinner, so I'll say goodbye for now.

Yours truly,
Roy

On Saturday morning, Clare decided to go to the diner for breakfast. Nell was there, of course, looking as fresh as always. As she waited for Nell to scramble some eggs for her, Clare picked up the newspaper lying on the counter. The headline proclaimed: "Bitter Fighting on Sicily's Shores" and in smaller letters: "Allies Invade Island in Moonlight Attack." Clare eagerly scanned the July 10th edition, hoping for some word of Roy's division. The article detailed the midnight paratrooper assault, the early morning naval bombardment, and the amphibious landings by American, Canadian, and British troops earlier that day, but did not mention exactly which divisions were involved.

"Did you see the news?" Clare asked anxiously as Nell placed the scrambled eggs before her.

"Yes, I heard it on the radio this morning, too," Nell answered.

"I'm afraid Roy's there," Clare said glumly.

"Yes, I think Johnny is, too. I know he was in the Mediterranean, so I'm sure his destroyer must have been part of the invasion fleet."

"You don't seem too worried."

"Oh, I'm plenty worried, Clare, but that doesn't help anything."

"I guess you're right," Clare said as she toyed with the eggs. "Still, I don't think I can go to the dance tonight. It just doesn't seem right to go and have a good time while some men are out there fighting now."

"Clare, you have to go. What about all the boys who'll be there tonight? And Kay would be awfully disappointed, too."

"Okay, Nell. I'll go. But I don't think I'll feel like dancing this time."

Clare got ready for the dance at Kay's house as usual. She wore the green dress again but left her hair down this time. After two weeks of dancing to records, she was happy to see a live band. It was not the Laurelhoppers but Jerry Cunningham and his Hot Seven. The band had the whole gym jumping, but Clare decided to serve punch for both halves of the dance.

All evening long, anxiety gnawed at her as she wondered about Roy's part in the invasion and when she would hear from him again.

CHAPTER 12

The days dragged on for Clare. She intently read the reports from Sicily every morning and listened to the news on the radio every night. She closely followed the progress of the Third Division, of which Roy's infantry regiment was a part, as it made its way along the northern coast of Sicily. She eagerly read each new column from Ernie Pyle, hopeful the war correspondent might mention Roy or at very least his regiment. The progress of the war, which had seemed so abstract to her before, was now very real. She began to notice casualty lists printed in the newspaper. She read the names carefully. She knew that she would not recognize any of the names, but she felt it was the least she could do for these men who were giving everything for her freedom.

On Friday, July 23rd, Clare read about the capture of Palermo by General Patton's army. She wondered if Roy were there now, being showered with flowers and fruit by cheering Sicilians. She had not received a letter from him since the beginning of the month, but she tried not to worry. Nell had not heard from Johnny, either. They both concluded that the men must be very busy, and delivering mail could not be a priority now. Clare forced herself to go to the dance each Saturday with Kay. Although she did not feel like dancing, she did not want to disappoint the young men who came each week, and she found she was thankful for the distraction.

Clare's anxiety was relieved in early August when Mrs. Dietrich handed her an envelope with Roy's familiar script. She put the letter into her apron pocket and slipped into the locker room to read it when no one was looking. She saw with disappointment that it was dated before the invasion and had taken almost a month to reach her. She read quickly:

> *July 8, 1943*
> *Dear Clare,*
>
> *I hope you are well. I am doing fine. We have been spending a lot of time training this past week. We just found out exactly where we are going next and it's a big deal. I wish I could tell you, but I know by the time you get this letter it will be in all the newspapers and you'll know where I am. You shouldn't worry about me though. I've had the best training, and they don't call me Trigger for nothing!*
>
> *I was very excited to receive two more letters from you today. I hope you'll keep on writing to me although I think it will be awhile before I get any mail again. I keep all of your letters with me and look at your picture before I go to sleep every night. I think I'm the luckiest guy in the world to have a girl as wonderful as you writing to me!*
>
> *Yours truly,*
> *Roy*

Clare continued writing to Roy, usually two or three times a week, hoping he would eventually receive the letters. They seemed dull to her, but she figured maybe he was having enough excitement and did not mind reading her mundane letters.

On August 17th, Clare excitedly read the news that Messina had fallen. The Americans had beaten the British in the race to liberate the important city closest to mainland Italy. The German troops had retreated across the Straits of Messina leaving the entire island in the hands of the Allies. Clare saw with great excitement that troops of the Seventh Infantry Regiment of the Third Division were the first to enter the city. That was Roy's regiment, and she eagerly scanned the pictures in the newspaper thinking she might spot him. She imagined him parading through the city to cheering crowds and hoped he would be getting some well-deserved rest now.

That night, Clare and Kay went to the diner to celebrate the end of the Sicilian campaign with Nell. Nell had received a letter from Johnny that day, and the three girls were in high spirits, although Clare wished she had heard from Roy. Her wish was granted the next day when a letter arrived at the store for her. She tore it open right away and read:

July 20, 1943
Dear Clare,

By now I'm sure you know where I am. I still can't give you too many details, but the landings were not as bad as I expected, not where I was anyway. In fact, the sea was so rough that I was real glad to go ashore! Since then the fighting on Sicily has gotten tougher, but we are making good progress. Not too many guys have been hurt. In fact, the mosquitoes are more dangerous than the Italian army! A lot of guys have gotten malaria, but I'm fine. A lot of Italian soldiers have surrendered, so we are fighting more Germans now. The local people are very happy to see us and are glad we are kicking the Krauts off their beautiful island. I'd sure like to come back here after the war and see this place under better circumstances. I'd like to bring you here, too, Clare, and we could go swimming in the sea together.

I hope you are well. I think about you all the time and carry your picture with me everywhere. I had a dream about dancing with you the other night. I can't wait until I can come home and take you dancing!

Yours truly,

Roy

Clare read the letter with great relief. Although it was dated almost a month earlier, she felt sure that Roy was safe now that the fighting was over. Once more she had the feeling that she was watching a movie with a happy ending. She was able to enjoy her days at Kingsley's and the Saturday night dances with renewed enthusiasm.

The following week, Mort Lester and the Laurelhoppers played at the dance again. Clare was wearing the green dress and half expected to see Roy walk through the door of the gym. Of course he did not, but Clare did notice something unusual. A man in civilian clothes, his expensive pinstripe suit incongruous amidst the sea of uniforms, was earnestly talking with Mrs. Prescott. At first Clare thought he might have been a new member of the band, but later she saw Mort Lester introduce him to Betty Wilton. When the music started, the man retreated to Mrs. Lincoln's side. He watched the proceedings with interest but did not dance.

At ten o'clock, the notes of the last song faded, and the servicemen filed out of the gymnasium. Clare saw the man approach Betty Wilton again. He gave her a card and they shook hands. Clare wondered if he might be from a record company. *She is awfully good,* Clare thought. *Maybe she really will become famous.* As Clare and Kay cleaned up the remains of the refreshments, they were surprised to see Mrs. Banks leading the well-dressed man toward them.

"Girls, I'd like to introduce to you Mr. Hastings from the USO's New York headquarters," Mrs. Banks said as the man reached for their hands. "This is Kay O'Neill and Clare Carlyle."

"It's a pleasure to meet you, girls. I'm here tonight recruiting performers for a new USO tour we're putting together. I've asked Miss Wilton to join us and am very hopeful she will agree," said Mr. Hastings. "And that brings me to you," he continued with a smile.

Clare looked at him with confusion.

"You mean you want us to be performers, too?" Kay asked eagerly.

"Well, no, not exactly. We're looking for some regular girls, hometown girl-next-door types, to come along on this tour. Of course, the boys enjoy seeing Marlene Dietrich, Betty Hutton, and the like, but what they really want is a real girl they can talk to and dance with for a while. I've been watching you both tonight, and I think you're just the kind of girls we're looking for," Mr. Hastings explained.

"Where will the tour go? When do we leave? Will we meet Bob Hope?" questioned Kay.

"We haven't worked out all the details of the tour yet. All I can say right now is that it will be a little different from the other tours we've had so far. Of course, it's a volunteer position. But all your expenses will be covered. And your real reward will be in knowing how much you are helping with the war effort. Dancing and talking with the men may seem like a small thing to you, but it means a great deal to them. You see how much the men passing through Laurelmont appreciate these dances, so you can just imagine how much the men in the field will appreciate it when they see you."

"Okay, sign us up!" Kay cried with delight.

"I don't need an answer tonight. You think about it, and I'll be back in two weeks from tonight for your decision. I hope I'll have more details for you then, too," Mr. Hastings said as he handed each of them his card.

Kay was bursting with excitement as she and Clare left the YMCA.

"I can't believe it! We're going to have a wonderful time! Aren't we, Clare? You haven't said anything. What's the matter?"

Clare had been silent during the whole exchange with Mr. Hastings. At first she felt the same pulse of excitement as Kay, but then she thought about her father and her former life. Admittedly, she had not tried very hard at all to return to her own time for the past two months. Yet she had not left Laurelmont, and she felt that if she left the town she would never find her way back home; leaving would mean giving up on ever going back.

"Gee, Kay. I don't know ... " Clare said hesitantly.

"What's not to know? Think of the adventure, the excitement, all the fun we'll have!"

"I guess you're right," Clare conceded. Part of her *did* want to go.

"Plus my parents will never let me go if you don't go, too."

By then Clare and Kay had arrived at the diner. They entered and Kay told her sister about the USO tour with a great rush of words.

"Well, Kay, that does sound like quite an adventure, but you know Mother and Pop will never let you go," Nell warned.

"They can't stop me. I'm eighteen now. And Clare's

coming, too."

"Okay, you can try, I guess."

Kay chattered on about which movie stars they would probably meet, where the tour would go, and how many men they would see. At closing time, Clare walked home in the darkness debating whether she should go on the tour. She concluded she would go if it meant Kay's parents would allow her to go. It obviously meant a lot to Kay, and she had done so much for Clare. She wanted to help her friend, and this was the least she could do. Besides, she thought maybe there was some small chance of seeing Roy. Clare wrote to Roy the next day but made no mention of the USO tour; it seemed premature.

On Monday morning, Clare found Kay waiting for her outside of the dime store. Her pretty face wore a pout.

"Hi, Kay. What's wrong?" Clare questioned.

"It's my parents," Kay said dejectedly. "Nell was right. They won't let me go on the USO tour."

"Even though I'd be going, too?"

"They didn't care about that. They said you could do what you wanted, but they wouldn't let *their* daughter go. You're so lucky you don't have anyone telling you what to do."

Not so lucky, really, Clare thought. "Well, you could just disobey them and go anyway."

"I thought about that, but who am I kidding? I'm not going. But you go and have a good time," Kay said, although she did not sound particularly sincere.

"Don't be silly. If you're not going, then I'm not going either," Clare said with a mixture of relief and regret.

"You really mean that?" Kay cried, giving Clare a hug.

"Sure I mean it. We'll just tell that Mr. Hastings to find a couple of other girls. That shouldn't be too hard."

The friends walked into the store arm in arm.

On Thursday, Clare and Kay decided to meet for dinner and go to the movies afterward. The Laurelodeon was showing *So Proudly We Hail*. Clare got to the diner before Kay and sat down at the counter to wait. She picked up the late edition of the newspaper that was lying there and looked at the date: September 2, 1943. The day before, the headline had marked the fourth anniversary of the start of the war. On September 1, 1939, Hitler's army had invaded Poland. But today only Clare knew that the war would be over in exactly two more years. She wished she could tell someone that Japan would officially surrender on September 2, 1945, but who would believe her?

Clare idly flipped the folded paper over and saw a large photograph near the bottom of the page. She recognized it as soon as she saw it. It was a well-known photograph; while not as famous as the picture of the flag raising on Iwo Jima, it was still important enough to make its way into her American History textbook fifty years later.

Clare had studied the photo closely in her textbook, and she looked at it again with interest now. The photo, taken on Sicily, depicted four figures – a little girl, a teenage girl, and two women, one older and one younger – all clad in rags and sitting or standing in the doorway of what might have been their home. The older women watched the scene playing out in the foreground of the picture with piteous expressions while the little girl, her hair a mop of Shirley Temple curls, looked on with downcast eyes, clutching a cross around her neck and curling her bare toes as if to prevent a flood of tears. Only the older girl looked off into the distance with hard eyes, as if she knew the scene in front of them was the least of their problems. Clare now focused on the figures in the foreground. Involuntarily she let out a cry, and the paper fell from her hands.

CHAPTER 13

When Clare came to, Kay was beside her, and Nell was splashing water on her face.

"Clare, what happened? What's the matter?" Kay cried.

"It's the picture. It's Roy," she answered.

Nell retrieved the newspaper from the floor, and she and Kay peered at the black and white photograph. In the foreground, an Army medic was administering blood plasma to a wounded soldier. Nell read the caption aloud: "Holding death at bay with plasma - Pvt. Harvey White, Army hospital corpsman from Minneapolis, Minn., holds death at bay as he tensely administers blood plasma to a wounded Yank in the street at San Agata, Sicily, which then was half a mile behind the front line. Feelings of the girl and women spectators are mirrored in their faces."

Kay took the paper and squinted at the grainy photograph. "It doesn't say it's him," she said skeptically. "You can't be sure. It could be anybody."

Yes, looking at the fuzzy image on the front page, it could be anyone. But Clare had seen the large, clear print in her textbook. How could she tell them that? How could she tell them that the nagging feeling she had seen Roy before had not been wrong after all?

"I know it's him," Clare replied weakly.

"Okay, well, what if it is? There's still nothing to worry about. The caption says 'holding death at bay.' That means he's all right, doesn't it?" said Kay. "They wouldn't print this if the soldier died, now would they?"

That logic *did* sound reasonable.

"I hope you're right," Clare said.

"Sure she's right," interjected Nell. "Eat this meatloaf. It'll make you feel better."

Obediently Clare ate the meatloaf while Kay tried to cheer her up.

"Do you still want to go to the movies?" Kay asked hopefully.

"I guess so," Clare said, thinking it might distract her. "But maybe we could see a different movie."

"Okay, I'll see what else is playing," Kay said and flipped to the back page of the newspaper. "How about *Watch on the Rhine? This is the Army? Stage Door Canteen? Bataan? Bombardier?*

Clare shook her head "no" after each title. "Isn't there something that isn't about the war?" she cried. "I'm so sick of it! I don't think I can take two more years of this!"

"Two more years? That's awfully optimistic, at least according to what my pop says," Kay said quietly. "Oh, here's one that doesn't sound like it's about the war. It's called *Song of Texas.*"

"Okay. I like musicals," Clare said.

"Me, too. It's got Roy Rogers and Trigger in it," Kay said brightly.

Clare began to sob.

"Let's skip the movie tonight," Kay said, putting her arm around Clare's shoulder. She walked her friend back to Mrs. Harrigan's and brought her upstairs to her room.

"Are you sure you'll be all right, Clare?" Kay asked with concern.

"Sure, Kay. I'll be fine. Thanks for taking me home. I'll see you at work tomorrow."

Clare climbed into bed. She did not feel like reading or writing in her journal. She had taken the newspaper with her and unfolded it now. She lay propped up on one arm and stared alternately between the grainy picture on the front page and the studio portraits in the frame on her nightstand.

Maybe it isn't Roy, Clare thought. *No, I'm sure it is.* She looked at the picture of the man on the stretcher receiving the blood plasma transfusion. His eyes were closed and his blond hair fell back from his face. Two streaks of what must have been blood trailed down his cheek. Yet she could see two arms and two legs, and his light-colored t-shirt showed no signs of blood. He did not look badly hurt, Clare concluded. *Kay was probably right. They wouldn't have published the picture if he had died. He's probably recovering now or maybe even on his way home.* Clare told herself not to worry and then tried to sleep.

The next day, the picture was the topic of much conversation. Almost everyone Clare saw, from Mrs. Harrigan and Mrs. Nelson to Polly at the lunch counter, was sure they knew the identity of the soldier in the picture. He was someone's cousin, neighbor, son, or nephew. They were all sure it was their loved one, but only Clare knew the truth. Beyond telling Nell and Kay, she decided not to tell anyone else that it was *her* loved one, since no one would believe her anyway. But was Roy really her loved one? She had to admit that she did not love him; she barely knew him, really. It was more the *idea* of Roy that she loved: a wartime romance played out in letters with the hope of a reunion at the war's end. Still, if they kept on writing to each other, maybe they really would fall in love. She knew it certainly happened. Clare wondered if Mrs. Humphrey had recognized her son when the picture was printed in the Toledo newspaper. Or perhaps she had even been notified by the Army already and was expecting Roy to return home soon.

Besides speculation, the picture produced another effect on the people who saw it: the desire to do something to help the war effort. All across the country, people flocked to Red Cross blood donation centers. There was such a surge in blood donors that the Laurelmont Red Cross had to set up an extra blood donation center at the YMCA. Mr. Winston even gave each qualified blood donor an hour off to make a donation the following week. After the dance on Saturday night, Clare asked Kay if she wanted to give blood with her on Monday.

"Well, sure I'd like to, but I can't give blood, and neither can you," Kay replied.

"What do you mean? Why not?" Clare asked.

"You have to be twenty-one, and neither of us is old enough."

"That's silly. I'm going anyway. I'll just lie about my age," said Clare.

"But what if you get caught?"

"I don't see what they can do to me. I've got to try, anyway. You can come with me if you want."

"Well, I'll think about it," Kay said.

After lunch on Monday, Clare and Ginny went to the YMCA to donate blood. Kay stayed behind to mind their departments. An hour later, the two young women returned with gauze bandages on their arms.

"How was it?" Kay asked.

"Fine," Clare said. "I just told them I was twenty-one. You should come next time."

"Okay, I promise," said Kay.

School had started again, so the days were quieter than before without children in the store. The week passed slowly until Thursday, September 9th, arrived with the news that U.S. troops had invaded Italy at Salerno, and Italy had surrendered. There was much rejoicing in the streets, and the Salerno Bakery even made a special pastry called sfogliatelle to celebrate the impending liberation of their hometown. Clare was surprised by the degree of jubilation, as she knew what was still to come. While it seemed as if one of the three Axis powers was defeated, in fact Italy was still occupied by the Nazis. Over a year more of hard fighting lay ahead for the troops there before the whole country would be liberated.

The following day was Friday, and after Mrs. Dietrich handed out the paychecks, she returned to Clare with a large envelope. It was addressed to her, but the handwriting was unfamiliar. Clare hoped it was from Roy and figured maybe he needed someone's help to send it out. She showed the envelope to Kay with excitement.

"Are you going to open it now?" Kay asked as they walked home.

"No, I'll wait until after dinner."

"Okay, you can tell me all about it at the dance tomorrow night," Kay said as they parted company.

Back at the boarding house, Clare placed the envelope on her dressing table and went downstairs to eat. After enjoying some cabbage and kielbasa with Anna, she returned to her room. Sitting down on her bed, she carefully opened the envelope and slid the contents onto the bedspread. A packet of smaller envelopes tumbled out, and she immediately recognized the handwriting. It was not Roy's lovely penmanship but her own childish scrawl. All the letters she had sent Roy lay before her on the pink chenille. Clare stared at them with confusion. The first thought that came to her mind was that Roy had found another girl and did not want to write to her anymore. But amidst the familiar envelopes was one she did not recognize. It was addressed to her in the same handwriting as on the larger envelope. With trepidation she opened it and withdrew two sheets of paper. On the first one she read:

August 11, 1943
Dear Miss Carlyle,
By now I expect you have received official word from the Army, but I wanted to send you a personal note. Private Humphrey was a very special young man, and I am truly sorry for your loss. As difficult as this must be for you, I hope it provides you with some small measure of comfort to know that Private Humphrey died defending our nation from the great evil that is threatening the good people of the world.

Private Humphrey was wounded by enemy shrapnel while his company was patrolling a roadblock at Militello Rosmarino on August 9th. Although he was evacuated to an aid station in San Agata some distance behind the front line and received the best possible care including blood plasma transfusions, his injuries were grave. While the doctors remained hopeful, Our Lord saw fit to recall Private Humphrey to His service the following day. He passed on peacefully and was not in pain. Private Humphrey's body has been buried in the American cemetery in Caronia, Sicily. A beautiful setting overlooking the sea, it is land that Private Humphrey himself helped to free from the Nazis.

The enclosed letters were among Private Humphrey's personal effects. Although it is customary to return all personal effects to the next-of-kin, his mother in this case, I thought these letters might be of a personal nature and saw no harm in returning them directly to you. Private Humphrey spoke of you often and was always eager to show everyone your picture. I've also enclosed a letter that he had started writing to you. I'm sure he would have wanted you to have it.

I know the grief you are feeling is profound, but you must remember what we are fighting for. Regrettably, our victory can only be achieved through the sacrifices young men like Private Humphrey are willing to make. May God grant you peace.

Very sincerely yours,
Capt. Chevis Horne, Chaplain
7th Infantry Regiment, 3rd Division

As Clare had read the first sentence of the letter, she felt her blood run cold. She read on, the words becoming blurrier and blurrier through the tears that welled in her eyes. Then, with tears streaming down her cheeks, she unfolded the second sheet of paper and saw Roy's handwriting. It was not as neat as before but looked as if he had been writing hastily:

August 8, 1943
Dear Clare,

I don't have much time, but I wanted to write you a short note. We are getting closer to our objective here and I think things will be over soon, but there is still some hard fighting ahead of us. Most of the Italians have surrendered now and we're fighting the Germans. Some of my buddies have been wounded, but the docs here are real good. My pal Harvey is our medic and he gets them fixed up right away. I'm sure nothing will happen to me, though. Not when I've got a girl like you back home. I hope you don't mind that I think of you as my girl. Try not to worry about me.

The letter was unsigned and perhaps even unfinished. Clare read both letters over again several times. It seemed there could be no mistake. Roy really had died. The lifesaving power of the blood plasma transfusions had not saved him. Maybe it had saved others but not him. Clare sank her head into her pillow and wept. *Why him?* she wondered. *The casualties had been so light. Why did he have to be one of them?* This was not the way it happened in all the movies she saw. *This wasn't supposed to happen.* Amidst her grief, Clare found herself thinking, *it's all my fault. I could have stopped him. If only I had realized where I recognized him from in time, I could have stopped him from going, and he'd still be alive. Maybe if I can find a way to go back in time again I can stop him …*

Presently, Clare heard a soft knocking at the door. She looked at the door but did not move to open it; she did not want to see anyone now. However, the unlocked door opened slowly, and Anna peeked into the dimly lit room.

"Are you all right, Clare? I thought I heard the sound of crying," she said with worry in her voice.

Clare sniffled and held out the chaplain's letter to Anna, who read it quickly.

"Oh, Clare, I'm so sorry. You never told me you had a boyfriend."

"I … we met at the dance and started writing to each other. We weren't supposed to write to the boys, but he asked me so nicely that I couldn't say no," Clare choked out between sobs.

Anna sat down on the bed and put her arms around Clare. That act of comfort only caused her to weep harder as it reminded Clare of her mother's embrace and how much she had missed that. After a while, Anna gave her a clean handkerchief, and Clare blotted her eyes.

"You must draw comfort from the chaplain's words, Clare. Roy did not die in vain. He's a hero."

"Yes, but he was so young, only twenty-one." As Clare said the words, she realized that Anna's son was only eighteen and facing similar danger. Anna's eyes clouded, and Clare was sure she was having the same thought.

"He was old enough to make the decision to enlist on his own. Old enough to value freedom above his own safety. There was nothing that could have stopped him," Anna said with finality. Clare wondered if she were talking about Roy or her own son, now.

"I'm going to bring you some warm milk from the kitchen," Anna said as she left the room, dabbing at her own moist eyes with her handkerchief.

"Do you want me to stay with you tonight?" Anna asked when she returned with the milk.

"Oh, no, but thank you for your kindness. I'll be all right," Clare answered.

"Well, I'll be just downstairs if you need me," Anna said as she squeezed Clare's hand. Clare wiped her eyes again and tried to muster a smile. When Anna had left, Clare carefully put all the letters back into the envelope along with the folded-up newspaper with the picture of Roy. She got into bed, pulled the covers tight around her, and began to cry again, softly so no one would hear.

CHAPTER 14

When Clare awoke the next morning, she found she had no appetite and no motivation to get out of bed. The shock of Roy's death was still too much to bear. She stayed in bed all day, alternately crying, wishing she could change what had happened, and staring at Roy's picture. Around five o'clock, Anna knocked on Clare's door and let herself in, carrying some freshly baked poppy seed bread and a cup of coffee. She set the small tray down on Clare's nightstand and sat down next to her on the bed.

"Clare, I'm worried about you. You missed breakfast and lunch. That's not like you. I know this is a sad time, but you must go on. You know Roy would want you to."

"Yes, I know you're right. But everything seems so pointless now."

"No, you're mistaken. It's just the opposite. Everyone must do all they can to help the war effort. Nothing is too small. And now it's even more important. Were you going to the dance tonight?"

"Yes, I told Kay I'd meet her there, but I just don't think I can go and pretend to be cheerful after what's happened."

"You have to go. The boys need you more than

ever. And won't Kay be worried if you don't show up?"

"I guess you're right," Clare said as she began nibbling at the bread.

"Good. You'll go and you'll see that it will make you feel better to do something to help," Anna said as she rose from Clare's bed.

Clare eventually got up, washed, and put on her yellow flowered dress. She walked dejectedly toward the YMCA, debating about what to tell Kay. She was afraid if she told her about Roy right away she would start crying again and would not be able to stop, so she decided to wait until after the dance.

When Clare entered the gymnasium, she found Kay already setting up the refreshments. Her friend waved cheerfully to her, and Clare donned her apron and came over to Kay's table to help.

"What's the matter?" Kay asked immediately. She could tell Clare did not look quite like herself.

"I twisted my ankle on the way over," Clare lied.

"Oh, are you all right? Do you want to sit down? Do you need some ice?" Kay asked with concern.

"No, but I think I'll just serve tonight instead of dancing," Clare said, already regretting lying to her friend.

"Okay. Say, what did that big envelope have in it? Was it from Roy?"

"Uh, I forgot I sent away for some crochet patterns."

"Oh, my mother is always trying to get me to crochet or knit something for her, but I don't have any patience for that. I started a scarf once, but it came out all crooked. Of course, Nell is a whiz at all that domestic stuff, but I just can't sit still long enough. Except in the movies, but it's too dark to crochet there," Kay giggled. She chattered on as she and Clare set up the doughnuts.

The band began filing in and tuning their instruments. Mrs. Prescott and Mrs. Banks gave their now-familiar speech outlining the ground rules for the dance. The gym doors opened, and the tide of servicemen rushed in. Clare fixed a smile on her face, but as she served each boy, she kept wondering which ones would not be coming back. Finally the evening drew to a close, and the men reluctantly trickled out. As the room emptied, Clare noticed a man in civilian clothes standing next to Mrs. Lincoln. It was Mr. Hastings, from the New York USO. Clare had completely forgotten that he would be returning tonight to see if she and Kay would join the tour. She hoped maybe he had forgotten, too, and was there to ask some other girls. Kay came over to her table and began helping her clean up the refreshments.

"How's your ankle feeling?" Kay asked.

Before Clare could answer, Mr. Hastings was in front of them.

"Hello, girls!" he said, beaming. "You both look lovely this evening. I hope you remembered I'd be back to talk to you tonight. Do you have good news for me? Will you join the new USO tour? I can tell you more about it now if you need some convincing."

"I'm sorry, Mr. Hastings, but we're not going," Kay said. "We can't leave Laurelmont."

"Don't say that. It would mean so much to the boys. Won't you reconsider?" asked Mr. Hastings.

Even as she saw Kay resolutely shaking her head, Clare was astonished to hear herself say, "I'll go." Kay looked at her, dumbstruck.

"That's wonderful!" exclaimed Mr. Hastings. "I'd rather you came as a pair, but one is better than nothing. When you're finished cleaning up, we can sit down and talk about the details." He walked back to Mrs. Lincoln, and they began conversing enthusiastically.

Kay turned to face Clare with moist eyes. "You're going? Without me? And you didn't even tell me first? I thought we were best friends," Kay said, looking downward.

"Oh, but we are!" Clare cried. "I didn't tell you because I didn't know myself until that very instant. But I have to go. It's more important now than ever. I have to do more, do something to help. You'll understand when I tell you everything. Can we go to the diner when I'm done with Mr. Hastings? I want to tell you and Nell everything."

"Sure," Kay said curtly and shifted her focus to intently scrubbing a punch stain on the tablecloth.

Clare walked over to Mr. Hastings, and he led her to one of the tables in the lobby.

"I'm so glad you've decided to join us. But can't you convince your friend to come, too?" he asked.

"Kay would love to come, but her parents won't let her," Clare explained.

"But she's eighteen. She can do whatever she wants."

"I don't think she would defy her parents and risk displeasing them."

"That's too bad," said Mr. Hastings. "Well, there will be a lot of other swell girls going anyway. And Betty Wilton is going. She's going to be the star of the show."

"Oh, she's so beautiful and has such a lovely voice," Clare said, wondering if Betty would be nice or stuck-up and snobby because she was so pretty and talented.

"So this USO tour is going to be a bit different from the previous ones we've staged. They had a bunch of stars performing various acts, but this time we're going to stage a whole show. It's on Broadway now and is real popular. Maybe you've even heard of it. It's called

Oklahoma!, and it was written by a new team, Richard Rodgers and Oscar Hammerstein."

"Of course I've heard of it! I know all the words!" Clare said with excitement.

"You do? You must have seen the show a lot of times," Mr. Hastings said with surprise. "Do you sing, Miss Carlyle?"

"No, not really. Just to myself. I'll stick with the girl-next-door role and leave the singing and dancing to someone else."

"That's fine. We'll need you in New York in two weeks, on the 27th. We'll rehearse through December and plan to ship out right after Christmas. Will that be okay?"

"I guess so, but if I'm not in the show, do I need to be there to rehearse?" Clare asked.

"Well, not to rehearse the play, but there will be training and a lot of opportunities for service in New York. A lot of men leave from there to go overseas."

"Sure. And will we be going to Sicily? Or is that a secret?"

"No and no. We're headed to the South Pacific, Miss Carlyle. I hope that's not a disappointment for you."

"Oh, not at all," Clare said with wide eyes, the excitement welling up inside her.

"Good," Mr. Hastings said as he pulled an envelope from his briefcase. "This has all the information you need. Just sign the contract and mail it back to me when you've looked it all over. When we receive it, we'll send you a train ticket from Laurelmont to New York. Your room and board will be covered, and you'll receive a small stipend for essentials."

"Thank you, Mr. Hastings," Clare said, beaming. She watched him depart and turned back to the doors of the gym. Her smile vanished as she saw Kay scowling at her. She had momentarily forgotten her friend's anger and her own sad reason for this rash decision. She walked over to Kay, who turned away from her.

"Kay, can we go to the diner now?" Clare asked.

"Sure," she answered. They walked to the diner in silence, and Clare was certain it was the longest she had ever heard Kay go without talking. When they entered the diner, Clare was relieved to see that no one was there but Nell, drying some coffee mugs and humming.

"Why the long faces?" Nell asked as Clare and Kay sat down at the counter.

"Clare is going on the USO tour. Without me," Kay pouted.

"Is that true, Clare?" Nell asked. Clare nodded.

"But the worst part is she didn't even tell me first!" Kay said, her lower lip trembling.

"I didn't tell you because I didn't know. Honestly, I had forgotten all about it. But I did lie to you. I didn't twist my ankle. And I don't crochet, either," Clare said. Nell looked at her quizzically.

"I didn't get crochet patterns in the envelope. I got this," Clare said as she pulled the letter from the chaplain from her purse and handed it to Kay. She unfolded the pages, and Nell came around the counter to read it over her shoulder. Both girls gasped and looked up to Clare's eyes brimming with tears.

"Why, you should have told me, Clare. I'm so sorry," Kay said gently while giving her a hug.

"I know. I wanted to, but I was afraid if I told you before the dance, I'd start to cry and wouldn't stop. Anna convinced me to go tonight, that it was important to do something useful, so I didn't want to let the boys down," Clare explained between sobs. "I didn't remember about the USO tour, but as soon as Mr. Hastings asked if we were going, I realized I need to do more than just dancing and serving doughnuts here in Laurelmont, and this is my chance."

"I understand now, and I don't blame you. I'd do the same if I could," said Kay with a sad smile.

"I wish you were going, too," Clare said. "Maybe you could ask your parents again. Or I could try talking to them."

"Maybe, but I don't think they'll go for it. Still, I wish I could see England or even Italy … "

"Mr. Hastings told me the tour is going to the South Pacific," replied Clare.

"Oh, my parents would never let me go *there*," Kay said. "It's full of malaria and headhunters."

"And Japs," added Nell.

"I'm sure it's perfectly safe," said Clare. "They wouldn't send a whole theater troupe and a bunch of girls into harm's way."

"I suppose you're right, but I'm sure Mother and Pop won't change their minds. You go and have enough adventures for the both of us. I'll hold down things on the home front," Kay said ruefully.

Clare nodded sadly. "I have to be in New York in two weeks. The tour is a production of the Broadway show *Oklahoma!* Of course, I won't be in the show, but I have to be there for training."

Neither Kay nor Nell had heard of the show, and it occurred to Clare that it had not been on Broadway for very long. The cast album must not have been released, and the popular recordings were not yet on the radio. That explained why Mr. Hastings was surprised to find she knew it well.

"I saw the show in New York, before I came to Laurelmont," Clare lied. "It has some lovely songs. I bet some of them will become popular when Frank Sinatra and Bing Crosby record them."

"I'm sorry about Roy," Nell said, changing the subject. "I know how special he was to you."

"Thanks, Nell. I still can't believe it's real. If only I could have stopped him from going, then he'd still be alive," Clare said dejectedly.

"Don't be ridiculous. You had no way of knowing. And if you had stopped him he would have gone AWOL and gotten in a lot of trouble. You can't think like that," Nell said. "It doesn't do any good. You can't change what's going to happen."

"I guess you're right. But sometimes I feel like I can change what's going to happen. What's already happened," Clare said.

"You're not making sense now. It's time for you and Kay to go to bed. I'll lock up and we'll walk home together," Nell suggested.

CHAPTER 15

The next morning, Clare awoke to see Roy's picture on her nightstand, and the sadness rushed back to fill her heart. Then she remembered the events of the previous evening, and the grief was replaced with a new feeling: terror. *What have I done*, thought Clare. *Now I have to leave the safety and comfort of Laurelmont and the only people I know in the whole world to go to New York – and then to the South Pacific.* The feeling of excitement from last night had turned to dread. *So much for "Courageous Clare,"* she thought. *I can always change my mind. Kay would be overjoyed.* Then she thought of Anna's words encouraging her to do something more meaningful. *I will go*, Clare resolved. *I can be "Courageous Clare." A lot of young men – and young women – are doing a lot more courageous things than going on a USO tour, anyway. It's the least I can do to help.* With that, Clare got up, dressed, and went down to breakfast. She told Anna all about her decision to join the USO tour.

"I think you made the right choice, Clare. It will mean so much for the troops. You'll meet new people and see new places. And I'll pray for your safe return along with that of my son, Gregory," Anna said.

Buoyed by Anna's encouragement, Clare returned to her room and carefully read the contract Mr. Hastings had given her. She signed it and walked to the mailbox to send it back to him. She told Mrs. Harrigan that she would be leaving in two weeks. The older lady was disappointed but wished her well.

The next two weeks flew by as Clare prepared for her departure. After receiving her train ticket to New York in the mail, she bought a second suitcase and more clothing with some money she had saved. She spent most of her free time with Kay, who had forgiven her for deciding to go on the tour without her. Kay was not able to convince her parents to let her go, too. She did, however, come with Clare to donate blood. She found it was no problem to lie about her age, and promised Clare that she would donate as often as possible.

On Clare's last day of work at T.F. Kingsley's, she was treated to an ice cream soda by Mr. Winston and presented with a silver wristwatch all the girls had chipped in to buy. This was a most welcome gift, as the battery of her old watch had recently died; she could not replace it since watch batteries had not yet been invented. Clare was especially touched when severe Mrs. Dietrich gave her a hat she had knitted herself. Clare promised to write to them and tell them all about her adventures.

The next day, Clare did all her laundry and began packing her few possessions. She stopped in the library to return the book she had borrowed and was surprised when Mrs. Brooks wished her *bon voyage*. It seemed her imminent departure was the topic of discussion around town, just as her arrival had been. Next she visited her grandparents' bakery to purchase a plate of cookies for Kay's family. While she waited to be helped, she studied the shop she knew so well and glanced furtively at her grandparents. She wanted to talk to them, to tell them who she was, but she knew that would be a mistake. When she left the store, the orange cat appeared from the alley and enthusiastically rubbed against her legs as if he, too, were saying goodbye.

That evening, Clare walked over to Kay's house with the tray of cookies. Eddie and some of his friends were playing ball in the yard and raced over to help themselves. Clare went inside with the half-empty plate and presented it to Kay's mother, awkwardly explaining it had been full moments ago.

"Oh, I know dear, thank you! Nothing can get past Eddie. I once baked a cake for Mr. O'Neill's birthday, and when I went to put the candles on it, a piece was already missing. I gave Eddie a good scolding, but it didn't do any good," Mrs. O'Neill said, laughing. "We're going to miss you so much, Clare. Will you come back to Laurelmont when the tour is over?"

"Yes, I suppose so," Clare answered. She had not thought so far in the future as to what she would do *after* the tour.

Kay came down from upstairs, and they ate a few cookies. Then they went to Kay's room to get ready for the dance. Kay styled Clare's hair in an elaborate arrangement and then fixed her own. They put on their dresses and walked over to the YMCA, knowing this would be the last dance they would attend together for a long time.

Mort Lester and his Laurelhoppers were playing again, and Clare saw Betty Wilton talking with some of the band members. Then she was surprised to see the pretty blonde walking toward her.

"Hi, I'm Betty," she said with a warm smile. "Are you Clare?"

"Yes, I'm Clare Carlyle. I've heard you sing here a few times, and I think you're wonderful."

"Gee, thank you," Betty said, her cheeks reddening. Clare had never seen her this close before; she was even more beautiful than Clare had realized, with turquoise eyes and a slightly upturned nose. "I heard you're going on the USO tour, too, so I wanted to meet you. It will be nice to already have a friend there. I'm pretty nervous about it."

"Me, too," Clare confessed with relief.

"I've never been to New York before," Betty added. "Have you?"

"Yes, a few times," Clare said, grateful for some class trips to the natural history museum and art museums. "But I don't know my way around too well."

"We'll discover the city together. It will be such fun! Oh, that's my cue," Betty said as the musicians began tuning their instruments and darted back to the band.

Clare and Kay served refreshments for the first half of the dance. After the intermission, they jitterbugged and fox-trotted with the servicemen. As the evening drew to a close, Mort Lester addressed the crowd.

"We have just one more song for you this evening, but before I bring the beautiful Betty Wilton out to sing for you again, I want to tell you that this will be her last performance with the Laurelhoppers." The crowd made sounds of disappointment. "Miss Wilton will be departing on Monday for New York City to star in the USO's new traveling production of the Broadway smash, *Oklahoma!*" The crowd went wild. When the noise died away, Mort added, "but that's not all! Laurelmont's own Clare Carlyle will also be joining the tour to serve up some of that girl-next-door charm she's known for to our fellas in the South Pacific! Clare, honey, raise your hand so everyone can see you."

Clare, her cheeks burning, raised her hand. Her other hand was still being held by the soldier with whom she had just danced, and he suddenly twirled her around and dipped her. She was dimly aware of applause and even some catcalls.

"Without further ado, here's the lovely Betty Wilton to sing 'We'll Meet Again,'" Mort said, and the crowd cheered. As Betty sang, Clare danced with a procession of soldiers and sailors, cutting in one after the other. When Betty neared the last chorus, the room of moving couples stilled, and everyone sang along with her. After the last note faded, Mrs. Lincoln presented Betty with a bouquet of red roses, and Mrs. Prescott gave Clare a smaller bouquet of pink carnations.

The men reluctantly began filing out of the gymnasium, and Clare started to help clean up the tables of refreshments. Betty came over again and told Clare she would look for her on the train Monday morning. Other girls came over to wish them both good luck and *bon voyage*. Clare was uncomfortable with all the attention and worried that Kay would be upset, but her friend was stoically smiling in spite of the sadness and envy she must have been feeling.

When they finished cleaning everything up, Clare suggested they go to the diner. As they discussed the dance with Nell over their milkshakes, Kay commented on how talented Betty was. "She really can sing. I bet she'll be as famous as Betty Grable and Betty Hutton someday."

"Maybe you're right," Clare said, knowing this was not the case. "Anyway, she seems like an awfully nice girl." Clare noticed that Kay's face had fallen. "But no one could ever be as nice as you and Nell have been to me," she added. "I'll miss you both so much."

"We'll miss you, too. Come to breakfast here on Monday morning, and we'll see you off at the train station," Nell said. Clare could see Kay's eyes beginning to glisten.

"That would be swell," Clare said, forcing a smile to prevent the tears she could feel forming in her eyes.

Clare spent most of the following day with Anna, talking and helping her bake. She finished packing her two suitcases. Only the framed pictures of Roy were left on the nightstand. She suddenly realized that she really should send a letter to his mother, although it would be a difficult one to write. She unpacked her stationery again and began to compose the letter. It occurred to her that Roy's mother might not know it was his picture in the newspaper, so she decided not to mention it. Instead, she expressed her sympathy, told her she would never forget Roy, and explained that she was joining a USO tour to help cheer boys like him and remind them of home.

Clare slept restlessly that night, the mixture of excitement and anxiety producing strange and vivid dreams. She was relieved when the dawn came and was happy to bathe and dress. Clare looked around her room one last time to see if she missed anything. She closed the hinged frame containing Roy's photographs, carefully wrapped it in a handkerchief, and placed it in her purse. Then she slipped the heart-shaped charm, which had also been on the nightstand, into the pocket of her skirt. Now the room was just as she had found it when she arrived in June.

Clare went downstairs and bid goodbye to Anna, Mrs. Harrigan, and the other women in the parlor. She promised to come back to the boarding house when she returned to Laurelmont. She walked to the diner, stopping to mail the letter to Roy's mother on the way. Inside the diner, she found Kay already there, sitting at the counter. Clare ate a hearty breakfast of pancakes that Nell insisted was on the house. Nell arranged for the dishwasher to cover for her while they walked Clare to the train station. As Clare left the diner, she felt herself tense and held her breath. She was relieved to still see Kay and Nell beside her as they stepped out onto the sidewalk. They walked the few blocks to the station and saw that a train was already at the platform. The conductor was outside collecting tickets.

"Is this the train to Pennsylvania Station, sir?" Clare asked.

"Yes, it is, miss. Ticket, please," answered the conductor. Clare gave him the ticket while a porter took her luggage. She turned back to Kay and Nell, who each hugged her.

"Good luck, Clare. We'll miss you," Nell said warmly.

"Don't forget to write! And get me Bob Hope's autograph if you meet him!" Kay added.

"I won't forget to write. And I'll tell Bob Hope to send you a letter, too! Thank you both for everything you've done for me. I'll miss you!" Clare said as she began to climb the steps of the train. Once she reached the top, she turned and waved to them both. Inside, the train was already crowded with an assortment of servicemen, women with children, and older businessmen. Several men stood up to offer her their seat, but Clare spotted Betty at the back of the car. As she made her way toward her, she heard a few whistles from the young men. She wanted to scowl at them but could only muster an embarrassed smile. She sank down into the empty seat next to Betty.

"Boy, am I glad to see you!" Betty exclaimed. "I felt like Red Riding Hood – in a pack of wolves!"

The whistle blew to signal the train's departure, and it slowly began to pull away from the station. Clare leaned out the window to wave at Kay and Nell, who vigorously waved back. As the train snaked its way toward New York City, it stopped often. At each station more passengers embarked than departed, so the train became more and more crowded as the morning wore on. Servicemen were sitting on trunks in the aisles as they gave up their seats.

Eventually, Clare and Betty found themselves with two children sitting in their laps after a mother with three children boarded the train. She explained that her husband was just drafted, and she was moving in with her parents while her husband was in basic training.

"Oh," said Clare with surprise, "I didn't know married men with children could be drafted."

"Me neither until he got the letter," the woman said bitterly.

"I'm sure they won't make him do anything dangerous," Betty said brightly.

"I hope you're right," she replied, the worry evident in her voice.

To lighten the mood and entertain the children, Betty began singing "Three Little Fishies." They were clapping along and laughing at the silly lyrics. "Sing another one!" the children cried, and she obliged them with "A-Tisket, A-Tasket."

Clare was enjoying the impromptu performance as much as the kids. "Sing 'Mairzy Doats,'" she suggested.

"What?" said Betty.

"You know, 'Mairzy Doats,'" Clare insisted, beginning to sing the first few words. Her voice trailed away at the blank look on Betty's face. "How about 'Chickery Chick?'" Betty continued to look at her with confusion as Clare started to sing the lyrics.

"Now you're just teasing. Those aren't real songs," Betty said.

"Oh, yes they are. I guess they're not popular here yet," Clare said, realizing her mistake.

"Well, where *are* they popular then?" Betty asked.

"Uh, Schenectady … that's where I'm from," Clare said, falling back on her old lie. "But I know they'll become real popular all over the country someday."

"I don't know if the rest of the country likes gobbledygook as much as Schenectady does! But you seem awfully sure of that. Do you have a crystal ball?" Betty teased.

Clare was grateful that before she could answer, one of the children tugged on Betty's sleeve and asked her to sing "When You Wish Upon a Star," which she did, beautifully. By now, the adults sitting near them had turned to listen, and servicemen sitting on trunks in the aisle moved closer to hear – and see – the lovely singer. The rest of the trip passed with Betty taking requests from the other passengers. Clare was careful not to suggest any more songs that had not been written.

Finally the conductor's voice boomed, "Next stop, Pennsylvania Station!" The train pulled into the station, and a rush of people moved to exit the compartment. Clare and Betty helped the young mother carry her children from the train to her waiting parents. Then they located their luggage and finally had the time to take in the grandeur of Pennsylvania Station. Massive Corinthian columns flanked the walls, and sunlight streamed in from a huge arched window. It was overwhelming as people rushed past them, each in a hurry and each seeming to know exactly where they needed to go.

"Where do we go now?" Betty asked Clare, with wide eyes.

"I guess we need to report for duty," Clare said as she took the letter from Mr. Hastings out of her purse. "When you arrive in New York, report to the YWCA, 610 Lexington Avenue between East 52nd and East 53rd Streets," she read.

The new friends gathered up their belongings and set off together, ready to begin their adventure.

PART II

NEW YORK

THE AMERICAN THEATRE WING STAGE DOOR CANTEEN. Born of stage, screen, radio, vaudeville and music world's joined, food, dancing and entertainment to service men—all free nightly.

CHAPTER 16

When Clare and Betty emerged from the cavernous train station, they found themselves on 7th Avenue at 33rd Street, several blocks west and twenty blocks south of the YWCA.

"Do you want to walk or take a taxi? Or maybe we can figure out how to take the subway there," Clare said.

"You lead the way, but I'm famished. I don't think I can wait until we get there to eat something," Betty replied.

"Me, too. Let's go to that automat," Clare suggested, pointing to a Horn & Hardart across the street.

"Okay, I've never been to one of those before. But I guess you know just what to do."

"Sure," Clare said uncertainly. She had been to an automat once, as a little girl, before they all closed. The thing she remembered most was that even the ladies' room required a token.

Clare and Betty crossed the street and entered the automat. The interior was gleaming white and chrome, spotless and streamlined. They found a table near the cashier, set down their luggage, and traded some coins for nickel tokens. After looking at all the food visible behind the small glass windows, Betty chose some creamed spinach, and Clare picked macaroni and cheese. They put their tokens in the slot, turned the knob, opened the door, and removed their selections. Behind the doors, workers quickly refilled the empty compartments. Afterward, they decided to share a piece of cherry pie and each got a cup of coffee, dispensed from the mouth of a dolphin-shaped spigot.

"This is the best coffee I've ever had," said Clare.

"Don't let your friend Nell hear you say that!" Betty replied.

When they finished their coffee, the girls decided to take a cab to the YWCA since they had suitcases to carry. They shared a taxi with two other women who were also going uptown. The driver left them off in front of a tall brick building with many small windows on the upper floors. Clare and Kay entered the lobby and introduced themselves to the receptionist. The woman had a clipboard with a typed list of names, which she quickly scanned.

"Oh, yes. There you are. With the *Oklahoma!* production. You'll be staying on the fourth floor with the rest of the girls in the troupe. There's a cafeteria on the first floor where you can eat your meals, free of charge. Tomorrow you will get your uniforms, have your physicals and inoculations, and start your training. Or rehearsing. I see you're the star of the show," she said to Betty, which made her blush. "Dorothy," she called to a young woman typing at a desk behind her, "please show Miss Wilton and Miss Carlyle to their accommodations on the fourth floor."

Dorothy led them to the elevator, and they ascended to the fourth floor. When they emerged, they heard music coming from an open door and saw several young women crowded around a radio. "That must be Laurey!" one of them exclaimed as they looked up at Clare and Betty.

"What an odd thing to say," Betty said to Clare.

"But that's you. That's your character," Clare explained.

"Oh, of course. I've never seen the play. I bet you know it better than I do."

"No, I'm sure that's not true," said Clare, although she knew it was. "You'll learn your part in no time."

They arrived at the end of the hall, and Dorothy knocked on the last door. No one answered, and she opened it with a key. Inside were four single beds, two of which had suitcases on them.

"This will be your room," Dorothy said, handing them each a key. "The bathroom is down the hall. Dinner is from five o'clock until seven in the cafeteria. Breakfast is from seven in the morning until eight-thirty, and lunch is eleven-thirty to one." She also gave each girl a thick envelope. "This has all your paperwork and instructions in it. You'll have a meeting with the rest of the girls tomorrow at nine in the morning in the hall downstairs. Let us know if you need anything. You've got a couple hours to settle in before dinner."

Clare and Betty thanked Dorothy and looked around the room. Two twin beds were on one wall, and two were on the opposite wall. A nightstand with a lamp sat between each set of beds. Two closets were on either side of the door.

"It's so small," said Betty. "I never had to share a room before. Or a bathroom."

"It's not so bad. I never did either until I went to college," Clare said.

"You went to college?" Betty asked in surprise.

"Just one year. I don't know if I'll ever go back. It's a long story," Clare said, anxious not to explain further. At that moment, the door opened and two women entered. One was young, a pretty redhead about the same age as

Clare and Betty. The other woman was much older, at least fifty. Clare thought she might be the redhead's mother, although there was no resemblance.

"Are you Laurey?" the redhead asked Betty.

"No, I mean yes, I guess I am now," Betty said, laughing. "I'm Betty Wilton, and this is Clare Carlyle."

"I'm Ado Annie, and this is Aunt Eller," the redhead said, motioning to the older woman. "But you can call me Bonnie when we're not rehearsing."

"And I'm Florence," the older women interjected.

"I guess we'll all be roommates for now," Bonnie said. "What part do you play?" she asked Clare.

"I'm not in the show," Clare answered. "But it's one of my favorites, and I know all the songs."

"Good," said Bonnie, "you can help us practice our parts. It's always handy to have someone around who knows the show."

Clare and Betty unpacked their few belongings and sat cross-legged on their beds talking to Bonnie while Florence wrote a letter. Bonnie explained that she was from Chicago and had been in several musical productions there and in one on Broadway with a minor role. She hoped this tour would be her big break. Florence occasionally looked up from her letter, sometimes nodding approvingly and sometimes shaking her head slightly. The girls felt as if they had a built-in chaperone with Florence as their roommate.

At five o'clock, Florence put down her pen and shepherded the three young women downstairs to the cafeteria for dinner. There they saw the rest of the women from their floor. Most were in their early twenties, with a few older women here and there. After filling their plates with some simple fare, they sat down at a long table with the girls who had first recognized Betty to be "Laurey." Most of them were in the cast with small parts, but Clare was pleased to meet a few like her who were there just to improve the morale of the boys. After dinner, the girls milled around the lobby of the YWCA, getting acquainted with each other.

"Gosh," said Betty, "it's our first night in New York. Doesn't it seem like we should be going out on the town?"

Overhearing her, Florence said, "There will be time enough for that, but tonight we should all go to bed early and get a good night's sleep so we are ready for the day tomorrow." It was hard to argue with the motherly advice, so Clare, Betty, and Bonnie followed Florence back to their room. They talked for a while more, and then Betty and Bonnie read magazines, Florence read a thick novel, and Clare wrote in her diary before turning out the lights.

The next morning, Florence saw to it that her roommates were up, dressed, and at breakfast by seven-thirty. After eating some eggs, toast, and potatoes, all of the women went into the gymnasium for their meeting. Mr. Hastings was there, along with Dorothy and another woman they had not met before. Mr. Hastings introduced her as Mrs. Gladys Cummings, director of the USO tour program.

"Good morning, ladies," said Mrs. Cummings as she took the podium. "I believe you have all met Mr. Hastings as he hand-picked each of you to participate in this groundbreaking tour. I will be overseeing your training while you are in New York. Once you depart for the tour, Mrs. Florence Dunmore, our own Aunt Eller, will be looking out for you. There is, of course, a similar troupe of male actors staying at the YMCA. Those of you with parts in the show will be meeting them tomorrow to begin rehearsals. Mr. Hastings and his production team will be overseeing that aspect of things. The rest of you will stay with me and receive training in a variety of subjects including first aid, tropical diseases, aircraft spotting, and recreation.

"You will have some free time in the evenings, but you will be expected to help out at the Stage Door Canteen or other USO dance at least three nights a week. Of course, more is even better. You must remember that your primary duty, both while here in New York and while on the tour, is to raise the morale of the troops by wholesome means, to support and encourage them, and to remind them of what they are fighting for. Needless to say, romantic attachments, either with the soldiers or the male actors, are strictly prohibited, both for your sake and theirs," continued Mrs. Cummings. At this, several of the girls made sounds of disappointment. *You don't have to tell me that*, Clare thought sadly.

Mr. Hastings explained what the rehearsals would be like for the women with parts in the production. "And since *Oklahoma!* is a new show that many of you haven't seen, I've arranged for you to all attend the Wednesday matinee performance this week," he concluded with a flourish. A cheer went up from the audience.

Mrs. Cummings laid out more of the ground rules and announced that four Army doctors were there to give each volunteer a cursory physical and a series of inoculations. After that they would receive their USO uniforms.

Clare waited nervously with the other girls. When it was finally her turn, she was surprised to see a lineup of hypodermic needles that a nurse explained would prevent smallpox, tetanus, typhoid fever, typhus, yellow fever, and cholera. She began to wish she were going to England instead of somewhere so remote, but reminded herself that it was a small price to pay compared to what the soldiers were enduring.

Afterward, her arm aching, Clare went to the next room and was fitted with a new USO uniform. It consisted of a close-fitting olive green jacket and skirt with a khaki blouse and tie underneath. On the left shoulder of the jacket was a red patch with a white eagle and "USO Camp Shows" in blue stitching. The same insignia was repeated in smaller pins on both lapels of the jacket. She was also given a soft cloth cap like the soldiers wore called a garrison cap with the same USO patch on the left side. Clare admired herself in the full-length mirror and thought she looked quite smart. Once all the girls were outfitted, Mrs. Cummings instructed them on how and when to wear their hats and uniforms, as well as how to style their hair and what kind of make-up to wear.

After lunch, the girls received a geography lesson and saw the route they would take: first across the country to San Francisco by train and then by ship to Pearl Harbor. After putting on some shows there, they would continue on by plane to Christmas Island and Samoa, followed by Fiji, New Caledonia, the New Hebrides, and the Solomon Islands until they were almost to where there was still fighting. Nevertheless, Mrs. Cummings assured them there would be no danger from the Japanese, and that the actual risks were far greater from mechanical problems and tropical diseases, which did not make anyone feel less anxious.

The girls ate dinner at the YWCA, and no one even suggested going out on the town. They were all nursing their sore arms and wondering what they had gotten themselves into. The following morning was devoted to the study of the tropical ailments they might encounter including malaria, dysentery, dengue fever, and a variety of skin infections known collectively as "jungle rot." Clearly the vaccinations they had received were not effective against a host of unfamiliar diseases, and they learned about the yellow Atabrine pills they would have to take to prevent malaria and how to use mosquito netting.

In the afternoon, Clare and the other women excitedly made their way to the St. James Theatre on 44th Street for the matinee of *Oklahoma!* Clare could scarcely believe she was sitting there about to see a live performance by the actors whose voices she knew so well from the battered original Broadway cast record she had listened to countless times growing up. As the lights dimmed and the orchestra played the first notes of the overture, Clare felt a familiar rush of excitement. Then the curtain rose to reveal an elderly woman, Aunt Eller, churning butter. Off stage came the fine baritone voice of Alfred Drake's Curly, proclaiming it to be a beautiful morning. Clare was transported still further back in time to the beginning of the twentieth century, before Oklahoma was even a state.

Clare, along with the rest of the USO volunteers, sat enraptured until the curtain finally came down and the applause died away. As they left the theater and emerged in the fading daylight, Betty, grasping Clare's arm, said with anxiety in her voice, "Golly, that was something else. That Laurey is a tough act to follow … "

"Aw, don't worry. You sing better than she does, and you're a lot prettier, too!" Clare exclaimed, although she was relieved she did not have to worry about being in the show.

"So was this performance as good as the first time?" Betty asked.

"First time?"

"Yes, you said you saw it already."

"Oh, right. Yes, it was just as good. I'm sure I'll like the next fifty performances I see just as much," said Clare.

After dinner back at the YWCA, there was much informal rehearsing and practicing of lines, now that all the performers knew just what they had to recreate. Without the men, Clare and a couple other girls filled in. She had a passable singing voice and joined Betty in a duet of "People Will Say We're in Love" as Curly and then sang Will's part with Bonnie's Ado Annie in "All er Nuthin'."

"You're not too shabby, Clare," Bonnie exclaimed. "And you do know all the words. You could be Curly's understudy!"

"Thanks, but I'll stick to serving doughnuts," replied Clare with a laugh.

CHAPTER 17

After a day spent rolling bandages for the Red Cross, Clare and the other girls got ready for their first trip to the Stage Door Canteen. They returned to 44th Street, this time to the basement of the 44th Street Theatre. There they found a large room with a dance floor, serving area, and many small tables. They were each given a red, white, and blue striped apron to wear over their uniforms. A woman explained to them that the Stage Door Canteen had been founded by the American Theatre Wing as a recreation center for servicemen and was staffed by Broadway's most famous stars. Only five hundred men could enter at one time, and most nights there were four shifts, so they could serve only two thousand men a night. *Only?* thought Clare. *This makes Laurelmont's little USO dance look like nothing!*

The women were divided into groups and would rotate chores for each shift. Clare first found herself serving milk, juice, and cider. There was no alcohol, but that did not stop the men from flocking to the club. The chance to dance with a pretty girl and glimpse some stars was attraction enough. For the next shift, Clare served cake and doughnuts. Then she helped clear tables and finally spent the last shift behind the scenes helping to wash all the

Flying Time

glasses, dishes, and silverware for the next night. All the while, a variety of entertainers kept the servicemen occupied. A band played swing songs, and soldiers jitterbugged with the pretty hostesses while tap dancers, singers, and comedians filled in the gaps. Before they were released from duty, the girls were told that when they came back the following evening they would be serving as hostesses and dance partners and could wear a dress instead of their uniforms.

The girls trudged wearily back to the YWCA.

"I'm dog-tired," complained Bonnie. "And we didn't even have to dance tonight, just stand around handing out milk!"

"I bet the boys in Italy and New Guinea are a lot more tired than we are," chided Betty.

"I know, I know," said Bonnie sourly. "But that doesn't make my feet stop hurting."

"You're awful quiet, Clare," said Betty.

"It's just that I still can't believe I'm here," she answered.

"Me, too. I never thought I'd see New York. But you've been here before," said Betty.

"Yes, but it was different then. A lot different."

"A lot different when you saw *Oklahoma!* here a few months ago?" Betty asked.

"No, I don't know what I'm talking about. I guess I'm tired, too," Clare said with a shrug, and they continued their walk in silence.

The next morning, Florence turned over the page of the calendar tacked to the back of their door and revealed that it was October 1st. There was a definite chill in the air, and the leaves of the trees in Central Park were beginning to turn crimson.

As Clare was still tired from the previous evening's

activities, she was relieved to learn that the day would be devoted to aircraft spotting lessons rather than something more strenuous. When the lights were dimmed to show slides of black outlines of American and enemy planes, Clare was sure she was not the only one who felt her eyelids growing heavy. Later, the lights came back on with a jolt, and Mrs. Cummings handed out a quiz. Clare looked at the outlines on the sheet blankly and made a feeble attempt to fill in the correct name of each plane. After lunch, Mrs. Cummings returned the graded quizzes, and Clare was shocked to see a pattern of red slashes on hers, striking out her incorrect guesses. She had gotten just one right: the F4U Corsair with its distinctive inverted gull wing design. She looked around and was relieved to see everyone else had a similar design of red marks. Still, she had never failed a quiz before and vowed to study until she could recognize them all.

"Young ladies," Mrs. Cummings began, "I'm sorry to say you all performed abominably. We will repeat the slides with the lights on this time, and you will take a guidebook to study over the weekend. By Monday I expect each of you to be able to identify every airplane on the list. This may not seem important to you, but you never know when it may come in handy."

That night, Clare and the other girls put on their best dresses and dancing shoes. They returned to the Stage Door Canteen and were given the same patriotic aprons to distinguish themselves as volunteers. Instead of heading to the kitchen or serving tables, they greeted the men as they entered, led them to tables, chatted with them, and danced to Freddy Martin and his Orchestra when they were asked. A ballerina performed a dance routine to *Swan Lake,* and a comedian told jokes.

During a break from dancing, Clare spotted a

beautiful young woman with tawny hair and recognized her immediately.

"Betty," Clare whispered, "isn't that Lauren Bacall?" she said while trying to point inconspicuously at the tall beauty.

"Who?" asked Betty.

"You know, Lauren Bacall," she said despite seeing a genuine look of confusion on Betty's face.

"She does look familiar. I think maybe I saw her on a magazine cover, but I'm sure I don't know her name," said Betty. Before Clare realized what was happening, Betty was dragging her over toward the young woman. "Hi, Lauren. I'm Betty Wilton, and this is my friend Clare Carlyle. She says she knows you."

"Hello, but my name isn't Lauren. It's Betty, just like you. It's swell to meet you, though," she said with a distinctive husky voice. "Where do I know you from, Clare? Were we at a modeling shoot together?"

"Oh, no," Clare said, blushing. "You don't know me. I just recognized you from your movies."

"Movies? I haven't made any movies. But you know, I just heard about one my agent wants me to audition for. With Humphrey Bogart! Can you believe that?"

"Yes, I can believe it. I know you'll get the part," Clare answered.

"Well, thanks, but I'm not too sure. Lauren, huh? There are so many Bettys, but I don't know anyone else named Lauren … ," she said, lost in thought. Before Clare could reply, a sailor interrupted and whisked the soon-to-be Lauren away. Clare turned to face Betty, who was giving her a strange look.

"You know, it's nice to be encouraging, but you can't be sure she'll get that part. Acting is a tough field, and a lot of models never make the switch."

"True," said Clare, "but I just have a feeling about her."

Before they could discuss it any further, a pair of Marines came over and asked them to dance. When the evening finally drew to a close, the girls handed in their aprons and walked back to the YWCA.

"How are your feet tonight, Bonnie?" asked Betty.

"Oh, they still hurt plenty, but tonight it seemed like the sacrifice was worth it. I danced with so many men. Each one was dreamier than the last. It's something about those uniforms. A few guys said they'd come back to see me, and I even got a few addresses," Bonnie boasted.

"No, that's not allowed," Clare and Betty said in unison.

"The only time they should see you again is if they're in the audience at *Oklahoma!*" said Betty.

"You're not supposed to write to them. Trust me on that one," Clare said sternly.

"Jeepers, I can tell there's a juicy story there. Was he sitting under the apple tree with someone else? Did you get a 'Dear Jane' letter from a fellow you met at a dance?" Bonnie teased.

"No, just a letter from a chaplain," Clare said quietly.

Bonnie gasped and stammered an apology. "Gosh, I'm sorry. I had no idea. What happened?"

"It's okay, you didn't know. We met at a dance in Laurelmont. He asked me to write to him and I did. I guess I fell for him. Well, he got it in Sicily. Not right at the beginning but when it was almost over. The worst part is I should have stopped him."

"Stopped him from writing?" asked Betty.

"No, stopped him from going. To Sicily. I should

have known what would happen, but I realized it too late," Clare replied glumly.

"That's ridiculous! You think you can see the future? No one knows what's going to happen. Besides, even if you did know, he had to go. Uncle Sam said so," Bonnie said.

"If you would have stopped him, then he would have been AWOL, or worse, a deserter," said Betty. "You wouldn't have wanted that."

"No, but still. Maybe he could have been more careful. I can't help feeling responsible. And I've learned my lesson. No more romance for me," Clare said firmly.

Betty and Bonnie exchanged skeptical glances, and the girls continued their walk in silence.

CHAPTER 18

Clare spent the weekend studying her airplane spotters' manual. She began to see the subtle differences between the planes and was now sure she could tell B-24, B-25, and B-26 bombers apart, although she was not sure why she should need to know. She had a harder time with the outlines of the Japanese and German planes without their telltale rising suns and black and white crosses to give them away. Betty and Bonnie alternately quizzed Clare on the aircraft names while she helped them with their lines. Florence kept watch over everyone, making sure each was suitably occupied.

On Saturday evening, the girls prepared for their service at the Stage Door Canteen. They had been told to wear their uniforms, so they knew it was milk, doughnuts, and kitchen duty for them instead of dancing and making conversation. They decided to take a break on Sunday night and go back on Monday, Wednesday, and Friday of the following week to fulfill their duty, rather than three nights in a row.

On Monday morning, Clare went uneasily to her lessons, far more nervous about the airplane quiz than any subject she had studied in high school or college. Mrs. Cummings collected their finished papers and returned them after lunch. Clare was relieved to see only two red marks on her paper; she had mixed up an American P-40 Warhawk and a German Me 109 fighter, something she was sure she would not do in real life.

"Girls, I'm pleased to note that most of you took your assignment seriously, and your scores improved dramatically since last week," said Mrs. Cummings. "You will be quizzed periodically to make sure you remember what you've learned. Now we have a special guest, Army doctor Major Margaret Craighill from the WACs to present a special slide show on venereal disease," she said with enthusiasm.

When the lights dimmed and the first slide appeared on the screen, some girls gasped or made sounds of disgust. Clare instantly wished for more airplane slides instead, but the WAC officer competently explained each disease and how the conditions were rampant overseas. *At least no one has to worry about AIDS*, Clare reflected.

"Thank you, Major Craighill, for that most illuminating presentation. Of course, that won't be an issue for anyone here as all the girls understand the strict no fraternization policy with the servicemen and the other members of the cast," said Mrs. Cummings.

At dinner, Betty and Bonnie asked Clare what she had done during the day. She shared her success on the aircraft exam but assured them the rest of it was not suitable dinner conversation.

"Well, we spent the whole day on the same dance routine. A cowboy stepped on my feet twice! It couldn't have been worse than that!" exclaimed Bonnie.

"Trust me, it was," said Clare. "You wouldn't want a cowboy anywhere near you after what we saw today!"

The girls returned to the Stage Door Canteen that evening, with Bonnie carefully guarding her sore toes and

Clare warily seeing each man as teeming with germs.

Clare spent the rest of the week rolling bandages, assembling care packages, and learning basic first aid, while the cast practiced their lines, songs, and choreography. On Saturday night, the girls decided to attend a USO dance, although they had already fulfilled their three nights at the Stage Door Canteen. The dance was at the swanky Hotel Edison on West 47th Street. The grand ballroom was an Art Deco masterpiece, and throngs of servicemen and pretty young women danced to the sounds of Tony Pastor and his Orchestra.

Clare and Betty were taking a breather at a small table when two men came over to ask them to dance, an Army private named Leo and a buddy of his from the Navy named Sol. They explained they were from Brooklyn and had known each other for years. They were just lucky to be on leave in New York at the same time. Clare danced with Leo and Betty with Sol until a man from the ballroom interrupted them and led Betty away. Sol found a new partner, a pretty girl named Ruth, just in time for them to see Betty walk out onto the stage.

"Ladies and gentlemen," said Pastor, "we're pleased to have a special guest with us tonight, Miss Betty Wilton. Betty hails from Laurelmont, where she sang with Mort Lester and his Laurelhoppers. Betty is here in New York preparing for her first stage role as Laurey in a new traveling production of the smash hit *Oklahoma!* This USO tour will be traveling to the South Pacific. Just think, it would sure be a 'beautiful morning' to see this doll on a South Pacific isle!"

The men cheered, and Clare could just make out Betty's reddening cheeks as the orchestra began to play. She sang "Little White Lies" as the dancers in the room swayed.

"Wasn't she terrific, folks?" exclaimed Pastor. "I bet

you all hope you're headed to the Pacific now!"

Betty returned to the dance floor and had no more chances to rest as man after man cut in for a dance with the rising star.

CHAPTER 19

The next few weeks passed quickly for Clare and the girls as they settled into their routines. The days grew shorter and the temperature brisker. They planned to celebrate Halloween at the Stage Door Canteen and were told they could come in costume instead of in uniform. Bonnie found a devil's horns and pitchfork in the props department, and Florence was a very convincing Wicked Witch of the West. Betty and Clare did not know what to wear. Clare looked down at her USO uniform and reflected that in her old life she would have thought she was already wearing a costume.

"Clare, you should come to the theater for our rehearsal. Then you and Betty can pick out something from the wardrobe department. They have lots of old costumes left over from their past productions that you could borrow," suggested Bonnie.

"That's a good idea," said Betty, "But I've never seen the wardrobe department. How did you see it?"

"Let's just say I got a private tour from one of the stagehands ... ," answered Bonnie, her cheeks coloring. Florence glared at her. "He's not in the cast or a serviceman. I didn't think I signed on to stay away from every man for the duration," Bonnie said defensively.

At the theater, Clare sat unobtrusively in the back while the cast rehearsed. They had come a long way in the short time they had been performing together, and she was sure that with more practice their performances would be as flawless as the originals. Or maybe even better, in the case of Betty, who really was luminous as Laurey. When she sang, all the stagehands milling about the theater stopped to listen although they must have heard her countless times before.

After the rehearsal, Clare went backstage to the dressing room and found Betty and Bonnie taking off their exaggerated stage makeup.

"You were both fantastic!" gushed Clare.

"Just wait until you have to see that every night. You might not be so enthusiastic then," said Bonnie. "Let's go have a look at the costumes," she said, leading Clare and Betty down the hall to a door with a man standing next to it.

"This is Harry," Bonnie said, indicating the stagehand as he opened the door for them.

"You dolls take what you want. Just have it back by Monday morning. No one will notice," said Harry as he leered wolfishly at Bonnie.

"Gee, I don't know," said Clare. "I wouldn't want to get you in trouble."

"Trouble's my middle name, sweetheart. Besides, it'd be worth it to see you dames in these costumes," he said, pointing to a chorus girl outfit with sequined black tap pants and a plunging neckline.

"But you're not going to see us," said Betty. "These are for us to wear for the servicemen at the Stage Door Canteen." Harry scowled.

"Don't worry, Harry. You'll still see plenty of me," Bonnie said while leading him behind a rack of clothes.

Clare and Betty went in the other direction. Clare was immediately drawn to a rack of kimonos left over from a recent production of *The Mikado*. She selected a turquoise one with fuchsia peonies and gold embroidery.

"What do you think?" she asked Betty while holding the kimono up in front of her. Betty turned and gasped, the smile vanishing from her face.

"You can't dress up as a Jap. That's not funny!"

"Oh, I didn't think. The fabric was just so beautiful, I guess I forgot," she said lamely. She put the silken robe back on the rack, losing all enthusiasm for choosing a costume. "I don't think I want to pick out anything here. Not at the cost of Bonnie's virtue, anyway."

"I think it's too late for that," Betty laughed while selecting a flowing pale blue gown adorned with artificial flowers. She put on a matching crown of flowers. "Good night, sweet prince," she said brightly.

"I think you make a lovely Ophelia, but I don't think she said that."

"Oh, I never made it all the way to the end of the play when we had to read it in school. But I'll take it anyway."

They made their way back to the rack concealing Bonnie and her stagehand, clearing their throats loudly to make their presence known. Bonnie emerged with a grin, her hat crooked and lipstick smeared.

"That's a beautiful costume, Betty. Every GI will know the answer of 'to be or not to be' when he sees you in that! What did you pick, Clare?" asked Bonnie.

"I didn't really see anything," answered Clare, hoping that Betty would not mention her kimono *faux pas*.

"That's too bad," said Bonnie. By now Harry had reappeared, straightening his tie. They left the room, and he locked the door behind them. "Thanks, Harry," she said.

"Any time, sugar," said Harry, giving Bonnie a pinch that made her squeal.

As the girls walked back through the theater, Bonnie said, "I know, how about you wear one of my costumes from the show, Clare? We're about the same size."

"Gee, thanks, Bonnie. That would be swell," replied Clare. She did not really want to wear one of Ado Annie's frilly dresses but did not want to hurt Bonnie's feelings.

On Sunday, the girls got dressed in their costumes. Clare needed Bonnie's help to put on Ado Annie's dress, a profusion of ruffles and polka dots surrounding a tightly corseted bodice. She looked longingly at Betty's soft, flowing gown and even the shapeless form of Florence's witch costume and was grateful again not to be one of the performers. The dress even made the close-fitting USO uniform seem comfortable by comparison. Bonnie gave her a matching ruffled parasol, and they made their way to the Stage Door Canteen, the red pointed tail of Bonnie's costume peeking out from the bottom of her coat.

At the Canteen, Clare was happy to trade places with one of the servers so she did not have to jitterbug in Bonnie's dress. She enjoyed watching the crowd, seeing the line of men waiting to dance with Betty, and the indignant reaction of GIs change to delight when they saw the devil who had jabbed them with her pitchfork. While scanning the crowd, Clare was surprised to see another woman wearing almost the same dress as she wore. Their eyes met, and the woman approached the refreshment table.

"You must be the USO's Ado Annie. I'm Celeste Holm."

"Oh, Miss Holm, I know who you are! You were wonderful as Ado Annie! But I'm not in the show. I'm just borrowing the dress tonight from my friend Bonnie," Clare said, motioning to the redhead in the crimson dress with horns, tail, and pitchfork.

"My, she does look like a girl who can't say no!" exclaimed Miss Holm, laughing. "I should go talk to her. Maybe give her some pointers. Or maybe she can give some to me! Lovely to meet you, dear. Good luck with the tour. I wish I could go, but we're about to record an album of the show."

"Yes, it's one of my favorites. I've listened to it over and over," Clare enthused. "I mean, I'm sure I will listen to it over and over," she added at Miss Holm's bemused look.

Clare was relieved when Miss Holm departed and even more relieved when the band played the last song, and they were ready to go home. Back at the YWCA, her discomfort was finally alleviated when Bonnie released her from the confines of the frilly dress.

"Thanks for letting me wear your costume, Bonnie. I don't know how you do it. Miss Holm seemed very nice," Clare said as she sank down into her bed.

"Yes, she did. She gave me some good advice. Except the part about watching out for a stagehand named Harry! I guess I am just a girl who can't say no!"

CHAPTER 20

After another week of instruction in first aid, plane identification, and hostess duties, Clare decided to treat herself to lunch at the Horn & Hardart. She snuck out of the YWCA, hopeful no one had seen her. She had not been alone in ages and was looking forward to a break from the other girls. They were all congenial, but Clare had to watch everything she said, thinking carefully about whether some song, movie, or event she mentioned had not yet happened. More than a few girls had given her a curious look at her mistakes. Clare was relieved to blend into the crowds of people thronging the streets, each seeming to move with resolute purpose toward some important destination.

She ducked into the automat and scanned the room, seeing no one she knew. She carefully examined the entrees behind each glass door and passed by some of the more creative offerings like tripe creole and kidney stew, concocted to take advantage of the fact that organ meat was not rationed. Instead, Clare chose a small chicken potpie that proved to have very little chicken, but she did not mind. She also selected a slice of coconut cream pie and steaming coffee dispensed from the dolphin-shaped spout on the wall to complete her meal.

Clare spotted an empty table in the far corner and

settled down. Someone had left behind a copy of that week's *Life* magazine with a handsome fighter pilot on the cover, and she was happy to have some reading material. She idly flipped through the pages, reading stories about Frank Sinatra serenading an audience of WAVES, the execution of Nazi spies, and an incongruously peaceful article about ducks. Even the advertisements were interesting to Clare, as mundane items like socks, belts, and prune juice proclaimed how they were helping to win the war.

But Clare gasped audibly when she turned a page near the back of the magazine and found herself looking at the picture of Roy receiving the blood plasma transfusion which had appeared in the newspaper two months earlier. It was now part of an advertisement promoting blood donation. "The Gift of Life is Yours to Give!" the caption shouted. In smaller letters below the photograph it read, "Blood Plasma Saves an American Soldier in Sicily," and urged the public to call their local blood donation center for an appointment today.

Clare felt tears well up in her eyes as she looked at the picture. *Saves an American soldier, what a lie!* she thought bitterly. *I'm sure it's saved plenty of soldiers but not my soldier.*

The picture was much clearer than what was printed in the newspaper, and she studied it carefully. The more closely she looked, the more she suspected that the image had been altered; the shape of Roy's nose looked different. Then she noticed that the Folmer Graflex Camera Company had prepared the ad – who better to retouch an image? Clare wondered if they knew Roy had not survived or just thought to err on the side of caution.

Would Roy's family and friends recognize him if they saw the ad? I guess it's okay to use his picture if it gets more people to give blood. With that thought, Clare realized enough time had elapsed for her to donate again, drained the last of her coffee, and departed for the Red Cross blood donation center.

CHAPTER 21

Thanksgiving came and went with Clare and the girls doling out a turkey dinner with all the trimmings to the boys at the Stage Door Canteen. Clare helped assemble care packages to send to the troops for Christmas. Some of the girls slipped in a photo with their name and address on the back, hoping the recipient would write to her, but Clare knew better.

Clare received several letters full of gossip from Kay. She still had a host of pen pals, and Nell's Johnny would be home on leave at the end of the month. Clare went to Macy's to find Christmas presents to send them. She chose two scarves: one with an embroidered Naval insignia for Nell and one with a "V" for victory for Kay as she had beaus in all branches of service.

Rehearsals for *Oklahoma!* were going well, and the new cast was now as flawless as the original one on Broadway. Clare had become an expert on tropical diseases, how to make a shy soldier feel at ease, what to say to wounded men in the hospital, and how to handle a drunken sailor. She felt ready for action and was elated when Mrs. Cummings and Mr. Hastings gathered them all together in the gymnasium and announced that the tour would depart the following week, two days after Christmas. Cheers went up from the girls, all of them just as anxious as Clare to begin their adventure.

Christmas was spent quietly with a service in the YWCA chapel and a filling meal of roasted chicken with candied sweet potatoes and mince pie for dessert. The next day, the girls visited the Stage Door Canteen for the last time and bid farewell to some of the regular Broadway volunteers they had come to know. Aware that the USO tour was about to depart, Alfred Drake made a surprise visit to the Canteen and accompanied Betty in singing "People Will Say We're in Love," much to the delight of the audience. Clare noted that Betty now seemed more at ease spontaneously performing in front of the crowd. The months of rehearsing had certainly given her a new level of confidence.

Clare slept intermittently that night, knowing their journey across the country would begin the next day. It did not take long to pack up her clothing and possessions. She carefully bundled her diary, the framed photos of Roy, and the charm into a handkerchief before stashing them in her USO-issued leather handbag. A bus came to collect the troupe and their baggage for the ride to Pennsylvania Station where they boarded a train bound for San Francisco.

The journey took the whole week with stops at Union Station in Chicago, then Denver and Salt Lake City before arriving in San Francisco. The train was constantly crowded, but the troupe had been issued highly coveted tickets to comfortable Pullman sleeper cars. However, Clare, Betty, and some of the other young women readily gave up their berths to mothers and children, instead sleeping upright in the crowded passenger compartments. The unspoiled views of the Great Plains, Rocky Mountains, and the Sierra Nevada helped to lessen the passengers' discomfort.

It was New Year's Eve when the troupe arrived in San Francisco. The men were sent to a YMCA, and the women were shepherded to the local YWCA. They reconvened at a USO club, and the cast gave their first performance of *Oklahoma!* to a standing room only audience of servicemen. The men were enthralled, and Betty and Bonnie spent hours signing autographs afterward. Clare was content to serve milk and doughnuts on the sidelines.

When the master of ceremonies announced it was nearing twelve o'clock, the audience counted down the seconds. At the stroke of midnight, the orchestra began to play "Auld Lang Syne." The sailor to whom she was about to serve a doughnut pulled Clare from behind the table for a close, slow dance; she did not mind and wondered what 1944 had in store for her.

CHAPTER 22

After a day of rest, Clare, Betty, and Bonnie took in the sights of San Francisco, riding a cable car from Chinatown to Fisherman's Wharf. They had escaped the watchful eye of Florence, who was now responsible for all the girls, not just the three of them. There was a palpable excitement in the air with so many servicemen on leave or waiting to depart for duty overseas, knowing they had to make the most of their time. Still, Clare and Betty returned to the YWCA at the expected hour to get a good night's sleep before the impending voyage. They could not convince Bonnie to accompany them, as she had found a very handsome Marine who was keen to take her out to some of Chinatown's famed nightclubs. She was nowhere to be found when they awoke the next morning, yet still managed to show up in time for breakfast, assuring them there would be plenty of time to sleep on the ship.

That ship turned out to be none other than the Matson Line's glamorous *SS Lurline*, a luxury ocean liner turned troopship for the war. Once accustomed to ferrying the wealthy and elite from San Francisco to Hawaii, now she teemed with servicemen and war materiel crammed into every corner. Clare, Betty, and Bonnie were assigned to a cabin on a lower deck and soon found they would be sharing it with three other girls. Once a luxurious room for a vacationing couple, the cabin was cramped and uncomfortable for six. Or at least Clare thought until they walked past the Grand Ballroom and saw the accommodations for enlisted men. The lavish chandeliers had been removed and scaffolding erected to support layer upon layer of bunks to sleep many hundreds of men.

Their luggage stowed, the girls made their way to the deck shortly before the ship was due to set sail. A crowd had gathered to see them off, and a band played at the dock. The girls waved to the well-wishers on the shore, and Clare felt a jolt of excitement as the ship began to move away from the dock. They kept waving as the ship sailed under the Golden Gate Bridge, and the onlookers became tinier and tinier specks in the distance. As the mainland grew smaller, Clare thought about her father with a pang. She reflected that she thought of him less and less often and wondered if he, too, were finding it easier to go about his life without her. Finally the shore itself faded from view, with only the vast blue of the Pacific as far as the eye could see.

Clare and the other girls soon realized it was best to spend as little time in their cabin as possible. Not only was it cramped, but it also became hotter and hotter. The gentle rolling of the ship became unpleasant below deck with no airflow or view of the horizon to combat seasickness. After the first night, they decided to try sleeping on deck. They found they were not the only ones to have that idea, and space was at a premium. Nevertheless, the fresh air made even the crowd more tolerable than the stagnant cabin. The girls discovered they were not the only women aboard the ship, and were happy to meet WACs and Navy nurses heading overseas for the first time, too. Looking out for schools of dolphins and flying fish became a popular activity while chatting about home.

While the servicemen had nothing to do, the USO troupe was soon put to work. The performers gave several small concerts each day. Their costumes and scenery were all stowed away, so they did not perform the show but sang excerpts and other songs requested by the audience. Betty, especially, became the crowd's favorite with hundreds of men pressing close together to hear her sing. Clare and the other girls who weren't performers were also kept busy. They visited sick patients in the infirmary, played cards, and served refreshments at the movies shown in the dining hall each night. Clare was even tapped to help type the ship's daily newspaper.

Although life at sea was not unpleasant, Clare was thrilled when they received word that land had been sighted. The passengers flocked to the deck to watch the growing outline of the shore emerge from the horizon. The six days at sea had gone by quickly. Clare knew that most of the other passengers were not disembarking but continuing on for many more days to New Caledonia or even New Guinea, very close to the fighting.

Clare's elation at sighting land was tempered with sorrow as the ship docked in Pearl Harbor. Although a little more than two years had passed since the Japanese attack that plunged the country into war, signs of the destruction were still obvious, most notably the wreck of the sunken *USS Arizona*, only the barbette of a gun turret remaining above the waterline and a slick of oil that Clare knew would continue to emanate from the ship for many decades in the future. Despite the warm tropical air, Clare felt herself shiver as she thought about the thousand men still entombed in the wreck below the water. She had never been so close to so much death and destruction before and hoped she never would come closer. And yet she knew so many of those men remaining aboard the *Lurline* would be going on to face even greater horrors at places like Kwajalein, Peleliu, and Leyte. It was a sobering thought, but Betty and Bonnie took no notice of Clare's melancholy as they pulled her down the gangplank toward land.

PART III

THE PACIFIC

SO YOU
ARE GOING
TO THE
SOUTH PACIFIC?

PREPARED BY COMMANDER AIR FORCE PACIFIC FLEET
REPRINTED BY AVIATION TRAINING DIVISION
OFFICE OF THE CHIEF OF NAVAL OPERATIONS
U. S. NAVY   1944

13

CHAPTER 23

"This sure beats New York!" exclaimed Bonnie. "Yes siree, I could get used to Januarys like this," she said as a warm breeze ruffled their skirts. Clare and Betty looked around wide-eyed at the bustling action of the harbor, the swaying palm trees, and the lush green mountains in the background. "I wonder what kind of dump they'll put us up in here," Bonnie mused. "Well, it can't be as bad as that sardine can we just came from."

A bus arrived to collect the troupe, driving them along the coast toward downtown Honolulu. They approached a YMCA and felt certain they had arrived at their destination, but the bus kept on going past the center of town. The buildings became smaller and less numerous, the foliage denser. They could occasionally see the multihued blue of the Pacific through breaks in the trees. Then suddenly rising above them was an improbable sight: a vast Moorish-style castle in a most unexpected shade of pink.

"It's the Royal Hawaiian Hotel! The 'Pink Palace of the Pacific!'" exclaimed Clare. The Navy had leased the hotel to serve as a rest and recreation center for troops serving in the Pacific, and now the USO volunteers would make it their home in Hawaii.

"Don't get so excited," warned Bonnie. "Remember that floating tin can was supposed to be a luxury ocean liner." But the girls found that their accommodations were perfectly acceptable, not plush like the wealthy prewar guests must have enjoyed but a lot better than a barebones YMCA.

The girls were given some time to explore the surrounding area, known as Waikiki Beach. The expanse of white sand was beautiful, except for the barbed wire that lined the shore, protection against a Japanese invasion that Clare knew would never come. Nevertheless, it was still possible to swim, which the girls did under the watchful eye of Florence, who took her role as chaperone and lifeguard quite seriously.

The troupe's respite did not last long; after all, *they* were the recreation. The next day they began performing *Oklahoma!* at least once a day, sometimes more. They played at the Royal Hawaiian, hospitals, and many of the other military bases on the island, always to an appreciative audience. Clare usually spent the time visiting patients in the hospitals or helping at one of the USO clubs. She wrote countless letters home dictated by wounded men who could not write, read books to men who could not see, danced to records, or played cards and checkers. She was exhausted each night, falling into bed wearily and wondering where she would get the energy for the next day. Then she remembered the men she had met in the hospitals, wounded at remote places like Tarawa, Bougainville, and Cape Gloucester, and felt contrite.

The girls became accustomed to seeing planes overhead, singly or in groups. Squadrons of fighters, dive bombers, and torpedo bombers practiced maneuvers. Clare did her best to identify each one, but knowing they had to be American planes made that task easier. In time, she even began to associate the sound of the engines with a particular type of airplane.

The volunteers' stay on Oahu lasted two weeks. By then Clare was sure that everyone on the island had seen *Oklahoma!* at least once. She had seen it many more times than she cared to remember and had even begun to question if it really was one of her favorite musicals. By now she knew every line of the show and knew when an actor misspoke or ad-libbed. The only thing that had worn on her patience more than the show was the pineapple. It seemed to be the only food available in abundance there and was incorporated into every meal in some creative way. Again Clare had to remind herself that too much pineapple was not a great hardship to endure.

The day before they were scheduled to depart Hawaii, the troupe was called together for a meeting about the tour itinerary and an update on each island's conditions. Near the end of the presentation, a Navy doctor came around to remind them of what tropical diseases would be common, stressing that they would be in little danger from the Japanese, but mosquitoes, parasites, and fungus would be relentless foes. With that, he distributed their first dose of the antimalarial Atabrine, making sure everyone had swallowed the little yellow pill.

"Now I know where the saying 'a bitter pill to swallow' came from," said Bonnie with a grimace. "And it turns you yellow to boot!"

"It's not that bad," Clare chided. "I'm sure it's better than having malaria."

The next day a bus transported the volunteers to a nearby airfield. They found two cargo planes waiting for them, their sets, props, and costumes already loaded aboard. Clare recognized the planes immediately as Douglas C-47 Skytrains, the military version of a DC-3. Clare knew that commercial DC-3s could be luxurious with plush seats and stewardesses. But as they climbed into the airplane, Clare saw that the interior, like that of the *Lurline* and·the Royal Hawaiian, was a far cry from its prewar days. Metal bench seats lined each side of the fuselage so the passengers faced each other. The girls strapped themselves in with seatbelts of heavy webbing.

Clare, sitting across the aisle from Betty, noticed that her friend was looking decidedly green. "Are you okay, Betty?" she asked. "You can't be airsick; we haven't even moved yet."

"I'm okay," Betty replied weakly. "I'm just a little nervous, I guess. I've never flown in an airplane before." A chorus of agreement went up from the other passengers.

"Have *you* flown in a plane before?" Bonnie asked Clare.

"Well, yes, but not like this one," she admitted. No, the planes she had flown in had been larger, pressurized, heated, had jet engines, and stewardesses who served Coca-Cola and tiny bags of peanuts. It was more like sitting in your living room for a couple hours and then finding yourself someplace entirely different. As the door of the airplane was closed, Clare realized she could see light streaming in from the outside through chinks around the door. The engines whirred to life, producing a deafening sound. The smell of oil and aviation fuel permeated the cabin. "I guess I'm a little nervous, too," Clare added with a wan smile.

The Skytrain began to taxi and was soon airborne. The braver of the girls craned their necks to see the land shrinking below them through the small rectangular windows. The less brave squeezed their eyes shut tightly, and Clare even saw one girl clutching a rosary. But the plane soon evened out, and the passengers began to relax.

They flew low and slowly, and the ride was bumpy compared to the jet airliners Clare had flown in before. The cabin was cold, and they were glad to be wearing their full uniforms. Once in a while, the pilot or copilot would come back to check on the passengers.

"Golly, this is the best looking cargo I've ever delivered," said the young pilot with a whistle. Clare guessed he could not have been more than a year or two older than her. That would have made her nervous before, but she felt surprisingly at ease.

The hours dragged on with nothing below them but the Pacific Ocean. They alternately dozed, chatted, played cards, and griped about the hard metal seats. The performers began to sing songs, with Betty leading the way. Clare was grateful they sang nothing from *Oklahoma!*; they must have grown tired of it as well. Clare wondered if flying was really any better than taking another ship.

After what seemed like an eternity, but was really more like 10 hours, the pilot announced that they would soon land. Clare watched as an island emerged from the vast blue below. It was astonishing to her that the young pilot had somehow found this speck of coral without the aid of all the high-tech instruments common in Clare's time. The airstrip came into view, he made a couple of passes, and then set the plane down on the coral runway. Although the landing had been bumpy, the passengers applauded. When the plane stopped and the propellers were no longer spinning, the pilot and copilot helped them from the plane. Bonnie was so moved and grateful to be on the ground again that she kissed them both.

Clare, too, was glad to be on the ground again. She turned to look back at the airplane and was suddenly reminded of the diner back in Laurelmont; its neon sign depicted the same type of plane circling the globe. She felt in the pocket of her skirt and touched the heart-shaped charm. She pulled it out quickly and stole a glance at it. *You're almost home*, she thought. But they were not technically in the South Pacific. They were on a small island due south of Hawaii, just a little more than a hundred miles north of the equator. The Americans called it Christmas Island, but Clare knew the locals pronounced it "Kee-rees-mass" and would come to spell it Kiritimati.

The base commander and his staff came to meet them and take them to their accommodations, two sparsely furnished Quonset huts made of corrugated steel shaped to form an arched roof and curved walls. Enlisted men unloaded the cargo, and the troupe got settled in their new home. It was hotter but surprisingly not more humid than Oahu had been. The troupe played six shows in three days. Clare found the men, who had not seen a woman in months, were delighted to talk with her and were exceedingly respectful. Before she knew it, they were boarding the C-47 for their next destination, Samoa.

They had not been in the air more than an hour when the pilot came back to announce they had just crossed the equator, and a cheer went up from the passengers. The flight to Samoa was a bit shorter than the previous one, but the troupe was just as anxious to land as before. What they encountered was the stereotypical South Seas isle, with waving palm trees, white sand, and pristine water backed by mountains covered in lush tropical foliage. Despite the picture-postcard scenery, they were warned against its mosquitoes, which spread not malaria but the much more horrifying elephantiasis. Clare was diligent in her use of mosquito netting, despite the heat and humidity. She examined it each morning for holes that might let in a tiny assailant.

Again the troupe played to enthusiastic audiences.

Clare and the other "girl-next-door" volunteers were eagerly sought out by officers and enlisted men alike. Most were happy to talk about their families, the girls they left behind, and news of home. Some wanted a dance, and very few tried to get fresh with the girls. To Clare's surprise, it seemed the time away from home and women had actually made them more polite.

Traveling further south and west, they flew to Fiji and then New Caledonia, playing dozens of shows. New Caledonia, a territory of France, was much more developed and civilized than Clare expected. It teemed with men on leave and recuperating from wounds or disease. They were not far from Australia now but did not stop there. Instead they flew north, visiting Efate and Espiritu Santo in the New Hebrides. Both islands had huge military installations, hospitals, and airfields. The troupe performed for thousands of men over the next two weeks.

Flying still further north, they landed at Henderson Field on Guadalcanal in the Solomon Islands. When Clare emerged from the plane, she could tell instantly that something was different about this island. The palm trees around the airstrip had no leaves; they were bare stumps or poles. Incessant shelling, bombing, and strafing by Americans and then the Japanese had devastated the surroundings. Although the island had been captured from the Japanese and secured for a year now, the terrain still bore the marks of heavy fighting. None of their previous destinations had been occupied by the Japanese. None had seen the violence and bloodshed that had visited Guadalcanal, once home to tranquil coconut plantations supplying oil to the soap industry.

As the troupe stood on the airstrip waiting for an official to collect them, another difference emerged. It was clear this was an active airbase with planes taking off for and returning from missions against the Japanese. Clare saw a squadron of airplanes approaching from the distance and instantly recognized them as Lockheed P-38 Lightning fighters because of their distinctive twin tails. The first one landed, but the second plane made an impossibly low pass over the airstrip, the wash from its two propellers sending the girls' hair into disarray. To Clare, it seemed as if the big plane was just inches above them, but she knew that could not be true. Cries of protestation and mild oaths went up from their small group. Even Florence, typically reserved and unflappable, said a few choice words.

By then the recreation officer had appeared. "Welcome to Guadalcanal, ladies and gentlemen," the young lieutenant said, beaming at the men and women of the cast. He motioned to some SeaBees to start unloading the Skytrains.

"Lieutenant, that's not the kind of welcome we're used to receiving," said Florence, still trying to tame her wild hair. "Are you sure you want us here?"

"Oh, yes, ma'am. I'm awful sorry about that. That's just the Sarge showing off. I know all the fellas will be awful glad to have you here. Follow me to your accommodations."

As they walked off the airstrip, Clare found herself even with the lieutenant. She could not help asking him, "A sergeant was flying that P-38? I thought only officers were pilots."

"You're right, miss. Only officers are pilots. That 'sarge' is a captain. Captain Parker York. But they call him Sergeant York. You know, like the hero from the Great War. The one Gary Cooper played in that picture. It's a nickname. They just call him Sarge. I suppose it would be easier to just call him York, but they don't," he said with a sigh.

"I know," Clare said wryly. "Everyone's got a nickname." She looked over her shoulder and saw that the offending airplane had come to a stop. The pilot had jumped out and was walking in the opposite direction. A ground crew rushed over to the plane, which Clare could see had a distinctive design painted on the fuselage near its nose: a pretty brunette wearing only skimpy red satin shorts and boxing gloves, her gloved hands placed strategically in front of her bare torso. Above the figure, "KO Punch" was painted in red lettering.

CHAPTER 24

Clare and the rest of the troupe found their accommodations on Guadalcanal to be more primitive than they had previously encountered. Instead of metal Quonset huts, they were shown to a series of olive drab canvas tents in a coconut grove. Between the two rows of tents was a neat gravel path defined by palm logs.

"This is our company street," the recreation officer said proudly, but no one else seemed to share his enthusiasm.

Clare, Betty, and Bonnie found a tent to share with three other girls. They each picked a wooden folding cot arranged around the empty center of the pyramidal tent. There was no other furniture, and the sides of the tent could be raised or lowered to allow for ventilation or privacy.

"Jiminy Cricket, what a dump!" exclaimed Bonnie when the young lieutenant was out of earshot. "This is the worst place yet."

"Bonnie!" Clare and Betty cried in unison.

"What's the matter with you?" Betty chided. "Why do you think we deserve better accommodations than the troops? They risked their lives for this island, and all we do is sing."

"I know," Bonnie said, chastened. "I'm just tired. I guess I don't feel like myself. I'm sure a good night's sleep in one of these comfy cots will do the trick," she said with sarcasm creeping into her voice.

That night, the members of the troupe were guests of honor at a fine dinner in the Officers' Mess, a Quonset hut with several long wooden tables parallel to the sloping walls. Afterward, they sat around chatting and drinking in the Officers' Club, an adjacent Quonset hut with multiple round tables and a bamboo-trimmed bar at the back. Eager for company, the men talked of home and the progress of the war. Everyone speculated about when the war would be over.

"I bet it's like the saying goes, 'Golden Gate in Forty-eight,'" the recreation lieutenant offered resignedly.

"Oh, no, you're wrong!" Clare exclaimed; she had said little previously, but the warm beer served up at the bar had loosened her restraint. "The war in Europe will end in May of 1945, and the war in the Pacific will be over in August of 1945. You should all be home by the end of 1945," she added brightly.

The others at the table stared at her dumbly for a moment. Clare felt herself redden as all eyes focused on her.

"Well, miss, you seem awfully certain about that. Either you're really a high-ranking official in the War Department or you have a crystal ball. Which is it?" asked another lieutenant.

"I've said too much already. Loose lips sink ships," said Clare, coyly.

"Now wait a minute, sister. Who are you, anyway?"

"I'm Clare Carlyle. I'm from Schenectady, New York, and I'm just here to help with the show," she said weakly. "I don't know why I said that ... ," her voice trailing off. "I used to work at a five-and-dime store. I don't know anything about the war."

"Clare, don't be modest," Betty interjected. "Tell them about how you went to college for a year. That's why she's so smart."

"Oh yeah, which college?" someone asked.

"Penllyn," Clare replied.

The men at the table raised their eyebrows, but before Clare could decide if they were impressed or merely doubtful, she was interrupted by a clatter from behind. She turned around and saw that the table behind her was full of aviators. They had been eavesdropping on the conversation. The man behind Clare had been leaning back in his chair with his feet propped up on the table, nonchalantly it would seem, but really to listen in on the discussion behind him. He caught himself an instant before the chair tipped over, spilling the drink he had been nursing down his shirt as he regained his balance. He turned around at the same instant as Clare.

"You went to Penllyn?" he asked. "I went to Glenmere. I'm Parker," he said, smiling and extending a hand to Clare.

Clare's eyes widened involuntarily as she took in the man before her. He had blond hair, blue eyes, and a broad smile with even, white teeth that shone against his golden tan. He was older than her, maybe twenty-six or twenty-seven. She noted the silver captain's bars on his collar and the pilot's wings pinned to his damp shirt. His sleeves were rolled up, and she admired his muscular arms and strong, capable hands. On one wrist he was wearing a heavy sterling ID bracelet with a smaller version of his Army Air Forces pilot's wings and the name "York" engraved in large letters.

"Ooh, I know *you*," Clare said. "We met on the

airstrip this afternoon. Thanks for the warm welcome, Sarge."

"Aw, don't be sore. I was just having some fun. I couldn't resist ruffling some feathers. You Hollywood types take yourselves much too seriously. Anyway, you don't look much worse for wear."

"I'm not a Hollywood type," Clare said indignantly. "I'm just a regular, hometown girl-next-door type. Here to raise morale and remind the boys what they're fighting for."

"Now that you mention it, my morale could use a boost. Dance with me."

Before Clare could answer, York pulled her up and toward the back of the building. A tinny wind-up phonograph sat on one end of the bar, playing V-disc recordings by Dinah Shore, Kate Smith, and Tommy Dorsey.

"Sorry it's no orchestra, but it will have to do. Schenectady, huh? Never been there."

Clare was about to reply, "me, neither," but stopped herself in time and resolved to drink no more of the officers' beer. "So where are you from?" she asked, beginning her standard script.

"Connecticut," York replied.

"Have you got a special girl back home?" asked Clare, instantly regretting her customary question. Either he did or she would not believe him if he said no.

"No, not any more. Thought I did once. Didn't even send me a 'Dear John' letter. Just stopped writing to me. That's for the best, I suppose. Too much to do out here without having a gal to worry about, too."

"What did you do before the war?" Clare asked.

"I graduated from Glenmere in Thirty-nine. I worked at my father's firm on Wall Street for a couple years. I was in the flying club at Glenmere, so I already had a private pilot's license. I enlisted in Forty-one when it became clear we weren't going to stay neutral. Of course, I thought I'd be going to Europe. But it turned out they sent me here, and I've been on one forsaken rock after another since Forty-two."

"That's a long time!" Clare exclaimed. "Haven't you served long enough to go home?"

"Sure, but then I'd have to go back to my old life. I'd rather a Jap get me than die of boredom behind a desk on Wall Street. But don't tell my folks that."

"I understand. I don't know if I'd want to go back to my old life, either," added Clare. *I don't know how to go back to my old life anyway*, she thought.

"What about Penllyn? Don't you want to graduate?" York asked.

"Oh, I do. But it's complicated. Maybe someday."

"What were you studying there?"

"Anthropology," Clare replied. Of the thousands of men she had already met while with the USO, not one had asked her so much about herself. That was just as well, since she was not supposed to give out personal details. But she felt instantly at ease with York and sensed he genuinely wanted to know. Or maybe it was just because she still felt tipsy and was not thinking clearly.

"You could be the next Margaret Mead. How about *Coming of Age in the Solomon Islands*? I understand there are fascinating primitive mating rituals on these islands," York said with a wink.

Shocked, Clare pulled away from him, suddenly clear-headed. "That's not what I came here for. I'd better go. It's getting late. Nice to meet you, Captain York," she said coolly.

"Wait, I didn't mean to offend you. I was only teasing. Being out here for so long, I guess I forget what's proper sometimes. Let me walk you back to your tent."

"No, thank you, Captain."

"When will I see you again, Miss Carlyle? Let me make it up to you. We'll go on a picnic. I'll be the perfect gentleman, scout's honor."

"I can't. We're not allowed to fraternize with the men alone. It's against the rules."

"What if we're not alone?" York asked.

"I'll think about it," Clare replied, having already made up her mind to stay away from the tall, handsome aviator. Clare collected her companions, and they retired to their tent.

"Ooh, Clare that blond pilot was a real dreamboat. He was sure sweet on you," Bonnie said.

"A little too sweet. Besides, I've come this far and not been tempted by any fellas, and lots of them have been attractive. I'm not going to start now. It can only lead to all sorts of trouble," Clare said firmly.

"I think it's just the uniforms, anyway," Betty added. "I wouldn't give half these men a second look if I passed them on the street wearing civilian clothes."

"Maybe you're right," said Bonnie, "but I wouldn't mind seeing that one without his uniform and judging for myself!"

"You can have him," said Clare. "Let's get some sleep. Don't forget you two have a big day tomorrow." They sank down into their cots and arranged their mosquito nets.

"This is more comfortable than it looks," said Bonnie. "I'm sure glad they left us these wool blankets. Who knew it gets so cold at night on this island." Clare and Betty exchanged puzzled glances, the humid tropical night air even more oppressive under the mosquito netting.

CHAPTER 25

"Clare, wake up," Betty whispered. "Do you hear that sound? I think there's an animal in here. It sounds like a rattlesnake."

"I'm awake now. I hear it, too. That's no rattlesnake. That's coming from Bonnie's cot. I think it's her teeth chattering. She must have malaria!" Clare cried as she rushed to Bonnie's side. "She's drenched in sweat. We've got to get her to the hospital."

By now the other girls in the tent were awake, too. Clare instructed them to keep an eye on Bonnie while she and Betty went for help. Two litter-bearers accompanied them back to the tent. The commotion roused Florence from her slumber, two tents away. The medics carried Bonnie away on a stretcher, with Clare, Betty, and Florence trailing behind.

"I don't understand how she could get malaria; we've been so careful," said Clare.

"You know, her skin still has a rosy glow, and ours is starting to look awful yellow," Betty replied. "I bet she's been spitting out the Atabrine pills when no one's looking."

"Well, she'll have to take it now. That's the only treatment for malaria unless they have some quinine, but that's in very short supply," said Clare.

The medics got Bonnie settled in at the base hospital and assured Clare, Betty, and Florence that she would be fine in a few days. When they returned to their tents, all the members of the troupe were awake and had heard the news.

"What will we do now, Florence?" asked Bob, who played Curly in the show. "We're supposed to have our first performance at two o'clock today."

"We can't go on without an Ado Annie," said Jimmy, who played Will. "Who would I sing to?"

"If only we had someone who could fill in. Someone who knows the part. Someone who can wear the costumes," Florence said, looking pointedly at Clare. Clare realized everyone was staring at her.

"Me?" Clare said weakly. "Oh, no. I couldn't. I can't act. I can't dance. I'm not a very good singer. Can't one of the girls from the chorus do it?"

"Clare, we all know you can sing the part *and* wear the costumes. There's not much dancing. The chorus dances more than Ado Annie does, anyway. If we took one of the chorus girls away, you'd have to fill in for her, and that would stand out a lot more since you don't know the choreography," said Betty.

"I guess that makes sense, but I'd really rather not," Clare pleaded.

"Miss Carlyle, do I need to remind you why you — and all the rest of us — are here? To raise the morale for these boys who have done so much for us and everyone at home. Your little case of stage fright is nothing compared to what these men have felt when they stormed enemy beaches or faced anti-aircraft fire from Jap guns," Florence chided.

"You're right," Clare said, chastened. "I'll do it. But what if I'm terrible? What if I forget a line?"

"You'll be fine, Clare," Betty reassured. "They don't know what the lines are supposed to be. Besides, it's so rare they get to see a pretty girl. I'm sure they won't mind if you're not a regular Ethel Barrymore, anyway."

"I guess you're right," Clare said, despite an uneasy feeling in the pit of her stomach.

Clare spent the morning reviewing her lines and stage directions. At lunchtime, she and Betty went to the hospital to check on Bonnie. They found that her fever was diminished, and she was sleeping soundly.

"Gee, do you think Bonnie will be sore when she finds out I filled in for her?" asked Clare.

"No, I don't think so. Especially if you trip or forget the words to the songs," joked Betty.

After lunch, the actors got ready backstage. This was one of the most primitive outdoor theaters they had played, with seating made of coconut logs. But it did not stop the crowd from forming an hour before show time to get the best seats. Dressed in her first costume, the frilly polka dot dress with layers of ruffles, Clare peeked out from behind the curtain. Before her stretched what seemed like an endless sea of men.

"Betty, look at that crowd. I can't go out there in front of all those people," wailed Clare. Betty glanced out to judge for herself.

"That's nothing! We had more people in New Caledonia and Efate. Just don't look at the audience. Look at whomever you're talking to onstage, and you'll be fine. You know everyone in the cast. You'll soon forget all the people are out there," Betty advised.

"Okay, I hope you're right," Clare said, unconvinced.

From the wings, Clare watched the curtain rise, and Bob began to sing "Oh, What a Beautiful Mornin'." Betty and Jimmy sang the next two songs, and then Clare knew it was her cue. She felt the urge to run in the opposite direction, but she reminded herself of how Roy must have felt during the landing at Sicily and found the courage to go on. She was grateful that only Florence and Betty were onstage for her first scene and focused on them, willing herself not to look out into the audience. Florence exited and just Clare and Betty were left onstage for Clare's first song, "I Cain't Say No." To her delight, the audience broke into applause when she finished. *Maybe I could get used to this*, she thought. After the song, more of the cast entered, and there was a lot of dialogue. Clare only made one mistake, but no one seemed to notice, and the audience laughed after each joke. Still, she was relieved when she and Jimmy were able to run offstage after their scene.

After playing another scene, Clare watched the rest of the act from the wings, knowing she could relax until the intermission. She changed into her next costume, a blue and green striped dress with voluminous petticoats underneath. In the second act, she sang her other song, a duet with Jimmy's Will called "All er Nuthin'," to enthusiastic response. Nevertheless, she felt a wave of relief when the last note was played, the cast took their bows, and the curtain fell.

"Aw, Clare, you did a swell job," Jimmy said. "The audience loved you! How do you feel now?"

"Thanks, Jimmy. I guess it wasn't as bad as I expected. But I'd still rather hand out doughnuts and Coca-Cola. I don't know how you do it every day!"

"Sometimes twice a day," Betty added. "You're a natural, Clare. It will be even easier next time."

"Next time? I have to do it again?"

"There are still five more performances scheduled. I doubt Bonnie will be feeling well enough for a while."

"I guess you're right," Clare said dismally. "I'm going to make sure everyone in the cast swallows their Atabrine from now on!"

After changing out of their costumes, Clare, Betty, and Florence went to visit Bonnie. They found her much improved; her fever had broken, and she was weak but conscious.

"How do you feel?" asked Clare.

"Much better. First I was so cold, then so hot," Bonnie replied. "The doctors are real swell here, and they've treated me mighty fine. I'm sorry about the show today. I guess the boys were disappointed." Clare looked nervously at Florence.

"Don't you worry about it," Florence reassured. "You'll be back on the stage in no time."

As they walked back to their tents, Clare said, "Florence, I wish we'd told Bonnie about the show. What if she hears about it from someone else?"

"She'll understand. She's a professional. She knows 'the show must go on,' as we say."

"Gee, I hope you're right," Clare said doubtfully.

That night, the cast ate dinner in the Enlisted Men's Mess. Clare was overwhelmed by requests for autographs, and many men even wanted to have their picture taken with her. She was sure to tell each one that she was just filling in, and the real star was in the hospital with malaria.

The next day, Clare and Betty visited Bonnie in the hospital. Bonnie was sitting up reading a magazine when they entered.

"Hello, gals!" Bonnie cried. "I feel swell! This is the place to be. It's loads more comfortable than that tent they put us in."

"I'm glad you're feeling better, Bonnie," said Clare. "But there's something I have to tell you. We did perform the show yesterday. Florence made me fill in for you. I didn't want to. I wasn't anywhere near as good as you are. I made a few mistakes in my lines."

"Aw, Clare, I already know. I got to thinkin' about it when I started to feel like myself again last night. I realized the show had to go on. I wouldn't want anyone but you to fill in for me. I'm sure you did a fine job. In fact, I know you did, 'cause I heard a few of the medics talking about the show this morning."

"Oh, Bonnie, I'm so glad you're not sore. I can't wait 'til you're all better. Promise you'll take that Atabrine now?"

"I promise. See that handsome doctor over there?" Bonnie said, motioning to a captain at the other end of the ward. "Well, he says he's going to personally make sure I take it from now on, and I can't argue with doctor's orders!"

Clare and Betty left to prepare for the show. Although Clare still felt anxious, it was not the same stomach-churning feeling as the day before. The performance went well, with just one mistake by Clare. She was pleased to note that Jimmy had made two mistakes himself.

After dining with the officers again, Clare reluctantly followed the others into the Officers' Club. She looked around and was relieved not to see Captain York. Again they sat around talking, and Clare was careful to say little and drink nothing but Coca-Cola. She scanned the room periodically, half hoping to see York again and half dreading it. She wondered if he had seen either of her performances and hoped he had not. Eventually Clare noticed a lieutenant sitting at the other end of their table. He had been so quiet and was so nondescript that he blended right into the background. He was older than almost everyone else, close to forty years old if Clare had to guess, with thinning hair, a plain face, and round glasses. He sat listening intently, taking everything in but saying nothing. Periodically, Clare stole glances at him, and began to think there was something very familiar about him. He certainly did not seem to recognize her, so she doubted she had met him on one of the other islands. She thought she heard someone call him "Jim," but that still did not jog her memory. At the end of the evening, she was walking past him, trying not to stare at him, when he stood up.

"Excuse me, Miss Carlyle, I saw your performance today, and it was quite enjoyable," the unremarkable man said.

"Thank you," Clare replied. "Do I know you from somewhere?"

"Oh, I don't think so. I just flew in on a tour of the islands. Writing some reports for the Navy. I'm Lieutenant James Michener," he said, extending a hand.

Clare gaped at the older man for a moment. "You're James Michener! I can't believe it! I'm such a big fan of your work!" Clare cried, wringing his hand. Now it was Michener's turn to gape.

"I must say, miss, that's the oddest reception I've ever received. I've never met someone familiar with my work editing textbooks for Macmillan before," he laughed. With that Clare remembered the only book Michener wrote before the war had not been published until after his success with *Tales of the South Pacific*.

"Oh, I guess I read one in college. I went to Penllyn for a year before the war," Clare said, trying to recover her cool. "I always say editors make the best writers. Are you writing anything interesting besides reports for the Navy?"

"No, I'm always tied up with paperwork. But you know, one hears such fascinating stories out here from the pilots and the men who've moved from one island to another waiting for something to happen. Sometimes I do think about writing them down."

"Oh, you definitely should! I'm sure it would be wonderful!" Clare gushed.

"I don't know. Maybe someday. So that show you put on was awfully swell. I'm not sure if this pairing of Rodgers and Hammerstein will last, though. I don't know if that Hammerstein fellow can fill Hart's shoes."

"I have a feeling they're going to be very successful. You know, a book about those stories from out here would make a good musical," Clare suggested.

"That sounds ridiculous, Miss Carlyle. I don't know if anyone will want to read about this place, but I definitely can't imagine listening to someone sing about it. That's quite an imagination you have there. Well, good luck with your show."

"Thank you, Lieutenant Michener. Good luck to you, too," Clare said, wringing his hand again. They parted company, and she and Betty started walking back to their tent.

"Clare, who was that old guy you were talking to?" asked Betty. "He certainly wasn't dreamy like that Captain York from the other night."

"That was Lieutenant Michener. I think he's going to be a very famous writer someday."

"Oh, Clare, you and your predictions. I hope you didn't get that poor man's hopes up."

"No, just gave him some encouragement. He liked the show, anyway." *This really has been "some enchanted evening,"* Clare reflected dreamily.

When Clare and Betty stopped at the hospital to visit Bonnie the following day, they found her back to her old self. In fact, she was reluctant to leave as she had developed quite a crush on the doctor. She persuaded them to let her stay another night so she'd be in top form to return to performing the next day. That meant Clare had one more show to do, which went smoothly. The next day, she was very happy to give the costumes back to Bonnie and put on her apron to serve refreshments instead.

Clare and some of the other girls set up beverages in the mess hall while the troupe performed. She was just putting the finishing touches on a table of doughnuts when she felt a tap on the back.

"Oh, it's you," Clare said as she looked up into the handsome face of Captain York.

"Nice to see you, too, Miss Carlyle," York replied.

"Why aren't you at the show?" Clare asked.

"I've seen it three times already. I didn't need to see it again."

Clare blushed, realizing he had watched all three of her performances. "Well, that's a shame. I'm sorry you had to endure that. Bonnie's the real star. I was just filling in while she recovered from a malaria attack."

"On the contrary, Miss Carlyle. I think you're the better actress by far. I know firsthand that you're not a girl who can't say no. But if what I hear from a buddy at the hospital is true, your friend isn't acting at all!"

"Oh, that's a rude thing to say about Bonnie!" *True, perhaps,* thought Clare, *but still rude.*

"Aw, don't be sore at me again. Will you come on that picnic with me? I'll bring my commanding officer along as a chaperone, and you can bring a friend. What do you say?"

"I could bring Florence along, I guess," Clare teased.

"You mean Aunt Eller? I couldn't do that to Rick. What about Laurey?" York suggested.

"Depends what your CO looks like."

"The ladies think he's a combination of Errol Flynn and Clark Gable."

"That bad, huh? I couldn't do that to Betty. I'll pass on that picnic, Captain. Have a doughnut," Clare said, shoving one into his hand.

"If you change your mind, just come to the airstrip. They'll know where to find me." York walked out of the mess eating his doughnut. At the door, he turned to give her a wistful glance. Clare could not help the twinge of guilt she felt. *Oh, get a hold of yourself,* she thought. *You've come this far. You're not going to fall for one of them. But maybe just one picnic couldn't hurt ...*

Clare was relieved when the intermission started, and men began filing in for some refreshments. The overwhelming crowd took her away from her ambivalent thoughts of York.

At dinner that night, Bonnie was the center of attention. Her triumphant return was widely toasted, but Clare did not mind. She was much more comfortable serving the refreshments and talking to the men about home. Once back at their tent, they made sure Bonnie was tucked in beneath her mosquito netting.

"I miss the hospital. There were white sheets. And soft mattresses. And handsome doctors ... ," sighed Bonnie.

"Sweet dreams, Bonnie," Clare laughed.

"Clare, are you still awake?" Betty whispered after she heard Bonnie gently snoring.

"Yes, Betty. What's the matter?"

"Nothing's the matter. It's just ... well, after the show today, I met a nice fella. A man, really. He asked for my autograph. We had such a nice conversation. He asked me to go on a picnic with him. I said we really weren't allowed, but I'd think about it. There was something about him. And he was so attractive, too. He looked like he had all the best parts of Errol Flynn and Clark Gable put together," Betty sighed.

"Is he a pilot?"

"Yes."

"Does he fly a P-38?"

"Yes."

"Is his name Rick?"

"Why, yes. Have you met him?"

"No, I haven't met him. Did that Captain York put you up to this?" Clare asked.

"No, do they know each other?"

"Yes, your Rick is York's commanding officer. York tried to get me to agree to go on a picnic with him this afternoon. Said he'd bring him along as a chaperone if I wanted to bring a friend. He mentioned you specifically."

"He did?" Betty said eagerly. "He could chaperone me anytime! Let's go. What harm can it do?"

"Plenty," said Clare. "Besides, I'm not sure if I like that York anyway."

"I think you do. I saw how you looked at every man who came into the Officers' Club tonight and looked so disappointed when it wasn't him."

"That's not true. I could have been looking for Lieutenant Michener."

"That old geezer? I don't think you were."

"Well, maybe you're right. There is something about York," conceded Clare. "I'll think about it."

CHAPTER 26

"What did you decide, Clare? Will you go on the picnic?" asked Betty.

"What? Oh, that already?" Clare said, her mind still foggy from sleep. "How could I have thought about it? I was asleep all night."

"That didn't stop me. I had the craziest dream last night," Betty said and started to hum the song of the same name. "What do you say? Please?"

"Oh, okay. You're way more persuasive than York. If we see one of them today, we can tell them. If not, we'll go the airstrip tomorrow since there's no show. York said they'd know where to find him. I guess that goes for your fella, too."

Clare visited boys in the hospital in the morning and then served refreshments as usual during the show. Though she saw hundreds of men, there was no sign of Captain York. After the show, Betty reported that she had not seen Rick, either. Although they ate dinner in the Enlisted Men's Mess, they snuck over to the Officers' Club afterward but did not see either pilot.

"We'll try the airstrip tomorrow," promised Clare. "What's Rick's last name and rank, anyway?"

"I don't know," Betty admitted sheepishly.

"Did he have bars on his collar or a leaf?"

"I don't know. I wasn't really looking at his collar. He did have the most beautiful brown eyes, though."

"Well, I'm not going to ask for a Rick with beautiful brown eyes at the airstrip. We'll ask for Captain York and assume if we find one we'll find the other."

The midmorning sun glared overhead the next day as Betty and Clare made their way to the airstrip. There was a great deal of activity with planes of various types taking off and landing. Clare looked around for the P-38 Lightning with the risqué boxer on the nose but did not see it.

"Maybe he's on a mission," suggested Betty. "Let's ask that ground crew over there. One of them might know."

Clare and Betty approached a crew of five men working on a badly shot up Grumman TBF Avenger torpedo bomber. The men immediately took notice of the young women and came to attention as if a general were in their presence.

"Howdy, ladies. What can we do for you?" asked one man with a Southern drawl.

"We're looking for someone. A pilot named Captain Parker York. Flies a P-38 called something like 'Knock Out.' Do you know him?" Clare asked.

"You mean Sarge? Sure, everyone knows him. Whoo-wee, he's awful lucky to have two beautiful gals lookin' for him. Well, maybe not so lucky, I reckon, as his squadron moved out yesterday. Went north, I think. I dunno where, though."

"I think they went to Stirling Island, in the Treasuries," another man offered. "Aw, nuts! I wasn't supposed to tell you that. I sure hope you two ain't Jap spies."

"They ain't no spies, Joe!" a third man bellowed. "You two were mighty fine in the show, and we appreciate you comin' all the way out here to sing for us. It sure does mean a lot."

"Thanks for your help, boys. What you're doing means an awful lot to us and to everyone back home. Stop in the Enlisted Men's Club tonight and say hello," Clare suggested.

"We sure will, ma'am." As Clare and Betty walked away, they could hear one of the ground crew muttering, "Those pilots have all the luck. The dames are always after them. What they don't know is it's us who keeps those planes in the air. Those flyboys just get 'em all shot up and expect us to clean up their messes. Wouldn't be no pilots at all without us guys on the ground." The other men agreed.

"Well, I guess that problem is solved," said Clare with a mixture of relief and regret.

"Now I'll never see Rick again," Betty said dismally.

"Betty, it's better this way. You don't want to get attached to a guy and then have something happen to him. Trust me, I know."

"I know," Betty agreed, "but it was just going to be one picnic."

The next day after the show, Florence gathered everyone together and announced that there would be just one more performance on Guadalcanal. The tour organizers decided to add an additional stop before the troupe would return home. In two days, Florence said they would fly north to a small island with a new airfield and a PT boat base. Someone asked what it was called, and Florence replied, "Stirling Island." Betty let out a little squeal of delight, and Clare felt her heart start to race.

CHAPTER 27

The C-47 came in low over the coral airstrip on Stirling Island and landed on the second pass. The flat island was tiny compared to Guadalcanal; it was sheltered to the north by Mono Island, large and volcanic with steep, forbidding cliffs. Clare scoured the airfield but saw no sign of any P-38s. She saw Betty looking all around and guessed she was doing the same thing. A jeep came to take them to their new accommodations, swerving to avoid some large craters that still looked fresh. When asked, the driver of the jeep explained they were from a Japanese air raid on the island, but there had not been one in three weeks, and it was nothing to worry about. The girls exchanged doubtful glances.

While settling into their new accommodations, the girls heard the drone of engines overhead. "Japs!" cried Bonnie, ducking under her cot.

Clare recognized the sound but left the tent to get a better look anyway. Above she saw a squadron of P-38s coming in to land.

"They're ours. Nothing to worry about. Unless a certain someone decides to buzz our tents, of course," Clare said.

"Is it really them?" asked Betty, eagerly.

"I don't know if it's their squadron, but it's the right kind of plane."

"Let's go and see. No one will miss us for a while."

"Okay," Clare agreed, and they walked back to the airstrip.

By the time they reached the runway, most of the planes had landed, and ground crews were swarming over each one. Clare scanned the nose of every plane until she spotted York's Lightning. "He's here," she said with excitement. They walked over to the airplane and found York leaning up against the fuselage, telling a mechanic about the mission. Upon seeing them, he broke into a wide grin.

"Hello, ladies! Well, if it isn't the famous stars of the USO. If I'd known you were here I would have given you one of my special welcomes when I landed. Miss Carlyle, you sure came an awful long way to find me," York said with a sly smile.

"Not at all, Captain York. It's just a coincidence we were sent here next," Clare replied.

"I don't believe in coincidences, Miss Carlyle," York said, staring into her eyes.

"Actually, Captain, it's your commanding officer we're here to see," said Clare, turning away from his gaze. "It seems you weren't exaggerating about his charms, after all, and my friend Betty would like to see him."

"Ah, old Hollywood worked his magic on you, Miss Wilton," York said to Betty. "I guess you must have worked some magic on him, too," he said, looking her up and down appreciatively. Clare felt an unexpected stab of jealousy.

"Lou," York said to the mechanic, "please go get Major Overbrook. Tell him someone wants to see him. But don't say who. I want it to be a surprise."

A few moments later, a tall pilot with a shock of dark, wavy hair and a small, well-groomed mustache appeared. He broke into a radiant smile at the sight of the two women. Clare glanced at Betty and found her smile matched his. She had never seen Betty react to a man that way before. *She wasn't exaggerating,* Clare reflected. *He really could be a movie star.*

"Ladies, may I present Major Richard Overbrook, commanding officer of our squadron and five time ace, if I might add," said York. "This is Miss Clare Carlyle of the USO, and I believe you have already made the acquaintance of Miss Betty Wilton."

Overbrook took Clare's hand politely but did not take his eyes off Betty.

"Pleasure to meet you, Miss Carlyle. Miss Wilton, I'm delighted to see you again. Perhaps you'll take me up on that picnic I offered. This island is a lot more picturesque than Guadalcanal. I think you'll find there are many secluded beaches and coves for swimming. How about tomorrow afternoon?" Overbrook suggested.

"That would be lovely," breathed Betty.

"Hey, that picnic was my idea," said York.

"Of course I meant all four of us," Overbrook assured him. "Betty, come see my plane," he said, taking her by the hand and leading her away.

Clare found herself alone with York. Suddenly shy, she studied the P-38 Lightning on which the fighter pilot casually leaned. Up close she could see the nose art was expertly done, the painted figure titillating without revealing anything. The face looked familiar, and Clare concluded the artist must have copied it from a pinup calendar. Beneath the cockpit, Clare counted sixteen carefully painted Japanese flags.

"You've shot down sixteen Japanese planes?" Clare

said, impressed.

"Yeah, but that's nothing compared to Woody. He's a real pilot's pilot. Saved my behind more than a few times," York said modestly.

"Still, sixteen planes shot down. Just going up there at all makes you a hero in my book," said Clare.

"Nah, you're wrong about that. The real heroes are Lou and the rest of the boys here on the ground. Never get in the air at all without them. I come back all shot up and they get her fixed up right away. Of course, their job has been getting easier. Not so many Japs around now. They barely get any planes off the ground when we come over now. It's becoming a real 'milk run' like they say. We just deliver those exploding milk bottles and home we go. Starting to get as boring as a day on Wall Street. That's why it's especially nice you gals arrived to liven things up."

"I'm sure I'm not nearly as exciting as tangling with a Zero," Clare said.

"Maybe not, but I'd like to find out," said York with a wink. Clare knew she should not have felt as pleased as she did and was happy when Betty and Major Overbrook returned.

"So we'll pick you up at two o'clock tomorrow," suggested Overbrook.

"No, we'll meet you here," replied Clare. "It will be too obvious if you come to our tent. Florence would surely find out and stop us from going."

"Okay, here it is, then. See you tomorrow," Overbrook said while graciously kissing Betty's hand.

Back at their tent, Betty was beaming. "Oh Clare, isn't he magnificent? Those broad shoulders! That hair! Those eyes!"

"He does look like he stepped off a Hollywood set," conceded Clare. She preferred York's looks and was glad there was no competition.

"What are you going to wear? I'm so nervous! I haven't been on a date in ages."

"I don't know. I haven't either. I think I feel more comfortable with a whole roomful of men now, not just one. But I'm more worried about what Florence will do if she finds out," said Clare.

"Well, really, what can she do to us anyway? Besides, it doesn't seem to bother Bonnie. I'm sure Florence must have heard the rumors about her and that doctor."

"You're right. I'll try not to worry," replied Clare.

CHAPTER 28

Clare and Betty dressed for their picnic the following day, both choosing lightweight cotton print dresses and canvas sandals. They put on make-up and fixed their hair as well as the humidity would allow.

"Where are you two headed all dolled up like that?" asked Bonnie. Clare and Betty had not told her of their plans.

"We're going on a picnic with a couple of fliers we met on Guadalcanal. Please don't tell anyone. We don't want Florence to find out," Clare pleaded.

"Well, you two were certainly busy while I was in the hospital! Don't worry. Your secret is safe with me. As a matter of fact, I have a secret of my own. Remember that doctor from the hospital? Well, he arranged to be transferred here tomorrow, so it looks like I'll be occupied, as well," Bonnie said smugly.

Down at the airstrip, Clare and Betty found York and Overbrook waiting with a jeep.

"It's no surrey with a fringe on top, but it will have to do," Overbrook joked as he helped Betty into the back. York did the same for Clare, and the two men climbed into the front. They drove about a mile down the beach to a secluded cove ringed with palm trees. The girls watched with amazement as the two men spread out a blanket on the sand and set up an array of sandwiches, tinned peaches, Coca-Cola, and beer. They had even swiped some plates and napkins from the mess hall.

"You two went all out. I'm impressed," said Betty.

"Well it isn't every day we entertain USO stars," Overbrook replied.

"Or a budding anthropologist," said York, looking at Clare fondly.

"So, where are you from, Major Overbrook?" Clare asked.

"California," he replied. "Los Angeles. Call me Rick, by the way. Or Woody. The fellas call me that."

"What did you do before the war?"

"Actually, I made a few pictures. Just small parts. Did some modeling, too. Maybe you saw me in the 1940 Montgomery Ward catalog? In the men's robe section?"

"No, I'm afraid I missed that," Clare laughed. Overbrook struck a pose, as if holding a pipe in a pensive mood.

"How about now?" he asked.

"No, sorry. What movies were you in?" asked Betty.

"Nothing you've heard of, I'm sure," he replied.

"Will you go back to acting after the war?" Clare asked.

"I'm not in the habit of making plans for after the war. I don't usually make any plans even a day ahead of time now. Not in this business. So our picnic was a real stretch for me," said Overbrook.

"But you didn't fly today, did you?" asked Betty.

"Sure did. We were up in the air at four o'clock in the morning and over Rabaul by six. We were home before you sleepyheads were out of your bunks, I wager."

"I think I heard your planes come back. I didn't

know it was you. I'm glad I didn't or I would have been awful worried," said Betty. "You must be so tired."

"I'm okay," Overbrook replied. "Although I am missing my afternoon siesta."

"Clare, let's go for a walk down the beach," York suggested, pulling her up from the blanket. "There are some interesting seashells here. Not like you find on the East Coast." Clare gave Betty a questioning look, and she responded with a smile and a slight nod. York took off his boots and socks and rolled up his pant legs, and Clare left her sandals behind as they strolled down the beach, away from the base.

They walked at the edge of the surf, the clear waves lapping at their feet. Out further the water was every shade of blue from aquamarine to sapphire. At first they said nothing, and Clare was looking down at the sand, hoping to see some interesting specimens.

"Say, Clare, can I ask you something?"

"Sure, Captain York. What is it?"

"Please call me Parker. Or Sarge. Whatever you prefer."

"Definitely Parker. I don't think I care for all those nicknames much. So what's your question?"

"The other night, when we met on Guadalcanal, I heard you talking about the war. You seemed so awful sure of yourself that it would be over next year. Why would you think that?"

"I … I guess I'm just an optimist," she said, trying to laugh it off.

"I don't think so. I think you're a very thoughtful person. That's part of why I like you so much." Clare felt her cheeks flush and knew it was not from the afternoon sun.

"Thank you, Parker. And I like you, too. I wouldn't

be here with you if I didn't. Well, that and Betty would have killed me if I didn't go."

"But don't you think there's too much ground to cover for the war to end next year? We have to take back the Philippines and invade the Japanese islands. Those Japs put up one hell of a fight. They think it's dishonorable to be captured, so they fight to the end. I've even seen their pilots try to crash into a ship on purpose instead of bailing out after their plane's been hit. And then there's Europe. Almost the entire continent is still in Nazi hands. I just don't see how it's possible for a few more years at least."

"Parker, I can't explain it, but trust me, I'm pretty sure about next year. And I don't think it will come to an invasion of Japan."

"You're just a regular Cassandra, I guess."

"Something like that," Clare said, smiling mysteriously.

"So what about me then? Should I make plans for after the war?" Parker asked.

"Oh, Parker. I don't know what's going to happen. I wish I did. But I have a good feeling about you." His arm brushed against hers as they walked, and he reached for her hand. They walked hand in hand down the beach, stopping to look at an interesting shell or watch a hermit crab scurry past. The shore had curved, and they were no longer in sight of the spot where they left Betty and Rick. They paused for Parker to pick a showy pink orchid growing under a pandanus tree.

"Do you see a kiss in our future?" Parker asked as he tucked the flower behind Clare's ear.

"How about right now, instead?" Clare replied.

"That can be arranged," Parker said, putting his arms around her. It was a light, sweet kiss but not chaste by any means and full of promise.

"It's starting to get dark, Parker. We should head back."

"I suppose you're right," York replied, the disappointment evident in his voice. They walked back toward the jeep holding hands.

"Oh, look!" Clare cried. She bent down and picked up a small seashell: a shiny, oval cowrie colored blue-gray. On its back was a rust-colored mark that happened to be in the shape of a heart. "It's so pretty. You take it. It will remind you of me."

"I don't need a seashell to remind me of you, Clare. I'll probably need something to help me forget you. But I'll take it. You know, us pilots are very superstitious. We love our good luck charms, and this will be mine from now on." York slipped the little shell into the pocket of his shirt.

Soon they were within sight of Betty and Rick. They found Rick asleep with his head in Betty's lap. Betty was absently twirling a lock of the dark hair as she gazed out at the waves. Overbrook opened his eyes when the couple came nearer.

"Hey, what happened to you two?" he asked. "It's almost dark."

"I guess we lost track of time. Did you really mind, Woody? It looks like you got your beauty sleep anyway," said York, winking.

"No, I didn't mind," Overbrook said. "Did you mind, sweetheart?" he asked Betty.

"I didn't mind, either, Rick," Betty said breathlessly. It was clear they only had eyes for each other.

Clare and York packed up the plates and blankets and stowed them in the jeep. The two couples piled in, Parker and Clare up front and Betty and Rick in the back. The sun had set by the time they reached the base and parked the jeep.

"Let us walk you back to your tent," suggested Overbrook.

"But what if Florence sees us?" said Clare.

"Between the two of us, we've shot down more than forty Jap planes. Do you really think we're afraid of a nosy old woman?" asked York.

"No, I guess you're not, but *I* am," said Clare.

"Me, too," agreed Betty.

"Just leave her to us, girls," Overbrook said confidently.

Sure enough, Florence had noticed their absence and was waiting near their tent.

"Miss Wilton, Miss Carlyle! Where have you been all afternoon? Surely you have not been entertaining these two men alone. You know that is strictly prohibited."

"It's all our fault, ma'am," Overbrook said, giving her his most remorseful look. "The young ladies were quite clear in refusing our offer of a picnic. But we just couldn't take no for an answer. You see, ma'am, it was really like a business meeting. I don't want to boast, but I have some connections in Hollywood. Been in a few pictures myself, and I just thought after seeing these ladies onstage at Guadalcanal, that they could have quite a career in pictures. Now my agent is always looking out for new talent, and I'm sure these ladies have just what he's looking for. So you see, it was all purely innocent. There was no 'fraternizing,' as you might say."

"Major, you may be able to fool these girls, but I can see right through you. I know just what *you're* looking for, and it is unbecoming of an officer and a gentleman. You may have connections in Hollywood, but I have some connections in the office of a certain General Arnold. If I find that the two of you have been consorting with my girls again, I will have some choice words for Lieutenant

Colonel Adams of the 18th Fighter Group."

"We're awful sorry, ma'am. It won't happen again," said Overbrook. Betty looked crestfallen.

"And you, Captain? What do you have to say for yourself?" Florence said to York.

"I was just following orders from my commanding officer, ma'am," York said, motioning to Overbrook. "I knew it wasn't right, but what could I do? If I disobeyed, that would be insubordination, ma'am." Both Florence and Clare glared at him.

"You may be dismissed now, and I don't expect to have any more trouble from the two of you," Florence said as the two pilots retreated. "And that goes for the two of you, too," she said to Betty and Clare as she stalked off to her tent.

"Jeepers, Clare, how will we see them again?" asked Betty.

"I don't know. They sure didn't stand up to Florence. She *is* scarier than the Japanese. How does she even know who their superior officer is, anyway? From the looks on their faces, I don't think she was bluffing."

"Oh Clare, we made so many plans. Woody was going to give me a ride in his airplane. We were going to fly over the volcano on the next island."

"How? It's a one-person plane. Besides, I didn't think you were too keen on flying anyway," said Clare.

"He said he could give me a piggyback ride. I'd sit right behind him and hold him real tight so we could both fit in the cockpit. Doesn't that sound dreamy?" Betty said with a sigh.

"That does sound appealing," Clare said and wondered if York would offer her a ride, too. "It's a small island, Betty. I'm sure we'll see them again."

CHAPTER 29

The troupe gave their first performance of *Oklahoma!* on Stirling Island the next day. Clare eagerly looked for York in the crowd but did not see him. After dinner there was a dance at the Enlisted Men's Club. Clare had not danced in a while and was enjoying herself, until she saw Florence heading her way.

"I have a surprise for you," said Florence, leading a pleasant-looking young man by the hand. "This is Corporal Jacob Van Flynt. From Schenectady!"

Clare groaned inwardly. *I guess this was bound to happen*, she thought. *People really do live in Schenectady. Next I'll meet someone who actually has got a gal in Kalamazoo!*

"You can call me Jake," the corporal said while extending his hand. Clare clasped his hand and introduced herself.

"I could tell right away you were a Schenectady girl!" Jake proclaimed. "GE Realty Plot, I bet?"

Clare had no idea what he was talking about, so she made a vague noise of agreement.

"I'm so happy to meet someone from home," Jake continued. "When were you there last?"

"Um, June of last year," Clare replied, her voice rising as if asking a question.

"I can't believe I never saw you downtown. I'm sure I would remember a girl as pretty as you. I sure miss home. Do you remember – ?"

Before Jake could finish his sentence, Clare exclaimed, "Oh, I love this song! Let's dance now!" and dragged the corporal to the middle of the floor. Lionel Hampton's "Flying Home" blared from the speakers, drowning out their conversation. When the music died down, Jake gestured to the tables along the wall. Although the young corporal seemed like a very nice man, Clare did not want to "reminisce" about Schenectady. Before she could make up an excuse to leave Jake, one walked right up to them.

York strode up behind the pair and said, "I hate to pull rank on you Corporal, but I really must have a dance with Miss Carlyle now."

Clare smiled and shrugged her shoulders apologetically as the tall aviator whisked her away. This time, the stirring melody of "Moonglow" flowed from Artie Shaw's clarinet. Clare reflected that it was much more than just moonglow that had brought them together.

After two more dances, Parker led Clare toward the punch bowl for a drink. She saw with relief that Corporal Van Flynt was jitterbugging with one of the other girls. Hopefully he had forgotten all about her. Still, she felt quite guilty, not just about Van Flynt but about all the other boys she was ignoring. Yet how could she tear herself away from Parker? She knew this was just the kind of behavior she had been chided about. "Don't let yourself get too attached to one man – or let one man get too attached to you. You're there to boost morale for all the boys," she could still hear Mrs. Cummings telling the girls.

"Parker," Clare began with resolution in her voice, "I can't let you monopolize me like this. You're not even supposed to be here. This dance isn't for officers."

"Clare, you're absolutely right. I shouldn't be at this dance for enlisted men. That's why you'll have to come with me to the beach right now," York answered while leading her out the door and into the night air.

"Oh, no, Parker, I can't do that. It's too risky. I might get in trouble," Clare protested.

"Too risky? Well, *I'll* be flying escort for a bombing run over Rabaul tomorrow morning. I might get in trouble, too, but I don't have much of a choice about that, do I? You mean you won't risk some sharp words from old Aunt Eller to spend the evening with me?"

It was unfair of Parker to pressure her like that, Clare thought. Any one of these men might be off on a dangerous mission tomorrow. That was part of the reason the girls were warned not to get too close. Of course, Clare did not really believe that anything would happen to Parker. Sure, he probably was flying in the morning, but he seemed like one of those people to whom nothing bad ever happened, as if they have a guardian angel looking out for them. But he really did look hurt. And she certainly would rather spend the evening with him than dodging the heavy feet and wandering hands of the enlisted men.

"Well, okay," she agreed reluctantly. "When you put it that way, how can I refuse?"

York brightened at her words and led her to a jeep half-hidden in the bushes. He helped her in and then sped away from the cluster of Quonset huts toward the beach. Instead of slowing near the spot where they stopped the day before, he continued on.

"Where are we going?" Clare asked nervously.

"I found a better beach. Even more secluded," York replied with a wink.

As they drove farther and farther from the base,

Clare grew more and more concerned. She had forgotten about getting in trouble with Florence and was now worried about getting into a different sort of trouble. How could she go off with a man alone at night? A man she barely knew, really. She would be a fool to trust him or any man who had been out here for months on end with no girls in sight and only some faded photographs and dog-eared letters to remind him of feminine virtues. Clare chastised herself for these thoughts. *Parker has always been a perfect gentleman*, she scolded herself. He wouldn't do anything she didn't want him to do. But what if she *did* want him to? Perhaps that was the real crux of the problem. *No*, she resolved, *I'm just a girl who* can *say no*.

York slowed the jeep and eased it into a clearing in the bushes. "Wait here," he instructed mischievously as he took a bundle from the back of the jeep and disappeared toward the shore. A few moments later, he returned and helped Clare out of the jeep. He led her through the foliage toward the ocean. The almost full moon illuminated the sight before her. She was astonished to see that he had laid an olive drab blanket under a palm tree and had arranged a spread of fresh papayas for dessert and a sort of brandy the men had made by fermenting the juice from the canned peaches. York pulled her down onto the blanket, and she did not resist.

"Are you sure you're not just following orders, like yesterday," Clare teased. "I hope you're braver with the Japanese than you were with Florence!"

"She is rather intimidating. But she can't do anything to Woody and me. Funny she knows Adams, though. Well, even if she told him, I suspect he wouldn't do anything. Except maybe see if we could get him a date, too. Too bad your friend Bonnie has taken up with that doctor."

They sat talking, sipping the peach brandy, and

staring up at the immense sky full of unfamiliar constellations.

"How about we go for a swim?" suggested Parker.

"Oh, no I don't think so," said Clare.

"Don't worry about the sharks. I'll protect you."

"It's not the sharks I need protection from, is it?" Clare said, looking into York's intense eyes.

"I gave you my word I'd be a gentleman. I won't do anything you don't want me to do."

"Ah, there's the rub," said Clare, wistfully. "I think we'd better go back to base now."

"Can't I have a good night kiss first?" asked York, and Clare consented to one, which turned into many. They drove back along the beach, York steering with one hand, his other arm around Clare and her head on his shoulder. She would not let him walk her all the way to her tent. They parted company in the shadows with another tender embrace.

Clare's bubble of euphoria was burst at the sight of Florence waiting at her tent.

"Miss Carlyle, where did you disappear to tonight? I already know with whom. That nice Corporal Van Flynt said a blond captain took you away. After I expressly said you were not to see him again. I'm especially disappointed in you, Miss Carlyle. I didn't think you were flighty and weak-willed like some of the other girls. I thought more of you. And what would your parents say if they knew you were sneaking about alone with some man you barely know?"

"I don't know, Florence," Clare said with downcast eyes.

"Suffice it to say, if you go off with that flier again – or anyone else – I'll have to suspend your duties as hostess. That's the closest punishment to a dishonorable discharge that I can give you. What do you have to say for yourself?"

"I'm sorry, Florence," Clare said, burning with shame. "I'll focus on my duties from now on, I promise."

Clare went into her tent and found that Betty and Bonnie had overheard the whole scene.

"Ah, Clare, that's bad luck. You will still see him again, won't you?" asked Betty.

"I don't know. I don't see how I can," said Clare. "Did you see Rick?"

"Yes, he snuck into the dance, too. Took off his insignia so he wouldn't stand out as an officer and wore his hat down low. I'm lucky Florence didn't notice him."

"You two should get malaria," suggested Bonnie. "I *had* to see my beau today to get my Atabrine. Florence would have been mad at me if I *didn't* go!"

CHAPTER 30

The next morning, Clare was in the infirmary helping to roll bandages when she heard the drone of planes taking off. Involuntarily, she went to the window and watched the bulky B-24 Liberator bombers rise into the air. A few moments later, the nimble P-38s followed. One, two, three ... twenty Lightnings, she counted as they climbed into the sky. They would soon overtake the slower Liberators they were bound to protect. Clare tried not to think about Parker flying ahead of the bombers. She knew Japanese opposition had been light compared to what it used to be. *There's no reason to worry*, she told herself. *It's a routine mission, and he's got that guardian angel, doesn't he?*

Clare spent the rest of the morning chatting with the boys in sickbay. Most of them were there with various tropical diseases. Just a few had wounds from combat. They were all eager to tell Clare about their hometowns and girlfriends.

In the afternoon, she heard the roar of the airplanes making their approach for landing. Again she was drawn to the window as the Lightnings descended from their mission. One, two, three ... eighteen, Clare counted. Eighteen? She was sure she had counted twenty taking off, but maybe she was mistaken. Or maybe there were really two fewer planes now? No, it was just a routine mission. Still, anything could happen. Clare felt her heart pounding in her chest. She tried to reason with herself: *two planes missing out of twenty. That's ten percent. That means ninety percent of the pilots are just fine. So there's a ninety percent chance that Parker is just fine. No, a one hundred percent chance because it's Parker.*

She resisted the urge to run over to the pilots' headquarters. If Parker were there, she might get him into trouble. Finally, when it was nearing dinnertime she wandered over to the Officers' Mess, confident she would see that shock of blond hair and those glinting blue eyes. She peeked in the doorway unobserved and surveyed the men. She saw some of the pilots from Parker's squadron but not Parker. *Maybe he just hasn't come to dinner yet*, she reassured herself.

A small circle of men stood near the door talking. Clare could just hear snatches of their conversation, but soon she realized they were talking about that morning's sortie. "Ack-ack," "Rabaul," and "two Zekes" were all she could make out at first. She listened more intently and heard one of the lieutenants say "Johnson and York" and "just one parachute." Clare felt her knees grow weak and her head swim. She grabbed onto the doorframe for support. When she felt steady enough, she backed out of the doorway and raced back to her quarters. Some enlisted men tried to stop her to say hello, but she responded rudely, "I really can't talk right now," and brushed past them.

Clare was relieved to see her tent was empty. *All the other girls must be at dinner*, she thought. She slumped facedown onto her cot and involuntarily began to sob. *How could this have happened? But they said there was one parachute.* Clare prayed it was Parker's and realized she was condemning poor Johnson to death. He was a tall, good-natured redhead from Georgia. Naturally, the other pilots called him "Red." She did not wish him dead, but if she had to make a choice … Of course, the choice was not hers to make. Before she could ponder this further, she felt a hand on her shoulder and looked up to see Florence gazing down at her with consternation.

"I see you must have heard about Captain York," said Florence. When the older woman had heard the news about York and Johnson being missing, she was instantly sorry that she had given Clare such a hard time the night before. And yet, she also felt vindicated. This was one of the reasons not to make attachments out here. "I'm very sorry," she continued, offering Clare a flowered handkerchief, "but I understand the other pilots saw one parachute. There's some disagreement about whether it was York's or Johnson's. I don't want to give you false hope, but there is a chance he made it. I heard Major Overbrook saying a PBY was dispatched to the area to look for survivors. When you've collected yourself, I think you should come to the Enlisted Men's Mess for dinner. That will take your mind off things. There are still a lot of other men here who could benefit from your companionship."

Clare nodded weakly. "I'll be there in a little while." When her tears had sufficiently dried and she felt she could face other people, she walked over to the Enlisted Men's Mess. They had saved her a seat, and she glumly ate some cold slices of Spam. She caught Betty's eye across the room and could tell that she had heard the news.

One of the men seated across from her called out, "Hey Sarge, over here!" as he motioned to an empty spot at the table. Clare whipped around, expecting to see York, but saw a stocky, bullet-headed sergeant walk in instead. It took all her effort not to start crying again. Finally, she could endure no more and excused herself, saying she was feeling ıll.

Clare headed for her tent but at the last moment decided to walk down to the beach instead. She sunk down beneath a coconut palm and looked out at the ocean, wondering if Parker were somewhere out there. She scooped up handfuls of sand and watched the grains slip through her fingers, as large land crabs scuttled about her. She wept again, thinking not just of Parker, but of Roy, and her father, who was as good as gone now, too. *This isn't fun anymore*, she admitted to herself and wandered back to her tent in misery.

Betty and Bonnie were there to cheer her up.

"Don't worry, Clare. Rick says they'll find him. They won't stop looking. Rick says they've picked up lots of men who've been shot down. And Parker's known for being lucky," said Betty.

"I hope you're right, Betty. But sometimes luck runs out," Clare replied bleakly. She tried to sleep but tossed all night long, tormented by dreams of sharks and crashing waves.

CHAPTER 31

In the morning, Clare felt no better but had to resume her duties. She served refreshments during the show like an automaton, closed off from the living world around her. Afterward, she was clearing away empty bottles and half-eaten doughnuts when Bonnie rushed in, still dressed as Ado Annie.

"Clare, I have to take my Atabrine! Come with me to the infirmary," Bonnie said while dragging her out of the Quonset hut. Bonnie pulled her through the door of the hospital, and they saw a crowd around one of the beds in the back.

Clare looked questioningly at Bonnie, and Bonnie grinned back at her. One of the men near the bed shifted, and Clare saw a snatch of blond hair. She started to run forward, but Bonnie held her back.

"Wait until the others leave," she advised Clare.

A few men dispersed, and Clare got a clear view of the patient. It was indeed York, pantomiming with his hands the dogfight that had caused him to ditch in the ocean. Clare was relieved to see his two hands appeared to be uninjured. From the distance she could see that he had a bad sunburn but appeared otherwise unscathed. After a few minutes, a doctor – Bonnie's doctor – came out from the next room and shooed the men away. He motioned to Clare to come forward. By now York had spotted her and was grinning broadly. Clare ran to his bedside and embraced him.

"Ooh, easy there, Clare. The doc tells me I've got a few bruised ribs," said York, and Clare released her grip. She looked at him carefully; up close a long, thin gash was visible over York's right temple. York followed her gaze.

"That's nothing. Didn't even need stitches. Doc said the salt water cleaned it out real good, although there might be a scar. That's okay. It adds character, don't you think? Clare, are you going to say anything?" asked York.

Clare's eyes had welled with tears, and she forced herself to smile to stop their further progress.

"I thought I'd lost you," Clare sniffed.

"Aw, now don't cry. Nothing to cry about. It'll take more than a couple of Zeros for you to lose me," York said while handing her a handkerchief. "I was afraid you weren't going to come see me, though, after that tongue-lashing I heard Florence gave you. You're awful courageous to brave her wrath."

"I don't care what Florence does to me now. Tell me what happened. I didn't think the Japanese were sending up more planes."

"I didn't think so, either! It was a textbook mission to start with. We didn't see any Japs until we got to Rabaul. Even then they didn't send up any fighters. There was just a little anti-aircraft fire from below. The B-24s dropped their eggs as usual. My squadron dropped a few bombs of our own, made a few strafing runs, and started back for home. We were in tight formation, but I saw Red Johnson was falling further and further behind. I hung back to see what was the matter. His fuel pressure was dropping. The ack-ack must have hit him. He was almost out of fuel, so he decided to ditch. The next thing, two Zeros came out of nowhere. One dove on me and the other on Red, not realizing he was going down anyway. I saw Red's chute open, and knew I had to get both Zeros. There's no target a Jap likes better than a pilot who's just bailed. Well, maybe a hospital ship. Those red crosses make a fine target. But anyway, I distracted both Zekes away from Red. So then they were both on my tail. I climbed and they were dumb enough to follow. Up that high I could easily outmaneuver them. I shot one down right away. The other one was tougher, but I got him. Not before he got a lucky shot in, though. I knew I couldn't make it back, so I radioed in my position, bailed out, and hoped the Japs didn't pick me up first.

"By then the fight had taken me so far away from where Red went down that there was no sign of him. Well, I inflated my raft and decided to enjoy the ride. A few hours later, I heard engines and was awful glad to see it was one of ours, a PBY Woody had sent to look for us. We went back to where I thought Red went down but nothing. They're still looking. The PBY brought me to Bougainville. I spent the night there and got a ride back here today. Doc said I had to stay here overnight."

Clare was so enthralled by York's tale that she had not noticed the doctor had placed a privacy screen around them.

"Doc's very accommodating," York said, nodding to the screen. *Yes*, thought Clare, *I bet he's accommodating Bonnie right now.* "Won't you just keep me company awhile longer? I know visiting patients is part of your job." York shifted to the side of the bed, wincing, and patted the empty spot beside him. Clare sat down gingerly. She stroked his cheek and brushed his hair back with one hand, the other holding his tightly.

"Hey, I see tears in your eyes again. Everything's fine now," York assured her.

"No it isn't. What about Johnson? He seemed like such a nice boy."

"You're crying about Red Johnson?"

"Yes. When I heard you and Johnson were shot down, and it seemed like only one of you made it, I wished it was you and not him," Clare confessed.

"You did?" York said, pleased. "Well, I would wish it were me, too. That's okay. They'll find him. He's a good kid."

"Do you have to fly again?" Clare asked.

"Of course, I do. That's my job. Just need a new plane now. Too bad about the *KO*. The old girl had a good run, but I guess she wasn't as trusty as I thought, either."

"Well, she didn't let you down; it was the Zero's fault," Clare said, defending the P-38 now at the bottom of the ocean.

Clare and York talked softly, lying together in the hospital bed. After a while, they heard Bonnie clearing her throat loudly. She peeked around the screen.

"Doc says visiting hours are over in five minutes. Glad you made it back in one piece, Captain. Don't know what I'd have done with Clare if you hadn't," said Bonnie.

Clare and York said their goodbyes. She promised to visit him in the hospital again in the morning. Clare and Bonnie left, defiantly walking past Florence, who thought better of stopping them. Back in their tent, Betty was waiting to hear what had happened. Rick told her York had been rescued, but she wanted all the details.

"Oh Clare, I'm so happy for you," Betty said after hearing the whole story. "It's too bad he has to keep flying, though."

"That's what he loves to do. I wouldn't want to

stop him even if I could. Don't you feel the same way about Rick?"

"Oh, no. I'd stop him if I could. That face belongs on the big screen," said Betty.

"Or at least in a Sears catalog," teased Bonnie.

The next morning, Clare eagerly visited the hospital but did not find York there. One of the medics explained that the doctor had already discharged him. Clare was forced to stay there anyway, playing cards with men suffering from dysentery and malaria. After that day's show, Clare served refreshments as usual. York entered and cut to the front of the line.

"Parker, wait your turn," whispered Clare. "If you make a scene, Florence will notice."

"She can notice all she likes. But she's not going to do anything about it. Not to you or me. Or Woody and Betty."

"Why not? How do you know?" asked Clare.

"Turns out Woody really does have some connections in Hollywood. And one of them happened to be an agent for a famous vaudeville performer who was very well-known about twenty-five years ago for an act involving some peacock feathers and nothing else, if you understand what I mean. 'Flora and her Feathers' they called her."

"No fooling?"

"Yes, your prim and proper Aunt Eller was once a girl who can't say no herself. Woody happened to mention this bit of information to her, and she agreed that we can see just as much of you and Betty as we like."

"You mean you're blackmailing her?"

"Well, technically it's Woody, not me. I'd prefer to think of it as reminding her of her youthful indiscretions. Speaking of indiscretions, let's get out of here," suggested

York.

"No, I can't leave now. You have your job and I have mine."

"Okay, that's fair," said York. "How about Woody and I pick up you and Betty after dinner? We'll go for a drive in the other direction this time."

That evening, Betty and Clare found the two pilots waiting for them with a jeep. They drove past the PT boat base, parking in a grove of coconut palms. The four friends sat and talked. Then Betty and Rick went for a walk, leaving Parker and Clare alone in the jeep.

"I have a surprise for you," York said. "You can see it tomorrow. Come to the airstrip when you can slip away."

"What is it?" Clare asked. "Will I like it?"

"I hope so. I haven't seen it myself yet, but it will be ready tomorrow morning."

When Betty and Rick returned from their walk, the two couples drove back to the base. The men walked Betty and Clare right to their tent. Florence was standing by but said nothing and turned the other way, allowing both couples to say good night for as long as they wanted.

CHAPTER 32

After playing what seemed like an interminable game of Monopoly, Clare finally escaped from the infirmary the next day and hurried to the airfield. She found York in a thatch-roofed shack that served as the squadron's ready room, shooting the breeze with some other pilots.

"Clare, there you are! I was beginning to think you wouldn't come," York said, jumping up and taking her hand. "Close your eyes." He carefully led Clare to the airstrip. "Don't peek yet. Okay, you can open them now."

Clare opened her eyes and saw that she was standing before a P-38, presumably Parker's new airplane. Her gaze moved to the nose of the plane and she gasped. There on the nose was painted a very lifelike portrait of her. Lifelike except for the fact that she was dressed as a scantily clad gypsy fortune-teller gazing into a crystal ball. In the crystal ball was a flaming Japanese plane. Above the figure was painted "Clare-voyant" in yellow script.

"Do you like it? It came out swell, didn't it? That Lou is a real artist, not just a whiz of a mechanic. What do you think?" asked York.

"It's ... wow, that was not what I was expecting. I'm very flattered," Clare replied truthfully. *Also terribly embarrassed*, she thought.

"Of course, Lou's original idea was missing a few key pieces of clothing, but I told him that was unacceptable," York said gallantly.

"Gee, thanks," said Clare, reddening. "Have you flown her yet?"

"Yes, just a quick flight this morning. Might take her up again this afternoon."

"Oh, Betty mentioned something the other day. About going up with Rick … "

"You mean a piggyback ride? You'd want to go for a ride?"

"Maybe if it's no trouble, it might be fun … "

"You bet, sweetheart! I would have asked you, but I figured you'd say no. Come back after lunch, and we'll put her through her paces," York said enthusiastically. He gave her a quick kiss, and she dashed back to her tent.

Clare borrowed a pair of khaki slacks from one of the other girls and put on the sturdy brown leather oxfords from her USO uniform. She ate little at lunch, as she was beginning to feel nervous about the flight. She was not worried about something happening but feared she might suffer from motion sickness if Parker tried any fancy maneuvers. When she returned to the pilots' ready room, she found York waiting for her. He had scrounged up a small helmet with goggles and a yellow inflatable life vest known as a Mae West for obvious reasons.

"Here, put these on," he instructed. "Just in case."

Clare noticed that York was wearing a shoulder holster with a pistol and began to wonder what she had gotten herself into. When she was appropriately suited up, they went to the plane. Lou was checking a few things over before the flight.

"How do you like her, miss?" Lou asked, beaming with pride.

"You're very talented, Lou. I never imagined I'd see myself on the nose of a plane," said Clare, trying to forget Lou's initial idea for the painting.

"She's all ready for you, Sarge," Lou said to York. "Here's a parachute for you, miss," Lou said while helping Clare into the harness. "You're a brave girl, miss. Sarge took me up once. Let's just say I'd prefer to keep both feet on the ground. But maybe you saw the future in your crystal ball and don't have to worry," he said with a laugh.

York led Clare to the back of the fuselage. A small metal ladder with a couple rungs hung down from the airplane.

"You'd better get in first," York said. "I'll tell you what to do. Just don't step anywhere where it says 'No Step,' okay?"

York gave her a boost to the first rung of the ladder and instructed Clare where to put each foot and hand. With some difficulty she made it to the cockpit and stepped in. York followed her up and retracted the built-in ladder behind him. Once Clare was settled as far back as she could go, York climbed into the cockpit in front of her.

"It's a tight fit. Sure am glad you're smaller than Lou," said York. "And prettier, too," he said, giving her a wink over his shoulder. York closed the Lucite hatch and rolled up the two side windows, the bubble canopy enclosing them completely. Then he began a lengthy preflight check. Clare watched from behind and marveled at the complexity of the airplane. She counted an array of at least twenty dials and gauges, each measuring an important parameter that could not be ignored. There were numerous switches, buttons, and levers, the most important ones marked with a big red ball. Instead of a stick like most fighter planes, this plane had a control wheel on a yoke, like a larger bomber. York flipped more switches, and first the left, then the right engine roared to life. They taxied into position at the top of the runway.

"Ready?" York shouted back to Clare, and she responded with a "thumbs up." After a few more manipulations of the controls, they began to move forward, accelerating rapidly. Before Clare knew it, they were airborne. York raised the landing gear, and they began to climb. Clare saw the speed was one hundred and fifty miles per hour and rapidly increasing. Soon they leveled off and were cruising at more than two hundred miles per hour. They were over the ocean, but York banked left and flew back toward Stirling. They made a few passes over the small island. Although the bubble canopy gave them a three-hundred-and-sixty-degree field of vision, the engines and wings blocked some of the view, so York alternately banked right then left so Clare could see the coral island below.

Then they flew the short distance to dark and brooding Mono Island. They flew low over the volcano a few times. Clare saw thatched huts on the hillside. On the second pass, crowds of natives gathered to watch the airplane. Children waved and jumped up and down.

"Mind if we give them a show?" asked York. Before Clare could even answer, she felt York raising the nose of the plane. Instead of leveling off, York kept going. Clare felt the blood rush to her head and dimly realized that she was upside down. York came out of the loop and climbed again, this time doing a barrel roll. The sensation of being inverted was bewildering, and Clare hazily wondered how York was keeping control of the plane.

"You okay back there?" York shouted.

Clare gave him a shaky "thumbs up."

"How about a spin?" York asked.

Turning her thumb downward, Clare responded

with a loud, "No, thank you!"

"Okay, show's over, folks," he said to the unhearing crowd of natives below. "Clare, I don't want to land with so much fuel. Okay if we keep flying for a while? No more tricks, I promise."

Clare agreed, and they banked left and flew away from Mono and Stirling. Soon they were out over the open water with no land in sight. The ride was smooth, and Clare looked around as best she could. There was nothing to see except the blue of the sky above and the ocean below. Occasionally, she saw dark shapes in the water, the outlines of sharks, dolphins, and even whales. She watched York's able hands on the wheel, impressed by the ease with which he handled the big plane.

"We'll head back now," York said after cruising for an hour. He began to turn the plane, and Clare got a better view of the ocean below.

"Parker," she said, tapping his shoulder. "There's something down there. In the water. It's yellow," she shouted. The plane tilted, and York dove down for a better view. By then they both saw it clearly. It was a life raft. Then they saw a flash of light from below.

"That's a flare. There's someone on that raft," said York. Going lower still, they made out a figure waving up at them. "My God, I think it's Johnson!" York eagerly radioed in their position. "They're going to send a PBY. We've got enough fuel to wait 'til they show up if we're careful. Do you mind?"

"Of course not!" said Clare, forgetting about how cramped and uncomfortable she was. York began to make slow figure eights over the raft. After what seemed like an eternity, Clare spotted a speck in the distance.

"Look, Parker. That must be the plane," she said, motioning to the spot on the horizon. York continued his pattern while Clare watched the speck increase in size. As it came closer, she squinted and soon realized it did not look at all like a PBY Catalina, a big twin-engine flying boat.

"That's not it," Clare shouted, tapping Parker's shoulder insistently. "It's a ... a ... " Her mind raced through the airplane silhouettes she had learned, rejecting each one until the last one on her list. "Zero!" she yelled at the same moment York saw the plane.

York swore under his breath. "Hold on tight, Clare. This could get rough." The Lightning climbed, and the Zero foolishly followed. The Zero was below and behind them. Clare saw streaks of light coming from underneath as the Zero's two machine guns fired at them. York continued to climb, looping over and putting the Zero in front of him, while the Lightning's four machine guns blazed. The Zero tried to outmaneuver the P-38, but at that altitude it was no match for the larger plane. Patiently, York waited until he had a clear shot and then fired the Lightning's powerful twenty-millimeter cannon, scoring a direct hit on the Japanese plane. Smoke and flames trailed from the Zero as it began a downward spiral. Although they were high enough for the pilot to bail out, no parachute came.

The P-38 leveled out. Clare could hear York breathing hard. She then realized she had been holding her breath and gasped for air.

"You okay, Clare?" York asked, turning to see her as best he could. Clare impulsively leaned forward and gave him a kiss. "I'll take that as a yes, but no time for that now. Let's check on that raft again." The plane descended, and they found the raft unscathed, its occupant safe and feebly waving.

"I sure hope that PBY shows up. That used up a bit more fuel than I was counting on. We'll have to skedaddle soon, or we'll need some rescuing, too," York said, mostly to himself. They flew circles over the raft for a few more minutes and then saw the big Catalina flying boat lumbering toward them. York dipped one side of the plane, then the other, waggling its wings. The PBY returned the greeting, and York flew off for home.

Clare felt immensely relieved when she saw the dark form of Mono Island come into view, knowing that Stirling lay protected just behind it. York lowered the landing gear but made a low pass over the cluster of tents where Clare and the rest of the troupe lived before landing. The landing was smooth, and York taxied the plane back to its place in the lineup of P-38s. The propellers gradually came to a halt, and York rolled down the side windows and opened the canopy. He stood up, finally allowing Clare to unbend from the contorted position she had adopted for so long. York hopped out of the cockpit and released the ladder. He helped Clare out of the cockpit and then descended from the plane. Clare scrambled down, careful not to step where she should not. York lifted her down from the ladder and set her on the ground in front of him.

"You can fly with me anytime, Clare. I think *you're* my lucky charm."

"Lucky? We got shot at by a Zero! How lucky was that?"

"Not too lucky, but we got him anyway. And found Johnson, too."

By now Lou and a couple more members of the ground crew had arrived.

"Hey Sarge, heard you had quite a flight. That PBY confirmed it was Red. They got him and say he's going to be okay. Said he had a front row seat to quite a show, too. I guess I gotta paint another one of those Jap flags again. How did you like the flight, miss?" Lou asked Clare.

"That was more than I bargained for," said Clare.

"From now on I'm with you. I'll keep both feet on the ground, too!"

York patted the plane affectionately. "She did real good up there. You did, too, Clare. You were the one who spotted the raft. And the Zero, too, come to think of it. We'll celebrate tonight. Come to the Officers' Club after dinner. I have to go make my report about the flight," York said, giving her a quick kiss.

Clare shed the goggles, helmet, life vest, and parachute. She walked back to her tent, still trying to fathom what she had just experienced.

"Clare, where have you been?" asked Betty. "We didn't see you after the show today."

"I went for a ride with Parker. In his new plane. That he named after me."

"What?" cried Bonnie. "You're so lucky!"

"Oh, that must have been fun," Betty said, sounding a bit jealous.

"I don't think fun is the word I would have used, but it was an experience, anyway. I thought we were just going to fly around the island for a few minutes. But then he didn't want to land with so much fuel, so we kept going. We found Johnson. But then a Zero found us, and Parker had to shoot it down."

Betty looked at Clare narrowly. "Are you sure you haven't been drinking some of that jungle juice the boys make?"

"I know it does seem unbelievable. I can scarcely believe it myself," Clare said. "Parker wants to celebrate in the Officers' Club after dinner. Will you both come?"

"Of course we will," said Bonnie.

After dinner, the girls found a boisterous group at the Officers' Club. York spotted Clare right away.

"There she is fellas! My best copilot," York

proclaimed. The men raised their glasses to Clare, who politely protested that she had just been along for the ride.

"I don't think Johnson would agree with that. When he gets back he'll want your picture on his plane, too!" Overbrook said, while presenting her with a miniature pair of pilot's wings, which he pinned to her blouse. Clare blushed, uncomfortable at being the center of attention. She was happy when Parker pulled her away for a dance. The men in his squadron cut in, one by one, congratulating her on spotting their comrade. Clare noticed that Betty was dancing with Woody and Bonnie with Doc. The danger she had experienced earlier in the day seemed positively surreal.

Later, Clare and Parker walked along the beach. She felt perfectly content holding his hand and listening to the waves crash on the shore.

"Clare," York said, breaking the silence, "I hate to ask this, but how long are you staying?"

"I don't know, Parker. I've been trying not to think about it. I know there are only a couple more performances scheduled. Everyone must have seen the show by now. After that I think they're sending us home," she said dismally.

"What will you do when you go home?"

"I have no idea," Clare replied truthfully. "I suppose I could join the WACs or something. I guess it's worth it for a year."

"A year?"

"Yeah, before the war's over," Clare said, slipping.

"Oh, right. I forgot," York said dubiously. "I know we haven't known each other that long, so I have no right to ask you this, but will you wait for me?"

"Of course, Parker. I'll wait for as long as it takes."

CHAPTER 33

Florence raised her eyebrows at the small wings pinned to Clare's blouse, but she said nothing, and Clare offered no explanation. Clare was sure the story would get back to Florence but did not care. She did resolve to spend her last days on Stirling fulfilling her USO duties more diligently, however. Clare was engaged for the next few days helping in the infirmary, handing out refreshments during and after the show, and socializing with the enlisted men. Only afterward did she allow York to monopolize her time. York reported that Johnson was being treated for exposure at the larger hospital on Guadalcanal but sent his gratitude.

Despite the fortuitous outcome of Clare's flight, the pilots had received word from higher up that civilians were no longer to be taken on rides for safety reasons. Betty was terribly disappointed, but Clare assured her she was not missing anything; if she just wanted to hold Overbrook tightly, then it was best done on the ground. Betty grudgingly agreed.

Bonnie's head was not in the clouds but firmly planted on the ground at the base hospital. That made it especially strange when she began to complain about feeling cold the next evening.

"Didn't you take your Atabrine last night?" asked Clare. "I thought Doc was supposed to make sure you took it."

Bonnie thought hard. "I think we forgot. I guess he got distracted," she said, giggling and beginning to shiver.

"Let's get you over to the hospital," Betty said. Once the patient was under the watchful eye of Doc, Clare and Betty walked back to their tent.

"You know what this means, don't you?" asked Betty. Clare had been dreading this, but she knew tomorrow was the last show, and there was no way Bonnie would be over the malaria attack in time to perform.

"I know," Clare said glumly. "I think I'd rather fight off another Zero than go back on that stage again."

Nevertheless, Clare donned the frilly Ado Annie costume the next day. When she peeped out from behind the curtain, she was horrified to see that York and Overbrook had front row seats. She whispered the news to Betty.

"I know. Who do you think told them to get here early enough to get the best seats today?" Performing clearly did not faze Betty, but Clare was sure she would never grow to enjoy it.

After the performance, the cast was treated to a standing ovation, with York and Overbrook clapping and whistling the loudest. When the noise of the audience died down, Florence took over the microphone and explained it was their last performance of the tour. She recounted all the stops they had played, and the crowd cheered again.

"Before you all leave, we have a very special announcement today," Florence said. "Major Overbrook of the P-38 Fighter Squadron based here would like to say a few words."

Clare glanced at Betty who looked as surprised as

Clare. As Overbrook took to the stage, Clare wondered if he were going to ask Betty to marry him. She wondered if Betty thought the same thing.

Overbrook approached the microphone carrying a bouquet of flowers and an envelope.

"Ladies and gentlemen, we received a very special message at communications headquarters today, and I'm very honored to be the one to share it with you. Miss Wilton, stand here right next to me if you please." Betty came forward, beaming at Overbrook. He handed her the bouquet and made a show of opening the letter. In his most theatrical voice he read, "Dear Miss Wilton, word of your success in the role of Laurey in the USO production of *Oklahoma!* has traveled far and wide. In addition to entertaining countless GIs, sailors, and Marines, your performance has attracted the attention of none other than Mr. Frank Sinatra. Mr. Sinatra requests your presence in New York City immediately following your return to the United States in order to record a series of duets with him for his upcoming album. Should you be agreeable, please wire me your consent at your earliest convenience. Very sincerely yours, Mr. George Evans, agent to Mr. Sinatra."

The crowd cheered and Betty looked thunderstruck.

"Well, what do you say, Miss Wilton? Is that a 'yes?'" asked Overbrook.

"Yes!" Betty cried. "Yes, of course!" She threw her arms around Overbrook's neck, and he lifted her up and twirled her around.

Like everyone else, Clare clapped and cheered. But then she was struck with a disconcerting thought. She'd never heard of Betty Wilton. *No one named Betty Wilton ever sang with Frank Sinatra. Those songs were never recorded.* She began to try to rationalize what could have happened. *Maybe she changed her name. No, that's not likely. Maybe he changed his mind. Maybe she changed her mind.* Clare was pondering this when Betty ran up to her.

"Oh Clare, I can't believe this! It's a dream come true," Betty said, beaming.

"It's swell, Betty," Clare said, forcing a smile.

"It's more than swell. It's marvelous!" said Betty. "Clare, what's eating you? You don't seem very happy for me."

"Of course I am, Betty. I'm thrilled for you," Clare said, trying to sound enthusiastic.

"You don't sound thrilled. You're not jealous, are you?"

"No, of course not. Nothing like that."

"Then what? Don't you think I'm good enough to sing with Sinatra?" Betty asked, crestfallen.

"Of course I do, Betty. You're terrific. If there's anyone I'd like to hear sing with him, it's you," Clare said with sincerity. "It's just, well, don't get your hopes up too much. Just in case it falls through somehow."

"Clare, what a thing to say to me. Why on earth would it fall through?"

"I don't know. I don't want to see you be too disappointed if it doesn't happen."

"You say the strangest things sometimes, Clare. I remember you telling that model at the Stage Door Canteen she was going to be a star. And you told that dull lieutenant on Guadalcanal he was going to be a famous writer. Now I've got a guaranteed offer to sing with Sinatra, and you tell me not to get too excited about it? You know, you don't *really* have a crystal ball," Betty said irately.

"I know," Clare said. "I'm awful sorry, Betty. I really am happy for you. Maybe I am a little envious," she lied.

"Aw, Clare. That's okay. I have to admit I was a

little jealous when you came back from that flight with Parker, and everyone was making a big fuss about it."

"I'm sorry, Betty. I didn't want them to. I really didn't do anything worth making a fuss over. Promise me we're still friends?"

"Of course, Clare. You're my best friend. I guess that's why what you think matters so much to me," Betty said while hugging Clare. "Come on, let's go get out of these ridiculous costumes. I won't miss wearing these dresses!"

CHAPTER 34

Clare visited Bonnie in the hospital the following day. She was feeling much better and did not seem the least bit disappointed at missing the final performance. Clare spent the rest of the morning talking and playing cards with the men at the hospital. After lunch, Betty rushed in excitedly.

"Clare, Rick's going to take me up in his airplane this afternoon!"

"I thought civilians weren't allowed as passengers anymore."

"I don't care and neither does Rick. We'll be leaving the South Pacific soon. When am I ever going to get another chance like this anyway?" Betty replied.

"I don't think that's such a good idea."

"What could possibly happen? It's such a beautiful day. And Woody's the best pilot in the squadron," Betty countered.

"Parker does say that. But still, I think it's a bad idea. Is it really worth the risk?"

"Why should you be the only one to have all the fun? Clare, I'm surprised at you. First discouraging me about the gig with Sinatra and now this." Betty looked at her watch. "I have to go. Woody will be waiting for me."

Clare watched Betty stalk out of the Quonset hut. She tried to go back to playing cards but could not focus. She excused herself and stepped outside. *I've got a bad feeling about this*, Clare thought. *No, I'm overreacting.* But the feeling of foreboding would not leave her. *I've got to stop her*, Clare thought and began running to the airstrip.

She dashed into the ready room, but no one was there. Then she scanned the field and saw Rick and Betty next to his plane. They made a striking couple. Overbrook gave her a life vest and goggles, maybe the very same ones Clare had worn. She saw Overbrook kiss Betty and then give her a boost up to the Lightning's built-in ladder.

"Betty!" Clare yelled as she approached the plane. "Betty, don't go! Please don't go!" Clare grabbed Overbrook's arm. "Don't take her up, Rick. Please don't," she cried.

"Clare, what's gotten into you? Don't worry. I won't get in trouble for taking Betty for a ride."

"That's not what I'm worried about. I don't think you should. It's too dangerous."

"Don't be silly," Overbrook said, pulling himself free from Clare's grasp. "We're just going to fly around Stirling and Mono. There's no chance of any Japs this far south. I'm not going anywhere near where York took you. *That* would be foolish," Overbrook said as he climbed up the ladder. "We'll see you later. You'd better stand back now."

Clare mutely watched Overbrook settle Betty in the cockpit. He gave her a kiss and took his place in front of her. He lowered the canopy and raised the side windows. Rick and Betty both gave Clare their best movie star smiles and a "thumbs up" as the propellers came to life. Clare knew Overbrook was checking all the instruments. After a few minutes, he taxied the P-38 to the head of the runway and began to pick up speed. Clare saw the twin tails of the plane rise, and it was airborne. She watched them fly away with a sick feeling in the pit of her stomach.

Clare tried unsuccessfully to locate York. She gave up and went back to the base hospital. She began to make small talk with some of the men but found she could not pay attention; her ears were intent on hearing the whine of the returning P-38's engines. Clare left after two hours, certain she must have been distracted when the plane returned and missed hearing it land. She went to her tent, but Betty was not there. She considered asking Florence if she had seen Betty but thought better of it. She went back to the airstrip and saw York walking into the ready room. She ran in after him.

"Parker, there you are! Where's Rick? He took Betty for a ride in his plane. Are they back yet?" Parker tried to embrace her, but Clare shook herself free. "Not now, Parker. Did they come back?"

"I don't know, Clare. I'll go check." Parker left and came back a moment later. "His plane's not here, and his mechanic said he's not back yet. But don't worry. The mechanic said there was enough fuel for a couple hours, and they weren't planning on going very far."

"But they left a couple hours ago!" Clare wailed. "I just know something terrible has happened!"

"Clare, calm down. Don't you think you're taking this crystal ball thing a little too far now? It's not funny."

"Parker, I'm serious. We've got to find them."

"Okay, Clare, if they don't come back in another hour, I'll go take a look. In the meantime, I'll check if Woody filed a flight plan or radioed anything after he took off."

Clare followed him anxiously. Overbrook had not filed a flight plan, just a brief entry of "local flight" in the log. No radio communications had been received from his P-38. They tried to call up Overbrook's plane but received no response.

"That doesn't mean anything," York reassured Clare. "Might just be maintaining radio silence. When I called in our position the other day that was probably what brought that Zero out looking for us."

"But he specifically said he wouldn't go anywhere near where you took me, just around Mono and Stirling."

"Okay," York said, starting to sound worried, too. "I'll go look for them while it's still light."

"I'm coming with you," Clare said with determination.

"Absolutely not," York replied, equally determined.

"Two sets of eyes are better than one. And I'm the one who spotted Johnson and the Zero."

Seeing he could not argue with Clare, York relented. He asked Lou to get the *Clare-voyant* ready. In a few minutes, York and Clare were in the cockpit and taxiing down the runway.

The Lightning circled Stirling Island, flying low over Blanche Harbor, which separated it from Mono. Then York began flying a zig-zag pattern over Mono, dipping the plane left and right to get a better look at the ground. Clare stared intently down at the dense foliage below them but saw nothing unusual. After two passes over the interior of the island, York began to circle the perimeter. A barrier reef ringed part of the island. As they approached the point farthest from Stirling, Clare cried out.

"There! Look!" she said, pointing to a slick of oil on the water. York dove closer and saw debris floating amidst the reef. He immediately recognized it as a fragment of a P-38's horizontal stabilizer. He turned the plane back toward Stirling and radioed ahead. He felt Clare clutching at him tightly, her face buried in the back of his neck; he felt her sobbing against him and her hot tears trickling down inside his flight suit. When they had safely landed, he turned to look at her. Clare could see there were tears in his eyes, too.

"There's still a chance they're okay, Clare. Or maybe it wasn't even their plane," York said, but Clare could tell he did not even believe himself.

"I'm sure it's them, Parker. If only I had stopped them … " Clare said, her voice trailing off into a sob.

The other pilots and men of the ground crews crowded around them, eager to hear what they had seen. York described the wreckage, and a few of the other pilots decided to go back for another look. Word traveled fast throughout the island, as Overbrook was well-liked by all. Two of the PT boat skippers set out to look for survivors.

When the commotion died down, Clare and Parker were alone again.

"It's all my fault. I should have tried harder to stop them. It's just like Roy all over again … " Clare said between sobs.

"Roy? Who's Roy?" asked York.

"It doesn't matter now. He's gone, too. Now it all makes sense. That's why I never heard of them. If only I had stopped them."

"Clare, you're most definitely not making sense. Let's see if they have something at the infirmary to calm your nerves." Clare leaned against York as he led her to the hospital.

Bonnie saw them enter and weakly tried to stand. Her cheeks were tearstained. The news had obviously reached her. Clare rushed to her side, and the two women clutched each other and wept. York stood awkwardly by and was relieved when the doctor appeared.

"I'm sorry about Woody, Sarge. That's a tough

break. Everyone thought he was a real swell guy," the doctor offered.

"Thanks, Doc. I never thought he'd get it like this. I guess his luck just ran out. It's bound to when you've been out here long enough. Say, Clare's taking this awful hard. Is there anything you can give her?"

Doc walked not to the medicine cabinet but to his desk. He opened the bottom drawer, pulled out a mostly full bottle of Scotch, and handed it to York.

"This is the best I can offer. I figure you could use some, too. Raise a glass to Woody for me, will you?"

"Thanks, Doc," York said, accepting the bottle. "Clare, let's get you back to your tent. Doc will look after Bonnie."

Parker led Clare away. It was almost dinnertime, but neither felt like eating. York poured her a drink of Scotch, and Clare obediently swallowed the amber liquid, grimacing as it burned her throat and then filled her chest with its radiating warmth. York tucked her into her cot and promised to return later to check on her. As he left, he passed Florence, who threw him a scornful, accusatory glance.

Thanks to the Scotch, Clare slept soundly. It was dark when she woke, and she could dimly make out a figure on the cot next to hers.

"Betty, is that you?" she cried while struggling with the mosquito netting.

"No, Clare. It's just me," York said softly.

"Oh," Clare said, disappointment filling her voice. "Have you been here long?"

"A little while. It's almost nine. Are you hungry?" York asked.

Clare thought about it and realized she was. "Yes, I guess so."

"Me, too. I saved us some dinner. Let's go down to the beach," York said, helping her up. They walked silently for some time.

"Is there any news?" Clare asked hesitantly.

York nodded and then added, "The PT boat crews came back. Recovered some of the wreckage. It's definitely Woody's plane. They say there are no survivors."

They reached York's jeep and drove away from the base. When they came to a cove they liked, York spread out the rough olive blanket on the sand. They ate some cold fried chicken York had taken from the mess hall.

"Do you feel better now, sweetheart?" York asked.

"No, not really. I should have stopped them," Clare lamented.

"Aw, don't start that again, Clare. You can't really see the future."

"Parker, you're wrong. I do know what's going to happen. Or not happen. Some of it, anyway," Clare said seriously.

"Clare, you're an intelligent, logical woman. Don't tell me you actually believe in that fortune-teller mumbo jumbo, do you?"

"I can't explain it to you. I wish I could," Clare said lamely, longing to tell him the truth.

"Well, maybe some things are just supposed to happen. Just because you think you know what's going to happen doesn't mean you can change it. Suppose you had stopped their flight today. Maybe Woody would have got it over Rabaul tomorrow anyway. Maybe Betty would have contracted fatal scrub typhus," York suggested.

"I never thought of it like that before," Clare said, slightly cheered. "Maybe you're right." *Maybe if I'd stopped Roy from going to Sicily, he would have ended up at Anzio, and the same thing would have happened anyway,* Clare thought.

"Let's forget about the future, Clare. And the past. All we've got is now," York said.

Clare saw the wisdom in that. She did not mind when York pulled her against his bare chest and caressed her with his strong hands. She responded instinctively, her mouth and hands exploring every part of the aviator's eager body. She felt his insistent grip as he pressed her against him. His hands slid down over her skirt, tugging at it impatiently.

Suddenly York stopped. His hand darted into the pocket of Clare's skirt and pulled out the heart-shaped charm with the Army Air Forces propeller and wings insignia. He squinted at it in the moonlight.

"Where did you get this?" York demanded, his voice suddenly hard.

"Nowhere. It's nothing," Clare said, panting. "I didn't get it from another man, I swear."

"I know you didn't," York said. "I made it."

CHAPTER 35

"What?" Clare cried. "*You* made it?"

"Where did you get this?" York asked again. By now he had struck a match to get a better view of the charm. "Answer me, Clare."

"I found it," Clare replied weakly.

"Where?"

In a box of junk. At a flea market. Fifty years in the future. I can't tell him that! Who would ever believe it? "I found it with some scrap. I couldn't believe anyone would intentionally discard it, so I took it."

"In Schenectady?" asked York.

"No, in Laurelmont."

"Laurelmont? You never told me you were in Laurelmont," York said, his voice still cold.

"Didn't I? I guess I didn't think it mattered. I was there for a few months before I went to New York. That's where I met Betty. What difference does it make?"

"My girl, the girl I made this for, she lives in Laurelmont."

"Oh," replied Clare, knowing she did not really want to hear the rest of the story.

"I made it from the canopy of my first plane. A P-40. Cracked her up in a real bad landing. I sent it to her in a letter. A letter where I asked her to marry me. But I never got a response. Not a yes. Not a no. Nothing. That was worse than a 'Dear John' letter. Didn't even have the decency to turn me down," York explained.

"Gee, I'm awful sorry," Clare said, not knowing how to respond. "Well, she was very foolish to let you get away," she added.

"Yeah, my folks thought she was too young and foolish, too. Her folks didn't much like me, either. Never understood that. But I thought she was the one for me. Even named my first P-38 after her. But she let me down, too."

"*KO Punch*?" Clare asked. "That was her name?"

"Yeah, Kay."

"O'Neill," finished Clare, suddenly realizing the racy boxer bore a certain likeness to her friend back home. York stared at her.

"You know Kay?" he asked in disbelief.

"She's my best friend in Laurelmont. But I swear she never mentioned you."

"What? Did she have a boyfriend?"

"Oh, not just one. A whole bunch," Clare responded, and York looked even more hurt. "No wait. That didn't come out right. She wrote letters to a bunch of fellas, but it was nothing serious. She's the person who convinced me to go to the USO dance in the first place. Without her, I'd never be here. In fact, she was supposed to come on the tour, too, but her parents wouldn't let her."

"And she never mentioned me?" York said.

"Let me think a minute." Clare gazed off into the distance. "No, but she did say a few things that make more sense now. I teased her about writing to so many different men. That she needed a pilot to complete her collection and she got upset. Yes, I remember now. She said she had one of those, and it was real serious, but he stopped writing to her. And her parents didn't like him because he was too old for her and from a different background."

"Go on. What else did she say?" asked York, eagerly.

"Hmm. Well, Kay's parents seemed to like her sister Nell's boyfriend Johnny an awful lot. They hoped Kay would find someone like him."

"Did she?"

"No, I don't think so. The last I heard from Kay was around Christmas, and she didn't mention anyone. I think she was awful hurt to lose you. She thought you took up with some island beauty. You broke her heart. I guess I can understand that," Clare added.

"Well, she broke mine. I was sincere in my desire to marry her. Clare, I'm sorry, but if I thought I still had a chance with Kay, well, none of this would have happened," York said, gesturing vaguely at the blanket.

"I know, Parker. I never would have tried to steal you away from Kay. Honest," Clare said sadly. "She's my best friend, and I would never hurt her."

The pair sat awkwardly, and Clare smoothed out her skirt and blouse.

"I still don't understand why she never wrote back to me," York said.

"She must not have gotten your last letter."

"But it made it to Laurelmont, obviously," York said, holding up the charm. "This was in the letter."

"Maybe her parents intercepted your letters," suggested Clare, "if they really didn't like you." How anyone could see the handsome, well-educated aviator as an unsuitable match for their daughter was beyond her, but she knew people harbored prejudices about the most inconsequential things. "I suppose they were just trying to protect her. How did you meet her, anyway?"

"I was stationed near there for a while, during my flight training. I used to go to the USO dance at the YMCA gym to see her. Or we'd meet at the movie theater when I could get away during the week. I didn't realize how old she was then. Maybe if I had, I wouldn't have pursued her."

"Well, she's eighteen now," Clare said. "Even if her parents object, there's nothing they can do to stop you."

"She's nineteen now. Her birthday was last week."

"Oh. Well, so much the better. She can make her own decisions."

"Do you think I still have a shot with her, Clare?"

"Yes, I think you do," Clare said, unable to hide the disappointment in her voice.

"I've got to give it one more try. Will you do me a favor, Clare?"

"Of course, Parker. What is it?"

"If I write Kay another letter will you deliver it for me? Can I put the charm I made back in the letter?"

"Yes, Parker, of course I will. The charm doesn't belong to me anyway. I guess I knew all along I had it by mistake. I'll personally deliver the letter and charm directly to Kay as soon as I'm back in Laurelmont. And I'll explain everything," Clare promised. "Well, maybe I'll leave out a few details," she added, laughing.

"Thanks, Clare. You're the best." York hugged her, and Clare noted that all the passion between them had evaporated. "Some special man is going to be very lucky to have you someday." Clare shrugged and they got back in the jeep to return to the base.

CHAPTER 36

Bonnie was released from the hospital the following day, in time to attend a funeral service for Overbrook and Betty. It seemed the whole population of the island was in attendance, as everyone knew the affable pilot and had seen the beautiful singer perform. Clare and Bonnie stood pressed together, with York and Doc supporting them on either side while the chaplain spoke. When the prayers were concluded, several of the pilots from the squadron, including York, came forward and paid tribute to their friend. Clare would have liked to do the same for Betty, but she did not trust herself to get any words out ahead of the flood of tears she knew would come. She was grateful that Florence, instead, spoke eloquently and fondly of the young rising star and dashing aviator, all trace of disapproval forgotten.

As members of the USO cast sang hymns, Clare realized that York and a few other pilots had slipped away. When the songs concluded, a bugler played taps, and the sound of engines came from above. Clare looked up to see four P-38s flying in a V formation. As the planes came in low over the crowd, the Lightning behind the lead plane in the longer arm of the V pulled up abruptly, rising until it was out of sight and leaving a gap in the formation. The three remaining planes continued on into the sunset, maintaining the empty space that had belonged to their missing man. It was a fitting tribute.

At dinner that evening, Florence announced that they would fly back to Efate in two days' time. Clare let York know when they were departing. He told her he would have the letter ready for her by then. He had also found out he would take Overbrook's place as squadron commander. In time it would come with a promotion to major.

On the day of their departure, York visited Clare in her tent. He entrusted her with a thick envelope addressed simply to "My Darling Kay." York helped Clare stow her luggage on the waiting C-47.

"I'm going to miss you, Clare. Have a safe journey, and thank you for taking my letter to Kay. I hope we meet again," York said, kissing her cheek.

"I'll miss you, too, Parker. Just be careful up there. I'll never forget you. I hope we meet again, too," Clare said, full of melancholy. She watched Bonnie saying a tearful goodbye to Doc but could not help feeling his affections would soon be supplanted by those of another.

Clare and Bonnie climbed up into the Skytrain, waving out at York and Doc through the small rectangular windows. The plane taxied and rose skyward. Clare felt it was positively luxurious after the two cramped flights in the P-38. However, it did not take long for Bonnie to start complaining about the hard metal seats.

After landing in Efate, Florence explained that there was no hurry to send them home, so they would have to wait for a ship rather than fly back the way they had come. They found that the ship was to be the *SS Matsonia*, sister ship of the *Lurline* in the Matson Line. In the intervening week, the performers gave impromptu shows, but no one sang songs from *Oklahoma!* Everyone agreed that it would not be right to sing them without Betty. Clare was occupied with the usual tasks at the base hospital, serving refreshments, and dancing with the boys at night. The week passed quickly, and before she knew it, Clare was packing up her few possessions again. Now the envelope from Parker held a special spot next to the photos and letters from Roy.

Once aboard the ship, Clare and Bonnie found their cabin was even more cramped and shabby than the *Lurline* had been. It was going to be a long voyage back to San Francisco. They were not scheduled to make any stops along the way. At least there were many men returning home who were looking for company. Visiting boys in sickbay, playing games, and serving refreshments during the nightly movies helped to pass the time. Clare was more than a little pleased when occasionally someone mentioned he had seen one of her performances as Ado Annie. Nevertheless, three weeks at sea dragged on interminably. Clare was sure that the orange girders of the Golden Gate Bridge were the most beautiful sight she had ever seen.

PART IV

RETURN

CHAPTER 37

The *Matsonia* docked with little fanfare. Clare and Bonnie spent a few days in San Francisco. The first thing Clare did after arriving in their room at the YWCA was to write a letter to Kay, telling her she had safely returned to the United States. She figured news of Betty's death had reached Laurelmont already, so she had to mention that in the letter, too. Lastly, she told Kay that she had something very important to give her and asked Kay to meet her at the Laurelmont train station. Instead of accompanying Clare back to New York, Bonnie decided to go to Los Angeles in the hope of getting her big acting break. The USO troupe had more or less disbanded, with some people heading directly to their hometowns, rather than returning to New York. Clare soon found herself on a train chugging eastward, surrounded by throngs of soldiers and other passengers but feeling utterly alone.

The days on the train passed slowly. Still wearing her USO uniform, Clare felt obliged to entertain the men as best she could. Even so, that left her with a lot of time to reflect on the events of the past few months and ponder what the immediate future would hold in store. She knew she would return to Laurelmont and fulfill her promise to Parker, but after that she could not decide what to do.

Going back to her old job at the five-and-dime seemed too anticlimactic after what she had experienced. *Maybe I should join the WACs or the WAVES*, Clare mused. *Or see if the USO would send me on another tour. Maybe I should do something really important.* She quickly rejected the idea of trying to kill Adolf Hitler but began to toy with the idea of trying to save Glenn Miller, who would be lost on a flight over the English Channel in December. However, she remembered Parker's suggestion that maybe some things are supposed to happen and abandoned the scheme. *I guess I should try to find a way back to my own time*, Clare thought. *Maybe I can find Albert Einstein. If anyone could figure it out, it would be him. Oh, who am I kidding? He would think I'm crazy. No one would believe me. I'd find myself locked up in an insane asylum if I try to convince people I'm from the future.* Clare resolved not to think about what to do anymore and would wait to see what opportunities arose.

Eventually the train pulled into Pennsylvania Station. Clare collected her belongings and rode the subway to the YWCA. Nothing had changed much since she left at the end of December, except a large photo of Betty now graced the lobby, its small plaque explaining how she had given her life while serving overseas with the USO.

Clare ate at the Horn & Hardart, the warm, familiar food so comforting after her long journey. She danced at the Stage Door Canteen one night and served refreshments the next. Despite the crowds, she could not help feeling lonely. She sent Kay a telegram saying she would arrive in Laurelmont the following day.

As she boarded the train, Clare hummed "Sentimental Journey," but she knew there would be no singing on the trip without Betty. When the train pulled into Laurelmont's station, Clare saw Kay and Nell waving from the platform. She raced down the steps toward them and threw her arms around Kay first, then Nell.

"I'm so happy to see you both!" Clare cried.

"We are, too, Clare! I've missed you so much," said Kay. "Look at you in that USO uniform. You look terrific. And that tropical climate really agreed with you."

"You look great yourself, Kay!" Clare had not seen her friend in over six months. She seemed more mature and sophisticated. "You, too, Nell!"

"Nell? I think she's letting herself go now that she's an old married lady," Kay joked while jabbing Nell with her elbow. Clare looked down at Nell's left hand and saw a thin gold band on her ring finger.

"Oh, Nell! Congratulations! I'm so happy for you and Johnny."

"Thanks, Clare. Johnny came home on leave after Christmas. He only had two weeks, so we decided to make the most of it. We were going to wait but then decided there's no time like the present."

"That's so true," Clare replied. "I'm very happy for you, Mrs. McMurphy. Are you still working at the diner?"

"Oh yes, harder than ever. I've got to save up enough so Johnny and I can get our own place when he comes home for good."

"What about you, Kay? How are things at Kingsley's?" Clare asked.

"Okay, I suppose. I don't work there anymore. I got a job at the factory two months ago," Kay said proudly. "I work the swing shift," she added.

"Kay, that's swell! I'm real proud of you. And your parents let you?"

"They weren't too happy about it, but I don't care. I'm nineteen now, you know. Let's go to the diner for lunch. We can sit and talk until I have to get ready for work."

Nell and Kay helped Clare with her luggage. The diner was bustling with the lunchtime crowd, but there was one booth left. Soon the girls were seated, and Nell took their orders. She brought out the food and sat down to join them.

"Okay Clare, tell me everything. I want all the details. Oh, but poor Betty ... We were so shocked. What happened? No, start at the beginning. No, wait. You said you had something for me. What is it? Is it that autograph from Bob Hope you promised me? You said you'd ask him to send me a letter. Is that what it is?" Kay asked eagerly.

"No, Kay. I didn't meet Bob Hope. That's not it at all. But I don't think you'll be disappointed," Clare said, reaching into her purse and retrieving the letter from York. "Special delivery," she said, placing it in Kay's hand. Kay looked down at the envelope and her eyes widened. She looked up at Clare incredulously.

"Aren't you going to open it, Kay?" Clare could see Kay's hands trembling as she tore open the envelope and withdrew the sheets of paper. The heart-shaped charm tumbled out and clattered on the table. Kay grabbed it and stared at it a moment before devouring the letter. Clare watched Kay's expression change from confusion to surprise to delight. Tears of joy welled up in her eyes, and she threw her arms around Clare.

"It's from Parker. He still loves me, and he wants to marry me. It was all a misunderstanding."

"Well, what's your answer?" asked Clare with a bittersweet smile.

"Yes! Of course, it's yes!" cried Kay.

"But what about your parents?"

"I don't care what they say. I can make my own decisions. They will just have to learn to like him," Kay said resolutely.

"You'd better write him back right now. I know he's anxious for your answer." Clare gave Kay a sheet of pink stationery and a matching envelope from her purse. Kay quickly scrawled out a reply, addressed the letter, and sealed it. Then she reapplied her lipstick and added a red kiss on the back.

"Oh, Clare, that's the best souvenir you could possibly bring me. Who cares about Bob Hope, anyway? I think I'm the happiest girl in the whole world right now. How about you, Clare? Did you meet any nice fellas on your trip?" Kay asked.

"Oh sure, there were lots of nice fellas but no one special in particular," Clare lied.

"Don't worry, Clare. You'll find the right one someday," Kay said reassuringly.

"I guess you're right, Kay. Tell me everything I've missed in Laurelmont."

Kay and Nell filled Clare in on all the gossip of the past several months. She told them about her trip and what happened to Betty but carefully left out her romance with York.

"That sounds like quite an adventure," said Nell. "Kay, don't you think you'd better get ready for work?"

"Oh, I almost forgot! I'd better go. Clare, we told Mrs. Harrigan you would be back today. She said your old room is empty if you want it."

"That's swell, Kay. I hadn't even thought about that. I'll go there right after I go to the post office. I'm going to mail that letter for you myself. I don't want anything to happen to it."

"Gee, thanks, Clare. It's great to have you back!" Kay skipped out of the diner as if floating on clouds.

"That was some special delivery, Clare. I don't know how you managed that. I've never seen Kay so happy. Our parents won't be thrilled, but they'll get over it. Besides, they'll soon be too distracted to care much. I have some news to tell them that I can't keep a secret much longer," Nell said, looking down. Clare followed her gaze and realized Nell's dress was not as form-fitting as she would normally wear.

"Oh, Nell, congratulations! You and Johnny will make wonderful parents, I'm sure. Does Kay know?"

"No, she's been too khaki wacky to notice anything else. I expect that will change now. I guess this Parker is a decent sort, though."

"He is, Nell. He comes from a good family, and he really loves Kay. I wouldn't have brought back his letter if I didn't think he was worthy of her. I'll go mail the letter and then head over to Mrs. Harrigan's."

Clare exited the diner and walked up the street, happy to be home. Not much had changed while she was gone. She had missed winter, and now spring flowers were peeking out of the ground here and there. Clare entered the post office and waited her turn to buy a stamp.

"Please send this as fast as you can," Clare said. "I don't care how much it costs." The slow-moving postal clerk painstakingly affixed two three-cent stamps for faster service.

"Say, you're Miss Clare Carlyle, aren't you?" the clerk asked.

"Yes, that's right."

"I've got a letter for you. It just came addressed to Laurelmont, no street. Lucky you came in here," the clerk said, riffling through a stack of letters and handing one to Clare. Clare looked at it and smiled. It was from Parker. She tucked it into her purse and departed.

Clare soon found herself in front of the brick façade of Mrs. Harrigan's Boarding House. It looked much as it had when she first saw it the previous June, but the sign said "No Vacancy." Clare feared Kay had been wrong about her old room being available. As she raised her eyes up to the window of the room that had been hers, she spotted another difference. The flag hanging in the second floor window, the window that belonged to Anna, now had a gold star in the center instead of blue. Clare clapped her hand to her mouth to suppress a cry and felt tears spring to her eyes. It could only mean that Anna's son, so proud to be a Marine, had given his life for the Allied cause.

When she had composed herself, Clare rang the doorbell and Mrs. Harrigan answered.

"Clare, it is you! We've been expecting you. Kay told me you'd be back, and it just so happens your old room was free, so I've been saving it for you," Mrs. Harrigan said while ushering her inside. "Come upstairs and get settled. Then you must tell us all about your adventures." Mrs. Nelson and Mrs. Ellis were glued to the radio in the parlor, but both ladies rose and greeted Clare with warm embraces.

Mrs. Harrigan unlocked the door to Clare's room on the third floor. It was just as she left it, although perhaps the chenille bedspread was a little more faded.

"I'll let you rest, dear. You must be exhausted after such a journey. You just let me know if you need anything," the older woman said, departing.

"Wait, Mrs. Harrigan? There is something. The flag. In the window. Anna's window. It's a gold star now, isn't it?" Clare asked with trepidation.

"Yes, dear, I'm afraid it is. Anna got the news just after Christmas. Seems it happened on Tarawa. They awarded him a medal, but that hardly helps. Anna's a strong woman, though. She started working at the factory. She'll be happy to see you when she gets home tonight."

Clare unpacked her luggage and flopped down onto the bed. Suddenly she remembered the letter from Parker in her purse and retrieved it. She withdrew the folded sheet of paper, and a photograph slipped out. It was of a handsome, smiling aviator standing in front of his plane. But it was not Parker. Clare recognized the pilot as Red Johnson. On the nose of his new plane was painted a pretty Southern belle wearing a very low-cut gown who happened to bear a strong resemblance to a certain gypsy fortune-teller. Above the figure was painted "I Do De-Clare." Clare laughed in spite of herself. *That Lou is certainly talented*, she thought and wondered if Johnson had to convince him to paint more clothes on her. She flipped the photo over and saw it was labeled "Lt. Raymond 'Red' Johnson" and included his serial number and address. Clare unfolded the letter and read:

April 18, 1944

Dear Clare,

I hope you are well and your journey home was a safe one. I wanted to thank you for conveying my letter to Kay. I am eagerly awaiting her response and very much appreciate you pleading my cause. I hope her reply will be favorable.

I thought you would want to know that Red Johnson rejoined the squadron after recuperating for a few weeks on Guadalcanal. He has a new plane, and as you can see from the picture, Lou fixed it up real nice for him. Red was very grateful to you for finding him. As he's rather shy and proper, he wanted me to ask if you would consider writing to him. I know it would make him very happy to receive a letter from you.

Things just weren't the same around here without Woody. I bet you feel the same way about Betty. I did get that promotion to major. I think we'll be moving north soon as the Japs are pretty much licked at Rabaul.

What will you do now that you are home? Go back to Schenectady? Maybe finish your studies at Penllyn? Whatever it is, I know you will be a success. I think you are the most courageous woman I know. Please give my love to Kay. I wait for her reply with bated breath.

Yours truly,

Parker

P.S. I didn't know where to send this letter, but I figured someone in Laurelmont would find you.

Clare sighed. *I still don't feel courageous*, she thought. *What do I do now?*

Clare ate dinner downstairs and entertained the other residents with stories of her trip. She excused herself and got ready for bed but could not sleep. The house was quiet as she tossed and turned, but then she heard footsteps on the stair. She figured only Anna would be coming home so late. She crept out of her room and down the stairs. A soft glow shone from under Anna's door, and Clare rapped on it softly. Anna opened it a crack.

"Clare, it's you! They said you were coming back. Come in, come in," Anna said, opening the door. The two women embraced.

"Anna, I heard about your son. I'm so sorry. I wish there were something I could say or do to help, but I know nothing can," said Clare, fighting back the tears.

"Thank you, Clare. He was awarded a Navy Cross for valor at Tarawa," Anna said, opening a small box on her dresser. Clare looked at the navy blue ribbon with a stripe of white and a bronze cross adorned with a sailing ship in the middle. She tried to smile.

"It's a small consolation, but at least I know he died saving the lives of his comrades. I know it's what he would have wanted," Anna said wearily. "I suppose Mrs. Harrigan told you I'm working at the factory now. I'm exhausted, but I want you to tell me all about your trip tomorrow. I'm so glad you are back." The women embraced again, and Clare returned to her room.

CHAPTER 38

In the morning, Clare awoke to a familiar aroma. She dressed hurriedly and found Anna in the kitchen making poppy seed bread. Over a breakfast of the sweet rolls and hot coffee, she told Anna all about her travels.

"Clare, that's a real adventure. You must be very proud of serving and making a difference for all those boys out there," Anna said.

"No, not really," Clare confessed. "I feel like there's so much more I could be doing."

"So what will you do now?"

"I don't know yet."

"You could work at the factory. They are always hiring. If you come today, I'm sure you could start working tomorrow," Anna suggested.

"Kay's working there, too. I don't even really know what they make," Clare admitted, envisioning herself riveting a bomber on the assembly line.

"They make all kinds of things. From huge turbines for battleships to the tiniest electronic parts for radar and radio equipment. I work on the turbosuperchargers. They're for the P-38 Lightnings, you know."

"Oh, Anna, maybe you worked on the ones in the P-38 I flew in!"

"That could be, Clare. You should think about it." Clare assured Anna that she would consider a job at the factory.

Clare promised to meet Kay for lunch at the diner. She left a few minutes early to walk in front of the Salerno Bakery. The familiar building had not changed. She paused in the alley a minute deciding whether or not to go in. The ginger cat appeared, twined around her legs a few times, and then went on his way. Clare opened the door, and the comforting scent of fresh bread filled her nostrils. She studied the offerings in the glass case while other customers placed their orders, peeking in the back of the bakery as best she could. When it was her turn, she selected some cannoli. As her grandfather handed them to her, she caught sight of her grandmother in the back room. Clare realized immediately there was something different about her. Her slender figure was punctuated by a swelling about her middle. The woman caught her eye and gave her a warm smile.

"Congratulations," Clare said to her grandfather. "Your daughter will be very lucky to have such wonderful parents."

"Daughter? That's what my dear Clara says, but I think maybe it's a boy, no?" her grandfather answered.

"I have a feeling your wife is right about that," Clare said, paying for her cannoli.

At the diner, Clare gave the cannoli to Nell and asked her to bring them home for Eddie and her parents. Kay soon arrived, already dressed in her coveralls for work. Clare told Kay she had mailed her letter the previous day and found a letter from Parker, now Major York, waiting for her at the post office. She showed Kay the picture of Johnson and his plane.

"Oh, he looks sweet. And you're so lucky to be

painted on his plane. I wish my picture were painted on someone's plane," Kay lamented.

Clare gathered she did not know about the *KO Punch*. She wondered if Kay would mind being depicted that way and concluded it would not bother her friend one bit. Then it occurred to her, with a heavy heart, that maybe the *Clare-voyant* would be renamed once Parker received the letter from Kay.

"Kay, I talked to Anna last night. She works at the factory, too. I think I'll see if I can get a job there," Clare said.

"That's wonderful, Clare! See if you can get the swing shift, too. I'll put in a good word for you. I'm sure they'll hire you."

After lunch, Clare walked down to the factory. She had never seen it up close before. It was like a bustling city. She asked some girls in overalls where the hiring office was, and they pointed her in the right direction. Clare entered the office and explained to the receptionist that she wanted to apply for a job.

"We don't need any clerical help now, hon. Just factory work."

"Oh, that's fine. I wanted to work on the floor anyway. Maybe on the turbosuperchargers," Clare suggested.

"Okay, we'll see. Stay here and I'll let them know you're waiting," the receptionist said, disappearing into the inner office. She came back out and sat down at her desk. A few minutes later, her phone rang. She answered it and then told Clare to go in.

Clare found two men waiting in the office. One was dressed in a suit and tie, and the other was wearing coveralls and had clearly come from the factory floor. Clare smiled at the two men and then said in surprise, "Mr.

O'Neill! I didn't know you would be here." The man in coveralls gave her a fatherly embrace.

"Mr. Monroe, this is my daughter's friend, Clare Carlyle. She's just back from a USO tour in the Pacific," Mr. O'Neill said.

"That's very impressive, Miss Carlyle," the well-dressed man said, shaking her hand. "Why would you want to work here now?"

"I want to do something to help the war effort, and this is very important work."

"Mrs. Burke told us you want to work on the turbosuperchargers. That's very specific, Miss Carlyle. Why would you want to do that?" asked Mr. Monroe.

"My friend Anna works on them, but the real reason is I know some special aviators who fly Lightnings. That way it would feel like I'm helping them," Clare explained. "And I've flown in one myself," she added. "I know what they can do."

Mr. Monroe raised his eyebrows. "Well, as a matter of fact, we could use another person in that line. Can you start tomorrow?"

"I sure can, Mr. Monroe," Clare said with excitement.

"Good. Come back here tomorrow at one o'clock. We'll get you set up, and then you'll work the swing shift. Mr. O'Neill will show you out." Clare shook the man's hand again and followed Mr. O'Neill out the door.

Once they were outside, Mr. O'Neill turned to face Clare. He did not look as friendly as he had in front of Mr. Monroe.

"Clare, Kay and Nell are very glad to have you back. But I must say, Mrs. O'Neill and I didn't appreciate that 'souvenir' you brought back for Kay. We worked hard to get her to forget about that pilot, and now she's intent on marrying him," Mr. O'Neill said sternly. "How did you get that trinket he made for her, anyway? We burned the letter it came in and threw the charm in Eddie's box of scrap. It seemed a shame to waste the metal."

"I found it. I guess someone at the scrap drive couldn't bring himself to destroy it. It was just a coincidence that I found the person who made it."

"That's an awful big coincidence given the thousands of men in the Pacific. Mrs. O'Neill always says there's no such thing as a coincidence. She saw it as some sort of a sign that we should let Kay marry the lad after all. What do you know about him, anyway?"

"Parker? Well, he's a major now. He's a wonderful pilot. He's shot down almost twenty Japanese planes. Maybe it's more by now. But he's not just brave; he's kind and intelligent, too. Any woman would be lucky to have him. And any parents would be lucky to have him as their son-in-law."

"You sound almost like you're sweet on him, too."

"No," Clare blushed. "I know how devoted he is to Kay. He really does love her. I know Kay loves him, and she's determined to marry him. Don't you think it would be better if you gave them your blessing? I know you're concerned about his background being so different, but you are more alike than you think when it comes to what really matters."

"Maybe you're right, Clare. You really think he would take good care of Kay?"

"I do, Mr. O'Neill."

"Well, then, so be it. Good luck on your first day of work tomorrow," Mr. O'Neill said, the friendliness returning to his voice. He embraced Clare again and they parted.

Clare returned to the diner and told Nell about her

new job but did not mention seeing her father. She asked Nell to tell Kay to meet her for lunch before work the next day.

Back in her room, Clare got out two sheets of pink stationery. She wrote a letter to York explaining that Kay's parents would not object to their marriage and telling him of her new job in the factory making the turbo-superchargers that gave the Lightnings superior maneuverability at high altitudes. Then she wrote a letter to Red Johnson, telling him how happy she was that he was safe and how flattered she was that he had named his new P-38 after her. At the last moment, she enclosed one of the leftover pictures she had taken in the photo booth and sealed up the letter to Red. Clare then wrote a note for Anna telling her she would start working on the same assembly line as her the next day and slipped it under her door.

CHAPTER 39

Clare awoke with excitement, eager to start her job at the factory. She had no idea what it would be like but was happy to try something new. Anna was downstairs already when Clare came for breakfast. She was delighted to hear Clare would be joining her and felt Clare would fit right in.

"What should I wear, Anna? No one told me that."

"Do you have any slacks? Don't wear any jewelry, and be sure to tie up your hair," Anna advised.

Clare went to her room and opened the chifforobe. The only slacks she had were her blue jeans. She contemplated buying something new but decided to just wear them. The heavy fabric felt strange on her legs after months of wearing skirts and dresses. She put her sneakers on and her green blouse. She tried to figure out what to do with her hair. She did not have a scarf to wear but then remembered the hat Mrs. Dietrich had knitted for her. She decided it would have to do until she could find something more appropriate. Clare still had some time to kill, so she wrote in her journal. Then she carefully replaced it in the drawer of her nightstand, along with the framed photos of Roy and her collection of letters received over the past months. She looked at her watch, the going-away present from her friends at the dime store, and placed it in the drawer, too; she did not want the silver bracelet to get caught on any machinery.

On her way to the diner, Clare mailed the letters to York and Johnson. She found Kay already waiting in the diner for her. They took seats at the counter, and Nell served them some hamburgers.

"Clare, my parents say they will let me marry Parker!" Kay said, beaming. "I was going to no matter what, but it's so much better if they approve of him. I don't know what made them change their minds, but I don't care. I can't wait until he comes home!"

"That's great Kay. I'm so happy for you," Clare said.

"And I'm so happy you're going to work at the factory. We can take our breaks together. It will be swell. You know, there are some nice fellas who work there. I could introduce you to a few," suggested Kay.

"Maybe," said Clare. "I think I'd better focus on learning how to do the work first, though." Clare looked at the clock above the chrome sunburst backsplash. "Oh, it's ten minutes before one. I don't want to be late on my first day. I'd better go now," Clare said as she left some coins on the counter.

"I don't have to start until two o'clock today," said Kay. "I'll stay here until then. Good luck, Clare," she said, giving Clare a hug.

Nell came out from behind the counter. "Good luck, Clare," Nell said, embracing her. "Thank you," she whispered into Clare's ear.

"I'll see you later," Clare said, smiling at her friends. She turned and left the diner. The instant she was outside, she realized she left her hat on the counter. She turned to open the door again but found it did not budge. She pulled on it with all her might, but it would not open. Clare rapped on the glass, but no one came. She cupped her hands around her face to see inside. The lights were dim. The counter was empty. Clare looked up and saw that the neon signs were dark. The "OPEN" sign was no longer flashing, and the airplane circling the globe was not illuminated.

"Oh, is there a power outage?" Clare said aloud, trying the door again. Then she realized how dirty the windows were. The once-shining chrome exterior of the diner was dull. Clare turned to face the street, and a car sped past her. Then a pick-up truck went by. It was not until the compact Toyota drove past that she grasped what had happened. Nevertheless, Clare banged on the door again, tears filling her eyes.

"Are you all right, miss?" a young man in a t-shirt and shorts asked as he walked by.

"No, I left my hat. I've got to get back inside!" Clare cried. The man gave her a peculiar look and hurried past. Clare sat down on the steps of the diner for a minute to regain her composure. She tried the door one last time but to no avail. Slowly she began walking back down the street, staring at the cracked and buckling sidewalk beneath her feet. She walked past the empty barbershop and shoe store. She peered into the candy store, but there was no sign of Mr. Tolliver. The windows of McCall's had no merchandise, just heavy curtains obscuring the offices within. She tried the door of Kingsley's and it opened. Inside a receptionist asked, "May I help you?" There was no trace of the lunch counter, racks of merchandise, or worn wooden floors. "Whom are you here to see, miss?" the receptionist asked.

"Mrs. Dietrich? Mr. Winston?" Clare asked feebly.

"I'm sorry, miss. No one by those names works here. Which office are you looking for?"

"No, no office. I'm sorry," Clare said, dashing out. She continued to walk up the street and soon found herself standing in front of the library. The concrete and glass structure could not be missed. The door slid open, and she went inside. Wide eyed, Clare looked around her. She caught sight of the head librarian at the circulation desk and rushed over to her.

"I'm back," she said breathlessly. "I'm sorry I've been gone so long. You must have wondered what happened to me." The librarian looked at her watch.

"You're only five minutes late, Clare. No need to be so hard on yourself. You always get here early, anyway. It's all right if you take a few extra minutes at lunch."

"Minutes? No, I was gone for ... ," Clare said, her voice trailing away. "Okay. Thanks. I'll get back to work now." Clare slipped into the stacks and found a cart of books to reshelf.

I don't understand, thought Clare. *How did I get back? The librarian didn't seem surprised to see me at all. Have I not been gone for all these months? I couldn't have just imagined it all, could I?* Clare pondered these questions while she absentmindedly shelved the books. She would not have been surprised if some ended up in the wrong place.

When her shift was done, Clare left the library. She was tempted to revisit the diner, but the prospect of seeing her father won out, and she hurried home. As she approached, no aroma of freshly baked bread greeted her. However, Reggie ran up to her and threw himself down at her feet. Clare stroked his belly, and the cat purred contentedly.

"Have you missed me, Reggie?" Clare asked, and the cat rubbed his cheek against her hand as if in answer. Clare looked up at the sign hanging over the storefront she had visited the previous day and knew she would find no cannoli inside. She pulled open the door and bounded across the creaking wooden floor. In an instant she was in front of her father and threw her arms around his neck.

"I'm so happy to see you, Dad!" she cried. "I've missed you so much."

"Uh, I'm happy to see you, too, Clare. Tough day at the library?" he asked, chuckling.

"Day?"

"You look exhausted. There must have been a lot of books to shelve! You run upstairs. I'll close up and be there in a few minutes."

Clare climbed the stairs to their living quarters over the store. She could hardly believe she was seeing it all again. Everything was just the way she left it all those months ago. She sat on her bed in a daze. Eventually her father appeared.

"I'll make dinner tonight, Clare. You seem pretty tired."

"Gee, thanks, Dad. That would be swell," Clare answered. Her father gave her a funny look and went to the kitchen. In a little while he called her to dinner.

"So Clare, tell me about your day. It must have been hectic."

"Well, I ... I did shelve a lot of books," Clare said lamely. "How was your day?"

"Nothing special. Well, actually a buddy of mine came in the store today. He collects antique military items, and I mentioned that charm you found yesterday at the flea market. He said if he takes a look at it he might be able to find something out about it. Leave it with me tomorrow, and I'll show him."

"Oh, I can't do that, Dad. I ... I lost it. It must have fallen out of my pocket sometime today," Clare said sheepishly.

"Aw, that's too bad. Well, easy come, easy go," Clare's father said with a shrug.

Easy? thought Clare. *That's an understatement!*

After dinner, Clare washed the dishes, and her father settled into his armchair. Drying her hands, she came into the living room.

"What record should we listen to tonight, Dad?" Clare asked.

"How about *Oklahoma!*? It's been a long time since we've heard that one."

Clare inwardly groaned but withdrew the old record from its sleeve and placed it on the turntable. She curled up on the couch and was lost in the music.

"That sure is a classic. The movie's great, but it must have been something to see it on Broadway back in 1943," her father remarked as the last note faded.

"Oh, it was. And in the South Pacific," answered Clare, dreamily.

"*South Pacific?* Yes, that's a good one, too," her father agreed.

Clare wished her father a good night and went to her room. She pulled her Twentieth Century American History textbook from the shelf and opened it to the chapter about World War II. She found the page with the picture of Roy receiving the blood plasma transfusion. The caption simply read, "Army medic administers blood plasma to a wounded soldier." Clare wept silently, lamenting that she had not recognized the handsome young man when she had the chance and wondered if his family ever discovered that he was the soldier in the famous photograph.

Full of sorrow, Clare undressed and got into her own bed, Reggie pressed close beside her. She read a few pages of *Coming of Age in Samoa* to distract herself. *Hmm, maybe I will write* Coming of Age in the Solomon Islands *someday*, Clare thought. *That doesn't seem so impossibly far away now.*

She set the book down on her nightstand and remembered the nightstand in her room at Mrs. Harrigan's. She mourned the loss of her journal, her photos of Roy, the silver wristwatch, and the collection of letters from Roy, Kay, and Parker, all left there for safekeeping. She reflected that she did not have any concrete proof of where – or when – she had been for almost a year. And she wondered if her friends would miss her or wonder what had happened to her. Then she had an unsettling thought: perhaps Parker had not even survived the war. Maybe she could use the library's microfilm newspaper archives to find out what had happened to everyone. Maybe her own disappearance from Laurelmont would even be reported. It was all too much to process, and Clare drifted off to sleep, dreaming of soaring above volcanic islands and shooting at Japanese planes.

CHAPTER 40

Tuesday mornings were Clare's turn to staff the circulation desk. She stood behind the counter, barcode reader in hand, waiting for patrons to bring her their selections. A slow but steady stream of library customers approached with their books, magazines, or videocassettes. She scanned each card first, made note of any outstanding fines, and then scanned each item. She printed out the receipt with the due dates and handed each patron his or her stack of books. She sometimes felt awkward performing this task when she saw the titles of some books people chose. She saw lonely women checking out romance books. She could see who was trying to lose weight, battle depression, or find a new job. Consequently, she had trained herself not to look too closely at the books she scanned out of respect for the borrower's privacy. Today Clare had no problem distancing herself from her task. She scanned the books robotically, barely noticing what she was doing. While her hands were busy scanning piles of books, magazines, and videotapes, her mind wandered back to the life she had left behind. Of course she was overjoyed to see her father again, but she could not help missing her friends and wondering what had become of everyone. After her months of adventures, life in the present day seemed very prosaic.

The morning wore on, and Clare scanned book after book until one finally caught her attention: *Guadalcanal Diary*. Then *Thirty Seconds Over Tokyo*. Next *Baa Baa Black Sheep*. Her curiosity was piqued, and she looked up to see who was borrowing these three books. Clare raised her eyes and saw a handsome young man, tall and blond, smiling down at her. "Parker," she whispered. The man's expression turned to confusion.

"Is there something wrong with my library card? I'm not from Laurelmont, but I thought I could use it anywhere in the state?" the young man questioned.

She studied the man before her and realized it was not Parker, of course. He was younger, maybe twenty or twenty-one. His sandy hair had not been bleached by the tropical sun. He wore no Army Air Forces uniform or pilot's wings. Clare glanced at the young man's card and then at her computer screen. Both read "Peter York."

"I ... I'm sorry," Clare apologized. "It's just that you look like someone I know. Someone I used to know. Your card is fine," she said, pushing the books toward him but not letting go of them. "These books you're taking out, well, I don't normally ask about people's book choices, but it seems like you have a special interest ... ," her voice trailed off.

"Oh yes, well I want to learn more about World War II. My grandfather was in the war. In the South Pacific. I want to find out what it was like for him, so I thought I'd read some books. My grandparents lived in Laurelmont after the war, so I thought I'd come here. Kind of a pilgrimage, I guess."

"Your grandparents, are they ... ?" Clare could not finish the sentence.

"Living in Florida now," Peter replied. "I don't see

them too much anymore." Peter glanced around and saw that a line had formed behind him. "Sorry about that. I'll let you get back to work. Bye."

"Bye," Clare replied weakly, watching him turn and exit through the sliding door. A little girl was next in line with a pile of picture books. Clare mechanically scanned them, staring out the door until she could no longer see his figure. When she had helped the last of the patrons, she rested her head in her hands to steady herself and contemplate what she had just seen. *Could he really be Parker and Kay's grandson?* Before she could ponder it any further, she was startled to hear someone in front of her say, "Hello." She looked up and there was Peter.

"I'm sorry to bother you again, but I don't know anyone in town, and I thought you seemed interested in the books I borrowed, and I thought maybe, well, would you want to have lunch with me?" he asked.

"Oh, I'd love to!" Clare said, beaming with delight.

"Great!" Peter replied. "Can you get away now?"

"Sure, let me just tell my boss I'm going to lunch." Clare hurried away and returned a moment later. They walked through the sliding door and out into the sunlight.

"This town must have been something once," Peter remarked.

"Oh yes, it really was," Clare agreed ruefully.

"Maybe you can show me a few things. My grandmother used to work at a five-and-dime store somewhere in town. And her sister worked in a diner. I wonder if the buildings are still there?"

"Yes," Clare replied, "we'll walk past both of them. And the drugstore where we had our pictures taken."

"Huh?"

"I mean an old drugstore, too."

Clare pointed out the five-and-dime when they

neared it. Peter peered in at the remodeled interior. "Oh, it's just cubicles now," he said with disappointment. Then they approached the diner, a "CLOSED" sign in the grimy window. Peter stood back to look at the building, then went to the door, and cupped his hands around his eyes to see inside. "It's in pretty rough shape," he said. "Still, I can imagine it must have been nice when it was all shiny and new."

"Oh, it was," Clare answered. "I mean I can imagine it, too."

"Too bad we'll only ever get to imagine what it was like. Oh, look – there's a lady's hat on the counter still. That's been there a long time," Peter remarked.

Clare cupped her hands beside his at the door and peered in, too. There on the counter was the hat Mrs. Dietrich had knitted for her! Although she had just left it there the previous day, she could see it was covered with a thick layer of dust. Clare discreetly tried the door, but it was securely locked.

They walked past the diner and found themselves at the pizza parlor on the corner. "How about here?" Peter suggested.

"Sure," Clare replied, and they stepped inside. After choosing their slices of pizza, they sat down at a tiny table in the window.

Peter smiled at her and said, "I just realized I didn't even ask you your name. I guess I was a little nervous."

"I'm Clare Carlyle."

"And I'm Peter. York."

"I know," Clare said, grinning.

"Oh, of course, you saw my library card. So did you read those books, too?"

"No," Clare confessed, "not those particular ones, but I want to. I have an interest in World War II. Especially in the Pacific, too."

"It's hard for me to imagine that guys my age or even younger were the ones fighting the war. It makes me wonder if I would have had the courage to do what my grandfather did."

"Oh, Peter, I think you would have had the courage to be a fighter pilot, too," Clare replied, gazing into his blue eyes and remembering the view of sky and ocean from the cockpit of the P-38 Lightning.

The young man stared at her for a moment. "That's nice of you to say, Clare, but I never told you my grandfather was a fighter pilot."

Clare felt her face reddening. "Just a guess," she replied.

"A pretty good one. Let me show you this." Peter reached into his pocket. He opened his hand to reveal the charm, Lucite worn and brass tarnished.

Clare smiled. "Your grandfather made that for your grandmother."

"Yes, you're right!"

"I'm so glad you have it now. It's important that someone treasures it and remembers what it means."

"I think so, too. My grandparents gave it to me when I left home to go to Glenmere."

"You go to Glenmere? I go to Penllyn!"

"That's great! Maybe we can see each other when classes start again," Peter said with enthusiasm. "Oh, but you probably have a boyfriend … "

"That would be swell, Peter. And I don't have a boyfriend," Clare said with a smile, thinking back to Kay's efforts to find her a "fella" and realizing she felt happy to be living in the present again, instead of the past.

AUTHOR'S NOTE

Although *Flying Time* is a work of fiction, some characters and events are based on real people and occurrences. While some details are accurate, in other cases I have invented personalities or changed dates and places to better suit the story.

Most notably, Pvt. Roy W. Humphrey really was a twenty-one-year-old welder from Toledo, Ohio. He was known by his middle name, Willis, to family and friends. Private Humphrey enlisted in the Army in June of 1942, hoping to become a paratrooper, but was placed in the infantry. He landed on Sicily with the Seventh Infantry Regiment of the Third Division on July 10, 1943. One month later, on August 10, 1943, Private Humphrey died of wounds he received the previous day.

The fight to save Private Humphrey's life with a blood plasma transfusion was immortalized in a photograph taken by Army Signal Corps photographer Lt. John Stephen Wever. This photograph did, indeed, appear in newspapers across the country in early September 1943, causing a surge in blood donations and was subsequently used for Red Cross ads. The caption of the photograph did not identify the wounded soldier and strongly implied that the plasma had saved his life. People across the country thought they knew the identity of the wounded man, and some other soldiers even took credit for being the man in the picture. Private Humphrey's own family and friends never knew he was the soldier in the famous picture. More than sixty years later, the picture was finally published online with a full caption containing his name. Only then did some members of his family come to know the truth.

By all accounts, Private Humphrey was a very kind young man who was deeply missed by his family and friends. While most of the details I included are accurate, I have taken a few liberties. He did not work at the Willys jeep factory in Toledo, but since he was known as Willis that seemed fitting. Also, Private Humphrey did leave behind a special girl in Toledo, one who misses him to this very day. I'm quite certain that had he actually met Clare, he would have delighted in showing her a picture of his pretty girl back home.

Photo courtesy of the National Archives and Records Administration

The USO did stage a traveling production of the Rodgers and Hammerstein musical *Oklahoma!* which toured the Pacific in 1945 (I have altered the date and itinerary). The parts of Ado Annie and Aunt Eller were played by

Bonita Bimrose and Florence Dunlap, respectively. There is no evidence that Ms. Bimrose really was a girl who couldn't say no or Ms. Dunlap was a strict mother hen with a secret vaudeville past! Betty Wilton is not based on a real person. The part of Laurey was played by Gloria Hamilton. Also, the USO troupe did not include "girl-next-door" types, but young women did serve overseas in the Red Cross performing similar functions.

USO troupe members braved dangerous conditions to entertain the troops, and twenty-eight died during World War II. USO entertainers and Red Cross workers were occasionally treated to piggyback rides in fighter planes, at least one of which was fatal for passenger and pilot.

The Stage Door Canteen was a real club for servicemen during World War II. Created by the American Theatre Wing, it was staffed by Broadway stars – or soon-to-be stars like Betty Perske (Lauren Bacall). Originally in the basement of the 44th Street Theatre in Manhattan, other locations opened in cities across the country and eventually in London and Paris. All that remains of the original location is a commemorative plaque on W. 44th Street now.

The P-38 Lightning fighter squadron to which York and Overbrook belong is loosely based on the 44th Fighter Squadron (known as the Vampire Squadron) of the 18th Fighter Group of the 13th Air Force. The character of Maj. Richard Overbrook was inspired by dashing four-time ace Lt. Col. Robert Westbrook, who was lost on a mission over Indonesia in 1944.

Other characters who were real people are Capt. Chevis Horne (Army chaplain), Maj. Margaret Craighill (the first woman to be a commissioned officer in the US Army Medical Corps), Lt. Col. Milton B. Adams (AAF 18th Fighter Group), Celeste Holm (Ado Annie on Broadway), Alfred Drake (Curly on Broadway), and, of course, Lt.

James A. Michener.

Laurelmont is a fictional town, but it was inspired by the many once-prosperous industrial cities of Pennsylvania and New York, particularly Bethlehem, Allentown, and Hazleton in Pennsylvania, as well as Schenectady, New York. As a college student in Bethlehem, I spent countless hours wandering through the town, looking for glimpses of life in the 1940s – or, better yet, a portal back in time!

Finally, the heart-shaped charm is real, found by me as a teenager in the 1980s in a box of junk at a flea market in Lambertville, New Jersey. However, the charm is engraved with "New Guinea" and "1944." Also, the collar insignia is that of an AAF enlisted man or non-commissioned officer, so it is unlikely that a pilot made it. It was more likely made by a member of a bomber crew or ground crew. Charms like this, as well as pendants, brooches, and bracelets were made as souvenirs, but also as part of occupational therapy for wounded men. Like Clare, I've often wondered about the person who made it and how it came to be in that box of junk. While it hasn't literally transported me back in time, it's still the best fifty cents I've ever spent.

Acknowledgements

I would like to thank my sister, Maria Esposito, for her expert help with editing and proofreading. I am also grateful to William R. Ross for his support and encouragement during the writing process, as well as proofreading and editorial comments.

I thank my parents, James and Jean Esposito, for encouraging my interest in World War II. My father's nostalgia for his childhood during the war years and his love of Broadway musicals had a profound effect on me. My mother always clipped out newspaper articles about the war for me whenever she found them.

I am indebted to the many veterans with whom I've had the honor of speaking over the years, especially those who allowed me to interview them for the Veterans History Project at the Library of Congress. In particular, I thank my dear uncle-in-law, Leo Ross, who actually saw the USO tour of *Oklahoma!* while serving in the Pacific.

I also thank Mr. Neil Weiser, nephew of Private Humphrey, for sharing photos and details about his uncle's too-brief life.

Finally, I thank my friends Donna and Stephen Tytko for encouragement, critical reading, and the conversation that initially inspired me to write this story.

ABOUT THE AUTHOR

Donna Esposito grew up in Bucks County, Pennsylvania, not far from the homes of James A. Michener, Margaret Mead, Pearl S. Buck, and Oscar Hammerstein II. She earned an undergraduate degree in molecular biology from Lehigh University (where she hosted "Sunday Swing" on the campus radio station,  WLVR) and a doctoral degree in genetics from Cornell University (where she enjoyed learning to jitterbug and Lindy Hop when she wasn't in the laboratory). Donna resides near Schenectady, New York with her two cats, Eliza and Alexander.

Although a scientist by training, Donna's interest in World War II stems from seeing a local production of the Rodgers and Hammerstein musical *South Pacific* when she was nine years old. Since then, she has had an avid interest in all aspects of World War II history and popular culture of the 1940s. She counts flights in a Douglas SBD Dauntless dive bomber, Boeing B-17 Flying Fortress, and a North American AT-6 Texan trainer as the biggest thrills of her life, so far. Donna volunteers at the Empire State Aerosciences Museum in Glenville, New York.

Flying Time is Donna's first novel. She is currently working on other fiction and nonfiction projects.

Made in the USA
Columbia, SC
04 February 2020